THE VILLAIN'S BEAST

THORNED VOWS
BOOK ONE

KATE HAWTHORNE

THE VILLAIN'S BEAST

KATE HAWTHORNE

The Villain's Beast
Thorned Vows #1
by Kate Hawthorne

Edited by | Jordan Buchanan

Cover Design | Amai Designs

DEDICATION

If you've ever read a why choose fairy tale retelling and thought, "That should be way gayer than it is."

This one (and the next) are for you.

CONTENT WARNINGS

The Villain's Beast is a dark academia adjacent retelling with secret societies, mafia ties, and five morally ambiguous heroes. There is rough/edge play, dubious consent, primal play, exhibitionism, ritualizing branding and whipping, and (spoilers) off-page child abuse and on-page patricide. Please proceed with caution if any of the above concern you.

PART ONE
THE FOUNDATION

CHAPTER 1

FLETCHER

For as long as I could remember, I hated Gideon North. Growing up, it had been a rule in my household—one of many, but a rule just the same.

Don't speak unless spoken to.

Never question authority.

The Sinclairs above all else.

And fuck the North family.

I hadn't even met him before, but high school brought us to the same boarding school and instead of my father sending me off with hugs and good wishes, he'd sent me off with a black eye and a staunch reminder.

Stay away from Gideon North.

So when the time came for us to actually cross paths, I swallowed down any feelings that might have belonged to me, making sure I kept myself in line.

Fuck Gideon North and his shining brown hair. Fuck

the way it fell to just below his ears, not like it had grown out too long in preparation for boarding school, but like he was allowed to wear it that way all the time.

Fuck Gideon North and his dark green eyes that looked like forest moss, and fuck his lanky swimmer's build, his long and delicate fingers that played piano better than I ever could. Fuck Gideon North and the way his cheeks flushed pink when he smiled at strangers.

But most of all, fuck Gideon North and his godforsaken last name.

Fuck Gideon North for sitting down beside me in the library the sixth week of school, smelling like flowers and grass, huffing out an annoyed breath when I ignored him.

"You're Fletcher Sinclair, right?"

He licked his lips, and I wanted to fuck his stupid mouth too. But not in the way I was supposed to. In the way I *wanted* to.

"You know who I am," I told him, trying not to look at his face. Even in profile he was too pretty, too much.

"My father said I'm not supposed to talk to you." He bobbled his head a little bit from side to side. "Don't talk to that Sinclair boy. The Sinclairs are bad news."

It didn't sound a thing like what my father had said to me.

"Then why are you?"

"I don't listen well."

He smiled, and I wanted to die.

Fuck Gideon North for making me want *anything* beyond what my father said I could have.

"No one will know," he said.

"You're an idiot." I looked at him finally, a fine-tuned poker face the only thing not giving away my interest in him. "Everyone will know."

"It's just us."

"Your father paid for the upgrades to this library," I reminded him. "My father built the new residence hall. They're everywhere."

"Do you think they installed cameras in the walls?"

I swallowed, thinking of home. "I'm sure of it."

"No one else here wants to be my friend," Gideon said with a casual shrug. He pushed some hair behind his ear sending another rush of roses into the way too small space between us.

"I find that hard to believe."

"Well, they pretend they do, but they're all just scared of me or they want something."

"I'm not scared of you," I said.

"Right. So, you must want something then. What do you want, Fletcher?"

Fuck Gideon North and the way he said my name.

I closed my eyes, turning my head toward the wall. Up until the North family had paid for library upgrades, it had been the second oldest part of the school. Barely outdating the administration building, which had started as the single classroom at Rose Hill Prep back in the 1700s or something. Now that building bore my surname in a plaque at the cornerstone, a hefty donation made by my grandfather years before I was born. There was a time when I knew the history of the school, when I remembered the name of the founding members, but they'd long been erased. If not with time, then with money.

The only names that mattered now were ours. North and Sinclair.

"I want you to go away."

"Fletcher," he said, almost pouting.

"That's what I want," I said again, even though it was the last thing I wanted.

And, fuck, I *wanted*.

"What's the motto?" he asked, no doubt changing course when he realized friendly camaraderie wasn't going to get him anywhere.

"*Sub rosa*," I murmured.

I knew it as well as I knew all the rules of my life. Some Latin meant to remind all of us that we had the things that were ours because of blood that had been shed for generations. Blood and money and war, and all it got anyone was me and Gideon sitting side by side in the library of a private school, one of us knowing the rules of the world far better than the other ever would.

Gideon was too good for this life. I knew that from the first time I saw him in the halls. My father had raised me to understand this life was luxurious, but never without cost. For my entire life, the Norths were always one step ahead of us, one more zero in their bank accounts than ours. Gideon's father had been better at playing the game than mine had been, but my father had made certain the change in our family's ranking would be a blip and not a constant. From the day I left my mother's womb, he'd been positioning me to take back everything he'd lost.

Whether I liked it or not.

"I'm good at keeping secrets, Sin," he said softly.

I didn't know which was worse—the way his shortening of my name made something new and inexplicable tangle into a knot of thorns in the middle of my stomach, or the fact I knew Gideon North couldn't keep a secret to save his life.

But I could.

"Leave me alone, Gideon," I said, shoving my chair back so forcefully it fell onto the ground. He didn't even flinch at the sudden movement, at the sound, and for what wouldn't be the last time in our lives, I wondered if I'd underestimated him.

Fuck him for that too.

CHAPTER 2
GIDEON

With the exception of our library run-in the second month of school, Fletcher Sinclair managed to avoid me and ignore me until the spring. An impressive feat considering how small the incoming class of freshman at Rose Hill was. The literal who's who of society, from the kids of politicians to the bastards of billionaires, Rose Hill educated and trained some of the worst the world had to offer.

I didn't want to be one of them.

"Mr. North." My English teacher caught my attention and I pressed my fingernail against the sentence I'd been reading in my book.

"Yes, sir?"

"I asked you a question," he said.

Quickly, I shoved my bookmark toward the spine and snapped my well-worn copy of *Hamlet* shut.

"I apologize. I didn't hear you."

"I imagine you didn't." His mouth quirked up at the corner, and we both knew even if he wanted to punish me for reading, it would have made him a hypocrite to do so. "I was assigning partners for the final project and it seems the only person you've not worked with this year is Mr. Sinclair."

I threw a sidelong glance across the room at Fletcher, not knowing whether to be proud or worried his almost yearlong avoidance campaign was about to come to an end. In the fall, I'd foolishly thought the two of us could maybe break whatever stupid competition our fathers had been waging against each other, but his easy dismissal of me had proven otherwise.

We had a couple of classes together since we were both first year students, English being one of them and Biology another. In both, he'd come into class after me, eyes scanning over the available seats, calculating angles and distances, then choosing the one farthest away from me. At first, it had bothered me, but as the year wore on, I found his dedication to ignoring me to be admirable.

I'd never wanted anything as badly as Fletcher wanted me to go away.

"That's correct," I said.

At my confirmation, Fletcher frowned at the chalkboard, jaw tense as he stared straight ahead.

"The two of you are the last pair then. Since you weren't listening, make sure he catches you up on the assignment." Mr. Smith snapped his folio closed just as the bell rang.

Fletcher was up and out of his seat before I even had time to think about how to best approach him. I knew he wasn't going to make it easy, but I also wasn't going to fail this class on account of him. There weren't many things my parents expected of me, but not failing out of Rose Hill was one of them. The course of my life had been very clearly telegraphed for as long as I could remember.

Get good grades.

Do all the extracurriculars my mother wanted.

Graduate from Rose Hill Prep and funnel myself right into Rose Hill University.

Ensure the longevity of the North name.

I figured the North name carved into stone over the doors to the library meant it would live on long enough, but that wasn't what my parents had meant and we all knew it. I came from a complicated family with a complicated life, and my father had spent years padding the pockets of senators and congressmen and CEOs to ensure he had enough money to continue the habit.

I'd never understood the incessant need my father had for control over everything and everyone around him, but my understanding had always come secondary. As long as I did what I was told, there was peace. I was left alone to read my books and swim and play piano. If I stepped out of line...all of those things went away. The first time I failed a class had also been the last time, the grade resulting in my piano being thrown into the pool.

My father hurt *things* to hurt people and I never

understood why. There had to be a better way to get what you wanted in life.

Wasn't it better to be respected than feared?

He didn't think so, and the North name ensured I'd never be able to find out.

"It's a book report."

Fletcher's voice from above drew my attention away from the memory of losing my piano. I looked up at him, breath catching in my throat the way it did every time I saw him. Fletcher was tall and broader than any fifteen year-old had a right to be. He had shiny black hair and piercingly cruel blue eyes, a mouth that always frowned, a jaw that always ticked.

"What is?" I asked.

"The assignment." His frown deepened.

"Oh, right."

"Have you read the book?" he asked.

"Probably."

"You don't..." Fletcher trailed off, groaning under his breath, the hot puff of his frustrated exhale blowing across the top of my head.

"I've read it," I told him.

It had been so much easier to approach him at the beginning of the school year, back when I thought the two of us might have had a chance at being anyone besides who we were. He'd made it clear he wasn't interested in changing the status quo, so I'd let him be. It was better for both of us that way.

"What's your phone number?" he asked, the words

sounding so foreign coming out of his mouth my brain struggled to make sense of the simple request.

"What?"

"Your phone number," he said again, slower. The tip of his tongue darted out of his mouth, worrying the place where his lips came together. "So we can meet up and do this assignment."

"I'm surprised you're going to work with me on it."

His jaw moved back and forth, eyes flashing. "I can't fail."

"Neither can I." I cleared my throat and stood up, clutching my book and my notebook against my chest, then I gave Fletcher Sinclair my phone number and ruined the rest of my life.

CHAPTER 3
FLETCHER

I could have completed the assignment on my own. With my eyes closed.

Because once, when I was younger, my father had told me to get good grades and that fell right under the third rule.

So, I could have done the assignment myself. I should have done the assignment myself.

I shouldn't have asked Gideon for his phone number. Even though Gideon had only managed to somehow get more good looking over the months I'd spent ignoring him, my attraction to him wasn't what had kicked me into gear. It was a burning hot rage toward my father and the video call we'd had over dinner where he'd laid out the details for the next eight years of my life for me.

"You'll graduate top of your class at RHP," he said, "and the same at RHU. Then you'll marry."

I hadn't even managed a protest. Hadn't gotten past

opening my mouth, which was clearly too much of a response on its own. No sound had come out, but my father's eyes narrowed just the same and that familiar cold fear raced through my bloodstream.

"And you'll marry," he repeated.

"Yes, sir."

One day I was going to crack a molar for how hard he made me grit my teeth sometimes.

"Who do you want to marry, Fletcher?" he asked me next.

I licked my lips slowly, knowing there was a right answer and I needed to get it on the first try.

"Whoever you tell me to," I said quietly.

"Even if it's a woman?"

My breath caught in my throat, and I bit my lips together between my teeth wishing we were on a phone call instead of a video one. But my father was a calculating man and he knew how to read people's tells, including mine. He always wanted the upper hand and he'd beaten the need for it into me at a very young age. The fact that I still slipped around him sometimes was my greatest weakness and we both knew it. My father made a habit of knowing everything about everyone around him, but I thought I'd at least kept that one revelation about my sexual preferences a secret.

"Whoever you tell me to," I repeated.

"What if I want you to marry a *woman*, Fletcher?" His words burned as he sneered at me, the intensity of his hate pushing against me with every word. "What if I wanted you to fuck her on your wedding night and knock her up? Ensure the Sinclair family an heir."

Choking on my spit, I blinked hard. "I'm a virgin, sir. I don't—"

He cut me off, raising a hand to silence me, even across state lines.

"I would strongly suggest you don't stay that way for long. Do you understand me?"

"Yes, sir."

He dragged his tongue across the front of his teeth. "Your mother wants to hear about school now."

And with that, I'd been dismissed.

After hanging up with my parents, I'd lost my appetite entirely and decided to instead pace my room until my heels ached. Years of biting back my feelings and my rage had narrowed down into a sometimes hours-long routine of talking myself off a figurative and sometimes literal ledge. It was nearly Saturday when the pain in my feet finally quieted the anger in my brain, and Gideon's phone number burned a hole in my pocket, because even though I needed to get over myself and call him, I didn't want to. If my father had any idea how his newest order to finish top of my class had fallen in direct contradiction to his steadfast demand of *fuck the North family*, he would have had me out of school so fast I wouldn't have even known which way was up.

At least at school I was under his control, but not under his thumb. I had room to reset, room to breathe, even if it didn't always feel that way. After all, I *did* have

Gideon North's phone number. Shoving my hand into the pocket of my navy blue chinos, I traced the tip of my finger over the frayed edge of his torn notebook paper. I didn't need to look because I'd already committed the number to memory. If I closed my eyes, I could see him scrawling the digits on the corner of the narrow-ruled page, including the weird and backward way he wrote his 5's.

I pulled Gideon's phone number out of my pocket and shoved it under my pillow, then I dialed it. It rang through to voicemail and I called him again. He answered on the fifth ring, voice scratchy and tired with sleep.

Good.

I'd woken him up.

"Hello?" he croaked, and I tried to not imagine him in a bed that looked like mine in a room of the same dimensions. I didn't allow myself to wonder what his pajamas looked like, his body.

"We should start this report," I said.

He breathed into the phone, loud, like his mouth was pressed directly against the speaker.

"What time is it?"

"Time to start our report." I was a bastard, just like my father. "I'm in room 703, Southern Annex."

I hung up before he could protest.

At least I'd given him the courtesy of letting him hide his face.

Or maybe I'd just been trying to hide mine.

GIDEON

I should have gotten dressed, but I was half-asleep and too angry to see straight. It was just like a Sinclair to expect the world to bend to his whim and operate on his timetable. My father had always told me the Sinclair family was a scourge on society, and every day I knew him, Fletcher proved him right. When we started school, I'd wanted to believe differently, even if he'd shut me down. Clearly, there was still a part of me that thought there could be a chance for change.

It was late.

It was for an assignment.

But Fletcher Sinclair had called me.

The spring air was warm and dry as I jogged across the campus from my room in the Northern Annex to Fletcher's in the South. I hadn't bothered to get dressed before heading out. Instead, I'd shoved my feet into a pair of beat up Golden Goose sneakers and set off in my plaid pajama pants and an old RHU shirt I'd picked up some-where along the line.

When I reached the Southern Annex building, I rode the elevator up to the seventh floor, walking slowly down the hall so I could catch my breath. I didn't want to look desperate, but now that I was wide awake, it was impossible to hide my exhilaration. The version of myself from the fall tried to push himself to the forefront of my mind, spouting off silly ideas about being more than our fathers and more than our names.

The door to Fletcher's room was propped open, the deadbolt latch engaged to stop the heavy wood door from closing all the way. I knocked anyway, kicking it open with the toe of my sneaker and peering inside. His room was—unsurprisingly—the same layout as mine, though he'd of course decorated differently. Even in the dim light of his desk lamp, I could tell his room was a wash of navy blue and gray, from the bedding to the...well...to the bedding. There wasn't any decoration to be found unless you counted the stack of books on his desk, which I didn't.

Books were a necessity, not a luxury.

"I'm not surprised your manners are lacking," Fletcher said from the bed, not looking up from the book in his lap. He was still dressed from class, navy pants and a white button-down, though he'd undone the top two buttons.

"It was open," I reminded him.

"For a draft." He closed his book and looked up at me warily, nostrils flaring when he took in the state of me.

For the first time, I thought maybe I should have changed into real clothes, though I didn't truly think *what* I wore would make a difference to *how* I felt standing in the entryway of Fletcher Sinclair's bedroom.

"These rooms get so stuffy at night," he said, setting the book on his nightstand and swinging his legs over the side.

"Open a window," I suggested.

He glanced at his window—closed—like the thought had never occurred to him before.

"Have you read the book already?" he asked, changing subjects and standing tall.

It was only a matter of time and hormones before I was taller than him, but until then it was clear he was going to take advantage of the height difference between us. Fletcher pushed past me toward his desk, smelling like clean cotton and lavender, and I stared at the indent of his body against his comforter instead of watching him go. That moment offered me the first glimpse of what the rest of our lives would be. Missed connections, brushoffs, and the weight of a thousand unspoken words between us.

Swallowing, I spun around, finding his stare focused on the back of my head, now my eyes. His were blue as ever, a sharp contrast to the darkness of his room, but they betrayed nothing more than boredom. He had a copy of *Hamlet* in his hand, looking like he'd bought it two hours earlier.

"I've read it," I told him.

"Did you read the assignment?" he asked next.

I hadn't, because after class I'd gone to swim, then I'd spent some time playing piano, and then I'd settled in for dinner and bed. Fletcher hadn't bothered to reach out, so I'd written him off until Monday, but then...

"I haven't."

The corner of his mouth flashed into what might have been a smile, but it was gone as fast as I'd seen it. Back was the mask of impassivity and annoyance, which was ironic considering he'd been the one to call me. He'd been the one to wake me up, to drag me across campus in the middle of the night to start on a report we had two weeks to complete.

He'd called.

And I'd come.

Fletcher turned back to his desk and plucked a stapled paper from the top of a pile and handed it to me. The syllabus.

"It's all in here," he said with a scowl.

"Thank you," I whispered, realizing things for me and him were never going to be anything besides exactly what they were.

"I have to piss." Fletcher fussed with the button of his pants, popping it undone before spinning on his heel. "Catch yourself up so we can get started when I'm done. We don't have all night."

I looked down at the syllabus, flipping to the back page that detailed the information about the end of term assignment. It didn't need to be a group project; it was barely enough work for one person let alone two. Group projects were meant to teach important life skills like delegation and time management. Skills that would never matter to men like me and Fletcher. When the time came, everyone would do whatever we told them to anyway.

CHAPTER 5
FLETCHER

We could have finished the project in two hours, but somehow we managed to drag it out for the entire two weeks. The first night, we argued about who would take what part of the project, a rendezvous which ended with Gideon storming out of my room just shy of one in the morning, face flushed and hands shaking. He showed up at eleven the next night, and we finished what we'd started the night before.

Sunday, again at eleven.

By Tuesday night, we'd drafted the barest bones of an outline.

We worked at a slow pace, maybe deliberately. Every second we spent together was a direct rebellion to the rules of my father and probably to his as well. North and Sinclair, side by side, working toward a common goal. In all the history of our families that I'd bothered to remember, I'd never heard a story like that. It had always been lying and cheating and conniving until one man came out on top. One day, someone would break the curse of our names, but I didn't think it was either of us. Gideon, maybe, but not me. There was too much fear inside me still, tangled in the marrow of my bones. I was my father's son, a soldier for him, and I always would be.

Wednesday Gideon showed up with two takeout boxes of curry in a crinkling plastic bag. He didn't say anything different, didn't *do* anything different. He was still in those well-worn plaid pajama pants, his hair twisted back into a messy knot at the base of his skull. When he lifted the bag of food to show it to me, his undershirt rode up, revealing the smallest sliver of his tanned, bare hip.

Swallowing, I stepped back, mind racing.

I was losing the upper hand.

"I hate curry," I lied, hoping he didn't hear the way my stomach growled at the scent of it.

Gideon didn't falter. He licked his lips, corner of his mouth twitching—almost indecipherably.

"More for me then," he said.

I didn't invite him in. I never did, but he came anyway. Gideon dropped the bag of food onto my desk and pulled out one of the containers. In one graceful motion, he dropped down into the empty seat in front of my desk and kicked his legs up, propping them up on the foot of my bed. He made himself at home and dug into his meal, ignoring me until he'd polished off the last bit of rice in the bottom, then he tossed the empty in the trash and fixed me with an amused look.

"Now we can get started."

Upper hand?

Didn't know her.

Not anymore.

"How gracious of you to join me," I said, rolling my eyes and flipping my notebook open to the outline we'd drafted the night before.

It was one sheet of paper, both our handwriting, and as I leaned down to review what we'd agreed on, Gideon sidled up close to me, shoulders touching.

"Teamwork," he said softly, almost under his breath.

I looked at the backward way he wrote most of his letters, just like the weird fives in his phone number, wondering what life had been like for him before he was sent off to Rose Hill. He didn't carry himself like he was scared of his father, like he got beat for falling out of line the way I did. He didn't look like his dad dictated every second of his life.

But I knew he had to. He was a North, after all.

Fuck the North family, I reminded myself. A rule like that couldn't come without a reason behind it. Maybe I'd underestimated him because he was nice to look at it. Maybe Gideon was a far more skilled predator than I'd ever be. He could throw me off my own goals just by batting his eyelashes in the right light.

"Do your parents know we're working together on

this project?" he asked, so close I could smell the coconut on his breath.

"No."

"Mr. Smith would get fired on the spot if my dad found out," Gideon said.

My mouth went dry.

"My father would probably kill him," I whispered.

Gideon tensed, then relaxed, huffing out an aborted laugh. The paper in my notebook fluttered. I smoothed it down, unhappy to find it cool to the touch. My skin burned when Gideon breathed on me—why should the paper get off easy?

"Do you talk to him often?" Gideon asked. "Now that you're here?"

I hadn't talked to him since the first time I called Gideon to come over. "Not often. You?"

"Not since Christmas," he said.

"Lucky bastard."

Gideon laughed, leaning back and stretching his legs out, so comfortable and casual. He threaded his hands together behind his head and tipped back, staring up at the ceiling of my room.

"He treats his second better than me," Gideon said.

"My father doesn't treat anyone well." I kicked my foot against the back of Gideon's knee and he dropped his hands down to my desk, arranging himself in some semblance of an acceptable posture for studying.

He reached across me to get a pen, the entire length of his arm dragging over my chest, across my nipples. I shivered, knowing the feelings weren't right, but I didn't dare pull away from him. I didn't know if Gideon noticed or not, but when he pulled back, pen in hand, he touched me harder, longer...only with the outside of his forearm, the back of his hand.

I couldn't breathe.

"Fletcher," he said softly, clicking open the pen.

"What?"

"Remember the first day we met? In the library?"

I nodded. "Of course."

"I can still keep a secret," he said, brushing away invisible dust or eraser shavings from the notebook between us. "If you ever wanted to."

CHAPTER 6

GIDEON

I made it back to my room Friday just shy of three in the morning, beyond tired.

Beyond horny.

As soon as I closed the door behind me and locked it, I had my hand down my pants, my fingers curled around my always hard cock. Screwing my eyes closed so tight I saw stars, I imagined Fletcher's mouth, his elegant fingers, and I came all over my hand in less than thirty seconds. My knees trembled, gave out, and I slid to the floor with a sigh. I pulled my hand out of my pants and rested my wrist on my knee, strings of sticky cum spread between my knuckles, warm and wet.

I needed to shower, needed to wash my hands, but I'd used up all my fight earlier, reminding myself of the repercussions that would befall everyone if either my father or Fletcher's found out what we were doing. The phone calls were risky enough. If my father checked the bill and realized who the late night calls were with. I crawled to my bed, rewinding my memories back to the beginning of the school year. I'd started off with so much hope, thinking there was a way for Fletcher and me to just...

Be.

He'd rebuffed me with practiced skill, which had made it easy for me to keep my thoughts to myself for the duration of the year. But I'd spent the past seven nights sharing the same space, the same pens, the same air as Fletcher Sinclair, and I didn't want to ignore him anymore. I didn't want to be better than him or ruin his life or anything like that.

I wanted to curl my fingers around his wrist and kiss his knuckles, and kiss his jaw, and his mouth. I wanted him to breathe on me, wanted to feel his chest heave against mine when our bodies got too close.

I wanted.

And I wanted, and I *wanted*.

And I had one week left on this assignment and then everything would go back to how it was before. More cold shoulders from a boy I knew burned hot, and I didn't think I could bear it. Not after *knowing* what it felt like to be close to him.

"It's a mistake," I said to myself, pushing to my feet.

It was the same thing my mother had said to my father when he pressed the issue about sending me to Rose Hill. I don't know what she knew about me that I didn't know about myself, but with every passing day, I started to wonder if she'd been right. My father assured her I'd be fine, that I'd get to campus and remember who I was—a North, that I'd make him proud. She hadn't wanted me to leave for school. She wanted me to continue with my tutors at home where she could keep an eye on me, but Father had said no. He'd raised his hand at her, and that had been that.

I didn't know much about Fletcher's father, not as much as I knew about mine, and I wondered about him. Often. Stripping out of my pajamas and stepping into the shower, I wondered if Fletcher's father was smart enough to only leave bruises and scars where they couldn't be seen if someone was dressed. I wondered if he even cared. Men like our fathers were beyond reproach and above punishment. Boys like Sin and me...not so much.

Closing my eyes, I let the water wash away any evidence of my own transgressions. I washed my body, washed my hair, touched my dripping wet fingers between my ass cheeks, then turned the water off. Trying to walk this fine line of whatever this temporary truce with Fletcher was exhausted me. One more week for it to go either way.

Did I really have a chance at making a better life for myself?

I couldn't do it alone, but I'd spent my whole life doing things alone, being alone. Being the North heir was an isolating thing, and with Fletcher I felt less alone. Even just being in proximity to the way he hated me was somehow comforting, and I was drawn to him because of it.

Seven days left in this project.

Seven days left to feel alive.

Out of the shower, I put my dirty pajamas back on because they smelled like his room, and I climbed into bed. Burying my face in the pillow, I screamed at the top of my lungs. Why was life so hard? So unfair? Why couldn't I just be normal and have the things I wanted? In another life, I could sit beside Fletcher in the library and tell him I thought he had pretty eyes. I could watch him blush from the compliment and I could ask him if he ever jerked off thinking about me.

Maybe not the last part.

I rolled onto my back and exhaled, letting out a breath so thoroughly the bed threatened to swallow me whole.

Inhale.

Exhale.

Inhale.

I was anything but tired, so when my phone vibrated with an incoming call, I was quick to grab it. Quick to curse under my breath when Fletcher's name flashed across the screen.

"Hello?" I answered, rubbing an invisible ache in the middle of my chest.

"I don't think we should text," he said. "Someone could read them."

"We don't text."

But he was right.

There was silence on the other end of the line, and I closed my eyes, trying to imagine where in his room he sat. Was he still at the desk, notebook open in front of him or was he in bed, under the sheets with a half-hard erection like me?

"Thank you for the curry," he said. "It was really good."

I opened my mouth, then closed it. Licked my lips. Tried again. "You're welcome, Sin."

"Don't tell anyone."

"*Sub rosa*," I reminded him.

"That's...It's..." He sucked in a breath and let it out, loud against the speaker. "Good night, Gideon."

I loved the way he said my name like he hated me.

CHAPTER 7
FLETCHER

"Have I told you how boring your room is?" Gideon asked me three days later. He sat on my bed with his legs half crossed, a Styrofoam container of chicken and rice from the cafeteria propped open on his lap.

I looked around from my desk chair, frowning at my room.

"It's just a room?" I said, voice tipping up at the end. "How should it look?"

"It has no personality."

I had no personality. At least, not unless my father told me to. But in these late night hours with Gideon, I started to wonder about who I could be without my father. What kind of person would I be on my own? If I could make my own choices? Set my own rules.

"I can't imagine your room is much different," I said,

rolling my eyes and dumping my empty dinner box into the garbage.

Gideon had brought us food every night since curry, and I'd finally begun to eat it with him instead of after he left.

"My room is completely different," he said.

Feeling bolder than I had any right to be, I stood up and shrugged at him.

"Prove it."

"What?"

"Prove it." I reached toward the bed and smacked the top of his foot. "Let's go work in your room tonight."

"It's messy," he protested.

"Says the guy whose worn the same pair of pajamas every night for the last week."

Gideon's throat flushed a violent shade of pink, straight up to the apples of his cheeks. If he thought I hadn't noticed the way he'd shown up in the same worn pair of pajama pants every night since our first study date, he had another thing coming. No matter how much I hated it, I was still my father's son, and that meant being more observant than most.

I'd also noticed the spattering of freckles on Gideon's collarbone, the cowlick on the back of his head that sent his messy golden waves askew, the way he never looked at his cell phone when we were together. I'd noticed everything about him.

That was what a good predator did. Tracked and observed.

How could I be better if I didn't know who I was up against?

Biting the inside of my cheek until my eyes watered, I turned away from Gideon and headed for the door.

"Come on," I called over my shoulder. "Let's go."

It took Gideon time to get off my bed, get rid of his food, get on his shoes. The delay gave me time to get a breath of air that didn't smell like him, gave me time to pretend I hadn't started to doodle stars in the shape of his freckles on the corners of my notes when I got bored in class.

Gideon joined me in the hallway, my notebook held loosely in his hand. He didn't offer it to me and I didn't take it. I followed when he headed down to the quad, across the campus, to the Northern Annex. His room was on the fourth floor, facing west, and his space couldn't have been more different than mine.

Our furniture was the same because Rose Hill was still a boarding school and even though he and I were far better than anyone else there, they didn't want us to know that yet. The rest of the space, though? He was right in his assertion about the boredom of my room.

"Is dark blue your favorite color?" he asked, tossing my notebook onto his desk. It was a mess, strewn with homework and sheet music, stacks of books balanced on every flat surface. His bed was unmade, crimson and gold sheets all askew like he'd just rolled out of it before coming over to my room.

"What?" I blinked, trying to tear my attention away from his bed. "Why?"

"Everything in your room is blue or gray."

"No, it's..." I couldn't stop looking at his sheets, the indentation in his pillow from his head.

Gideon stepped beside me, following my stare. Our shoulders brushed together and he let out a sound so guttural and low, it shocked me back into the present. Gideon had lulled me into a false sense of security with his golden hair and his lithe body, his simple questions and wide eyes.

He was as much a predator as I was.

He was a matched competitor.

Partner.

"What, Sin?" he asked, breathless.

"I underestimated you," I whispered.

"How so?"

"We're just...we're who we are, right?"

"Gideon North and Fletcher Sinclair," he said.

"Rivals."

"Enemies."

Swallowing, I tipped my head back, finding reprieve in the smooth plaster of the ceiling. My chest burned, a tight stretch with every attempt at a breath, and my palms were clammy and wet. I wiped them against the tops of my pants, hoping he didn't realize or didn't know why.

"We're just two boys," he said.

It was such a ridiculous idea.

I turned toward him, fire in my eyes. He was so close, our toes touched. I didn't know if I wanted to fight him or...

"You know that's not true," I snapped.

"It could be."

"You and your secrets again, Gideon?" I sniffed, vibrating with a thousand feelings I'd never have a name for, wishing I could throw up so this hope and this fucking *want* would get out of me for good.

"Our life is nothing but secrets," he said. "Most of them are kept from us, so why can't we have our own?"

I admired his optimism. My father had beat mine out of me years ago.

CHAPTER 8
GIDEON

When I stepped into Fletcher's dorm room for the first time, I saw him as he'd been that day. A cookie cutter version of his father, the next Sinclair heir. But when he came to my room, he'd seen...

Me.

He might have been the first person ever.

"Secrets will get you killed," he rasped, clearing his throat and backing away from me. "Where's your book, Gideon? We don't have all night."

"On my desk," I said, gesturing with my thumb toward a stack on the edge of my cluttered workspace. "But you're the one who wanted to come over here in the first place."

"A mistake," he muttered, shoving past me to get his notebook and my book from the desk. "Let's get this over with."

Dorm rooms at Rose Hill Prep were not designed for collaborative work. The desks came with one chair, the bed...a twin. Group work was meant to be done in the library or the classroom, but for as much as Fletcher and I followed the rules, that was one we'd never bothered with. Just as I had every night in his room, he climbed onto my bed and straightened his back against the wall.

His feet hung off the side and he tried to toe his sneakers off, but the laces had been tied too tight in his hurry to get over to my room. Without thinking, I plucked them both loose and then climbed onto the bed beside him. Fletcher looked at me with wide eyes, mouth twisted into a miserable-looking frown.

Thump.

Thump.

His shoes hit the floor, pristine white socks bright as day in the darkness of my room.

He flipped open the notebook to the page we'd left off on the night before and shoved my battered copy of *Hamlet* into my chest.

"Read the last chapter out loud," he said, pulling a pen out of his pocket. "I'll take notes on the metaphors."

I could have told him every metaphor and allegory in the book from memory alone, but he didn't trust me and I didn't blame him. I was a North, and whatever tentative truce we'd accidentally stumbled into didn't change that. Me getting myself off every morning with Fletcher's name caught in the back of my throat didn't change anything either.

I read the chapter to him, trying not to focus on the fact we were on my bed instead of his. I pointed out some symbolism he'd overlooked in his notes instead of pointing out how nice it felt to have the outside of his leg pressed against mine. It was the closest we'd ever been, and I was in the same pajama pants as always, the soft and worn cotton not doing much to hide my quickly growing interest in our proximity.

Adjusting the book on my lap with a grunt, I turned the page and kept reading. I focused on the sentences, the words, the letters, my attention so rapt I didn't even notice when Fletcher set down the pen. He shifted his weight, pressing harder into my side, and I barely managed to stifle a gasp.

"I'll read the rest," he said carefully, holding his hand out for the book.

"It's fine," I told him. "I like reading."

To you.

I like reading to you.

"I'll read the rest, North." He grabbed the book out of my hands, and I had a split second to decide if I wanted to try and hide my arousal or let it be seen. In the end, it didn't matter. The book had hidden more than I realized, and the knowing sound that fell out of Fletcher's mouth at the sight of my erection only made it worse.

"You don't have to..." I trailed off, letting my hands fall to my sides.

The room fell so quiet, I could hear the spit move

around in Fletcher's mouth as he opened it, closed it, swallowed, opened it again.

"Gideon," he said softly.

"Please, just…don't."

"Are you that into literature?" he asked.

I shook my head.

"Show me."

I choked on my own spit. "Sorry, what?"

He was dead serious, blue eyes dark as cut sapphires as he fixed his stare on me. Both of us ignoring the hard rod jutting up from between my legs.

"Show me," he repeated, slower, lips curling around every word the way my hand always curled around my dick. "Take it out. And show me."

Blinking hard, I shoved the waistband of my pajamas down and fisted the base of my shaft for him to see. But Fletcher didn't look down. He kept his eyes on my face.

"Stroke yourself the way you do when I'm not here," he said next, and I did.

It was impossible to tell him no, but even if it had been easier, I didn't want to. This…whatever this thing we were doing together was…it was the ultimate act of rebellion, the biggest secret either of us would ever keep. Mr. Smith wouldn't be the only one dead if either of our fathers found out how our assignment preparation had turned out.

I'd very likely find myself at the bottom of the pool alongside my piano.

I twisted my wrist and pulled my hand up my length,

my entire body shuddering with pleasure. Only half of it from the feel of my hand, the other from the weight of his attention on me.

"Are you going to watch?" I asked, my strokes quickening, breath coming harder.

"I am watching."

Fletcher swallowed and gently pressed the side of his finger against the bottom of my chin, tilting my face up so I had no choice but to look at him.

"Are you cut, Gideon?" he asked.

My balls hurt. They ached.

"Yes."

He hummed, lips pursed into a tight line.

"Are you?"

My head fell back and Fletcher grabbed me. One finger beneath my chin, the other hand fisted in the back of my hair, holding my face once again level with his.

"No," he answered, leaning close.

I could still see his face, his eyes, the pained stretch of his mouth. His breath burned against my cheek, and I was close enough to see the thoughts racing through his eyes.

"I'm going to come," I warned him.

"Good."

My entire body seized as I finished, jets of cum spilling over the top of my hand. Fletcher's fingers tightened in my hair and his other hand drifted down. I didn't look away, not even as I registered the sound of his zipper, the rough slide of dry skin against dry skin.

Another burst of cum leaked out of my slit when

Fletcher gritted his teeth together and grunted. He blinked hard, clenching his jaw and letting out an almost silent groan as he finished seconds later.

More than anything, I wanted to look down, to see what we looked like with our pants down and our arousal smeared and drying between our legs, but enough was enough and Fletcher wouldn't give me the chance.

He tucked himself back into his pants and released his hold on my hair. He never even looked down at my dick, not even as he climbed off my bed and put his shoes back on, and especially not when he looked back at me before closing the door and letting himself out of my room.

CHAPTER 9
FLETCHER

Sometimes, if I'm feeling particularly masochistic, I try to think of the ways my life might have played out differently had I only looked down that night. I didn't, though, and it's probably the only thing that kept me whole through the following weeks, the following years…

Gideon and I kept our pants on for the rest of our study dates, but the tension between us was suffocating. When we sat together, he inclined toward me, the rose scent of his hair wafting around us both like the most dangerous kind of tie. His hair would brush my ear, and if I was feeling particularly brave, I would reach for him and tuck it back. His skin always burned my fingertips, and I ached to touch him more.

Touch him harder.

Touch him with intent.

The night before our assignment was due, Gideon

didn't show up at my dorm. I waited until 11:15, then I called him. He didn't answer, so I put on my shoes and trekked across campus to his building. Gideon was half in the hall, half in his room, with his hand braced against the door frame while he tried to fight his sneaker onto his foot.

I cleared my throat and he looked up, face blanching at the sight of me.

"Sorry," he said, slamming his foot down to get his heel into the shoe.

"Everything okay?" I asked.

He scrunched his nose. "My alarm didn't go off."

"Your alarm?"

"To come over." The door to his room swung closed, bumping him on the ass, but not latching closed.

"Were you not..." I trailed off, remembering about the first night I called him to study. When I'd woken him up.

"I'm awake now," he said. "Did you want to go to your room?"

"We're both here."

"Right."

His throat flushed that pretty pink again, and he pushed the door open with his ass, moving out of the way so I could join him inside. I hadn't been in his room since the night we'd jerked off together, and I had to close my eyes to center myself after the door closed behind me.

Gideon's sheets were still crimson red, still rumpled, but now I knew they'd be warm from his skin. He'd just been asleep there, and while he fumbled around his desk for his copy of *Hamlet,* I walked over to his bed and pressed my palm against the sheets. It would have been too much for me to bend over and smell them, to see if I could detect a trace of our spend dried into the expensive cotton.

"I think we're all set for tomorrow," he said nervously.

I looked over my shoulder at him, eyes narrowing at the way he wrung the book in his hands like he was trying to twist the spine in half.

"I think you're right."

He worried his tongue across the front of his teeth. "We probably don't even need to go over it," he said, words dying off. "We know the content."

"We do," I agreed, sliding my hand down toward the middle of his bed. "Do you sleep on your back?"

"What?" Gideon squinted at me, brow knit with confusion. "Why?"

"Just answer me."

His gaze fell from my face to my hands where I had his sheets fisted into a ball.

"Stomach," he rasped.

I counted to ten and forced my fingers to unfurl, letting go and exhaling through my nose.

"I thought you were mad about it," Gideon said.

He didn't mean about sleeping on his stomach.

"Why?"

"You didn't say anything about it," he said, lips twisted into a sad smile. "You didn't ask to do it again."

"Neither did you." I wasn't a beggar, but maybe I would have begged him.

Fact of the matter was, I'd spent the whole week not just thinking about the sounds Gideon made when he came, but also about what that whole encounter could mean for me. What it should have meant. If my father ever found out, he would have beat me to within an inch of my life. I didn't think he'd forgive me for *wanting* to get into bed with a North, let alone actually doing it.

My handprint was in Gideon's sheets.

"Are you still a virgin?" I asked.

"Yes," he said quickly. "Are you?"

"Yes."

But I wouldn't be for long. Father's orders.

"Have you ever kissed someone?"

I put my hand back on his sheets, moved it up to his pillow. Everything was cold already. He'd been awake for too long. Gideon set his book down on the foot of the bed and stepped toward me, the heat rolling off of him in waves threatening to drown me right there in front of him. My phone vibrating to life in my pocket was a life boat I wasn't sure I wanted, and when I pulled it out and saw my father's name on the screen, I wished I had actually drowned instead.

"What are you really trying to ask me, Gideon?"

The phone went silent, but I knew it was only a matter of minutes before he called back. I wasn't sure what he wanted, but I knew what I wanted, and I knew I was running out of time. I put my phone back into my pocket and shifted to face him head on. Without a word, Gideon let his green eyes drag over every inch of my face like he was mapping every hair and blemish in my skin. He licked his lips, pulling the bottom one between his teeth, shuffling half a foot closer to me.

"I've never kissed anyone," he said.

My skin burned and I wanted to scream.

Don't speak unless spoken to.

Never question authority.

Family above all else.

And fuck the North family.

Stay away from Gideon North.

Stay away from Gideon fucking North.

I understood the warning now because, in less than two weeks, he'd wormed his way under my skin and I'd practically cut myself open to make room for him. He closed more space between us and instead of moving away, I stood my ground, shivering when his breath huffed out against my cheek.

He was so close.

My phone started to vibrate again.

I was out of time.

I fisted Gideon's soft and silky hair in my hand, then I crashed our mouths together and kissed him.

CHAPTER 10
GIDEON

The next day, I went to class with kiss-swollen lips and the promise of change strumming just beneath my skin.

Fletcher had kissed me until I came in my pants, then he'd left without a word. His departure hadn't worried me because it was the same way he'd left me the night we masturbated together. Besides, it wasn't like I'd never see him again. Our assignment was due after lunch, and then...

Who knew what would come next?

For the first time since finding out my parents had agreed to ship me off to Rose Hill Prep, I had an undeniable sense of optimism that maybe...just maybe...my life might end up different than I'd always feared.

I got to class early, and Fletcher was nowhere to be found. We'd agreed no texting, so I couldn't reach out, and when it was our turn to present, Mr. Smith leveled me with a sharp look and a promise to see me after class. That meeting never came because, midway through class, the dean arrived, escorted Mr. Smith out, and dismissed everyone early.

To call it weird would have been an understatement, but when Dean Malcom stopped me in the doorway, my earlier sense of optimism turned abruptly into foreboding dread.

"Yes, sir?" I asked, adjusting the strap of my bag with nervous hands.

"Your lack of classroom participation has been brought to my attention recently," he said with a frown. "It's unfortunate Mr. Smith let it go on as long as he did."

"I'm sorry. What, sir?"

"I've been made aware that you offered no participation in your group final."

"I spent the past two weeks with Fletcher, sir," I protested, stepping back into the classroom. "We've worked on it every night since it was assigned."

We'd done more than just work on our paper, but those were secrets between Fletcher and me that no one was supposed to know about.

"Mr. Sinclair turned the paper in before class today," Dean Malcom said, and the floor dropped out from under me. I had to brace myself against a table to stop myself from falling over. "He advised Mr. Smith that you'd made yourself unavailable to him for the duration."

I dug my phone out of my pocket, ready to show him Fletcher's name in my call log, to prove whatever he'd heard was a lie. My lips were dry, though, the wet heat of Fletcher's mouth long gone.

"We worked on it together," I said again.

"Can you prove it?"

"You can ask Fletcher!" I raised my voice, fisting my hands at my sides.

"I've heard his side and I've seen the work he did on his own so he didn't fail. What can *you* show me, Mr. North?"

This was absurd.

Dean Malcom was lucky I wasn't one of those "you'll be hearing from my father" kind of kids, but I did take the time to remind him who'd just paid for their new library while I fought my way into my bag to pull out the notebook Fletcher and I had been working out of for the last two weeks.

It wasn't there, of course. And somehow, in my bones, I knew it wasn't going to be in my room either.

"I can't," I said through gritted teeth.

"I'm going to personally review the rest of your coursework, Mr. North, and then I'll determine if you pass or fail this class."

I didn't have anything to say to that, so I slung my bag back over my shoulder and headed for the door. I was going to find Fletcher and find out what the hell had happened from the kiss to now.

"And Mr. North?"

I stopped, not turning around.

"Your family might have paid for the library upgrades,

as you so kindly reminded me, but my office isn't in the library."

I bit the inside of my cheek until it bled and stormed off toward Fletcher's dorm. He was there, because of course he was, leaning against the closed door with his legs crossed at the ankle and his arms folded in front of his chest. His backpack sat at his feet, zipped up neatly and undoubtedly housing the notebook with all of our work in it.

"What did you do?" I asked.

Fletcher looked up at me, eyes red-rimmed and expression heavy.

"I don't know what you're talking about," he drawled.

"You're outside your room waiting for me," I said. "You know exactly what I'm talking about."

"Oh." He tried to look casual, straightening his spine. "Are you talking about our little group project?"

"Oh, so you admit it *is* ours?"

"I didn't turn in our work," he said.

"Right. You told them it was yours. You got the Dean involved?" My voice lifted to an embarrassingly high octave, and my cheeks burned with embarrassment.

"I didn't get the Dean involved. Would you calm down? You're making a scene."

"The Dean escorted Mr. Smith out of class this morning so you did *something*."

A flash of—something—lit up Fletcher's face, but just like so much between us, it was gone before I could get used to it, let alone make sense of it.

"What did you do, Fletcher?" I asked again. "Why did you do it? I thought…"

He huffed a sad laugh, mouth twisting into the cruelest smile I'd ever seen on anyone, including my father.

Fletcher leaned down, bringing our faces close together and my first reflex was to kiss him. I could still feel his lips on mine, his hands in my hair.

"What did you think, Gideon?"

"I…" Tears welled up in my throat, and I snapped my mouth closed before I did something I'd regret more than the things I'd already done.

"I," he repeated, mocking me.

I screwed my eyes closed, taking a step away from him.

Fletcher laughed at the way I recoiled from him, a sharp-edged noise that had us both reeling away from each other at the sound of it.

"Did you think that because you got off in front of me that there was something special between us?"

"We kissed," I whispered. "I thought—"

"Whatever you thought, you thought wrong." Fletcher bent over and picked up his backpack, blinking hard and shifting his stare to a point on the wall behind me.

"I thought we were at least…friends."

"We're not friends," he sneered. "We're Fletcher Sinclair and Gideon North. That's all we'll ever be."

He was right, and I hated him for it. But nowhere near as much as I hated myself.

Fletcher gave me a fleeting look, his nose scrunched up at me in disgust. I blinked, hating the way a tear escaped from the corner of my eye, but there was no way he was telling me the truth. With my eyes closed, I could recall the touch of him against my fingers, the way he'd smile at me when he didn't think I was looking. I could remember the way his fingers felt in my hair, his tongue in my mouth.

He was right that we weren't friends, but for two weeks...we hadn't been enemies.

Or so I'd thought.

Before I could arrange the words to tell him that, he gave me one last look with those tired blue eyes of his, then he walked away from me without so much as a single glance back.

And I didn't see him again for six and a half years.

PART TWO
THE INITIATION

FLETCHER

The Black Thorn house at Rose Hill University sat on the top of a hill at the boundary of the school's property line. The Sinclair family—*my* family—owned the neighboring plot, which caused more problems for the school and less problems for me. It was difficult for the administration to dictate what we could and couldn't do when the lines about where we did those things weren't always clear. Besides, families like mine only got as powerful as we were by spending generations blurring those lines anyway.

Rose Hill University schooled the cream of the crop as far as power went. Personalities were often lacking, but that was to be expected when you were the kind of people who'd never been told no. I'd been told no quite often in my life, though, a bitter fact I carried very close to my chest and never spoke about. That was how I often found myself on the weekends at the house, surrounded by people who had never been told no and would rarely tell *me* no.

They were entertainment.

But I was still bored.

"Can you fuck a little quieter?" I asked, stepping over the tangled mess of sweaty bodies on the floor.

It was the fall of my senior year at Rose Hill, and everything was about to change. I'd spent the last three years like any other student, attending parties and classes, counting down the days until I flipped a tassel from one side of the mortarboard to the other. Except where other students would walk away from the rivalries and pettiness of college life, I'd only dip deeper into those trenches. The start of my final year in college meant I was finally ready to assume my role as president of The Black Thorn Society, an underhanded group of men with too much money and not enough boundaries.

The fraternity itself was a ruse. A complicated masquerade of men who knew better and men who didn't. I found myself envious of those who didn't because they were the ones fucking and sweating and hoping to get closer to those who did. They all believed these were childish games and hazing meant to build character, but only a handful knew the truth. The upcoming initiation was a test of loyalty, nothing more.

It was my welcome to a world that I would have rather burned to the ground.

Summer was on the way out and initiation weekend was coming. Everyone who wanted to pretend to be anyone was trying their hardest to impress us on the off-chance they could earn a spot in our house and among our ranks. Initiation weekend meant it was time for the Black Thorns to have a president on campus again because the spot could only be held by a Sinclair, and up until now, it had been my father. Even though I'd spent my whole life being trained for this moment, being so close to opportunity and control was an aphrodisiac… even for me. It was hard to not be drunk with power after a lifetime of having decisions made for me. RHU was my first tease of freedom. A trial run for one year before being released into the proper ranks of my family and the men my family controlled.

"Sorry, Fletcher," my second, Daren, said with a grunt, his back arching up like a cat as he came inside whatever little freshman had been stupid enough to get under him.

"You know the rules," I said.

It was a warning meant for his ears alone. Anyone who tried to fuck their way into my good graces was out.

Stupider men had tried that before and, once, I'd almost fallen for it.

Never again.

"I do," Daren said with a laugh. Sweat beaded on his forehead and fell down onto the younger man's back. "He doesn't."

"You're terrible."

"Thank you."

"I'm going for a walk," I said, "leaving my phone."

It was a warm night, still too much like summer for

my liking, but the air in the house was thick with the smell of sex and I needed a break from it. I needed a break from my life and what was about to become of it. Even though I was more than ready for the freedom, the path to get there was beyond daunting.

The man with a cock up his ass whimpered, his dick leaking cum against his belly, and Daren gave me a mock salute before wiping the mess onto his fingers and smearing it onto his dick like it was lube before sinking back in. I closed the door behind me on the way out, wishing I could be like Daren, wishing I could be like anyone who was able to separate their heart from their cock long enough to just get off.

Not to imply I was a virgin, because I definitely wasn't. I'd lost the right to call myself that my freshman year in high school when I'd walked Sarah Reynolds back to her room after watching her fail her math final. She was distraught, beyond consolation, and I'd never admit it to another soul, but so was I. I took advantage of her that day. Or maybe she'd taken advantage of me and she just didn't know it. We were both not the best versions of ourselves back then, only one of us hiding that truth from the other.

With trembling fingers and lips that tasted like cherries, she asked for a distraction and I gave her one.

It was over quickly, and I called my father on the way back to my room to tell him about it. He wasn't even impressed. He acted like I'd called to tell him I cleaned my room or showed up on time for a tutoring session. I supposed that, to him, it was the same thing.

A command being given and an order being followed.

Without another word to anyone in the house, I made my way down the winding old staircase and out the front door. Black Thorn house was a monstrosity of a building, with black siding, four gables, and a wraparound porch offering immaculate views of the valley below. From my bedroom on the third floor of the house, I could even see Rose Hall, all the way on the other edge of the acreage owned by the college. That was a view—and a reminder—I could live without, but my father told me once the placement of the president's private room had been on purpose.

"So you never wake up without remembering who you're fighting," he'd said.

My first morning as president, I'd stared across the property at Rose Hall, wondering if Gideon was there. If he was awake. If he was staring back at me.

My ribs burned and twisted at the thought of him, contorting like a gnarled oak tree in the middle of my chest. Shortly thereafter I'd ordered Daren to hang blackout curtains and I'd never opened them since.

Avoiding Gideon North at Rose Hill University had proved to be far easier than it had at Rose Hill Prep...namely because he'd fallen behind after taking an F in our first year English class. One term later, his father pulled him out of the school entirely, and I'd never known such relief. It was impossible to look at him without hating myself, without hating my father. It took months after his departure for my anxiety to settle, and months after that for my routine to reassert itself. The years passed, and that sixteen year-old boy I'd been—along with all of his dreams—was long gone. I moved on to college unscathed, made it through three years without so much as a hint of Gideon North, and then the summer before my last year started, he showed up on campus looking nothing like the boy I remembered him to be.

At some point, Gideon had finally hit a growth spurt, shooting up well past my six-foot-one frame. I hadn't seen him up close—or in person—but I'd heard enough rumors about the return of the prodigal North son, ready to take his seat of power opposite mine. There was some part of me that had tried to convince myself he'd be out of my life forever. After his disappearance from school and his lack of enrollment at the college level, I thought I'd be free of him for good. But as I often did when it came to Gideon North, I'd let my guard down.

A mistake.

Rumors began to swirl about his arrival for our last year of college, ready to take his rightful spot as the head of the Crimson Roses, but they'd been just that.

Rumors.

Until Daren showed up at dinner in the middle of summer with a streak of pictures on his cell phone that proved Gideon had, in fact, arrived on campus. His hair was longer than before, but just as golden and beautiful. He was taller, more muscular, but still fitted with that lean swimmer's build I remembered him having when we were younger.

"They call him The Beast," Daren had said, not even blinking an eye when I snatched the phone out of his hand to zoom in on the photos of Gideon at the pool. Wearing nothing more than a small and tight Speedo, he cut a sharp line through the water, leaving four other swimmers in his wake.

"Why?"

"Because he is." Daren snorted, like it was some kind of joke I wasn't getting. "He's been here two weeks and he's already obliterated every swim record the college has ever had. He's less than one second off the world record for the hundred meter freestyle."

I tried to give Daren back his phone with as much casual indifference as I could muster. "That's a stupid nickname."

"You should watch him swim."

"I don't want to watch him do anything," I'd snapped. "And neither should you. You may not be a Sinclair, but don't forget whose side you stand at."

That sobered him up.

His earlier admiration gone, Daren gave me a sharp nod and a quick apology.

That was the last we'd spoken about Gideon North. The boy whose heart I'd once broken...along with my own.

Gideon North.

The Beast.

CHAPTER 12

GIDEON

I knew it was only a matter of time until he found me.

There was no place to hide at RHU, but I also hadn't bothered to try. Even though I'd had a rash of nerves when my father demanded my return to school, hiding from Fletcher Sinclair was the last thing on my mind. I wasn't scared of him, and I definitely wasn't avoiding him. My father pulling me out of school so many years prior, was an act intended to save *his* face, not mine.

In hindsight, my punishment over the whole affair with Fletcher had been a driving force toward turning me into the man I was today. Not to imply my father knew exactly what had happened between the two of us; no, he thought it was a breach of privacy at best. If he'd known exactly what Fletcher and I had done together, the things we'd talked about...I don't think either of us would have made it to college in the first place.

He'd withdrawn me from Rose Hill Prep before the term ended. Then he'd locked me away. I didn't see another person, let alone a tutor...a friend, for months. It was a punishment of the cruelest form, meant to remind me that nothing in my life existed without the grace of my father. By the time he allowed me to reintegrate social relationships into my life, I no longer wanted any. I'd thrown myself into swimming, deciding it was easier to focus on my endurance than anything else. My life, I'd quickly realized, would be a game of endurance in and of itself. If I wanted to live, I had to outlast not just Fletcher Sinclair, I had to outlast my father as well.

Instead of sending me back to school, my father eventually hired tutors. I excelled with all my coursework, but the only thing I wanted to do was swim. Being in the water had become my escape. As I was finishing my grade twelve classes, I was able to hold my breath for two minutes. The day he told me he was sending me to Rose Hill for my last year of college education, I held it for three minutes and nineteen seconds.

And then I screamed.

Part of me had naively hoped that after being removed from prep school, I'd managed to avoid the most treacherous and formative years of the next generation of North and Sinclair rivalry, but I'd never been a lucky man. I could have lived a passable life having never set foot on the University property, but my father, as always, had other plans.

After the incident my freshman year, he'd made it a

point to position himself—and our family—on top of the Sinclairs. It was a shift of power, and I'd never understood how he'd managed it, but everyone in his life had become a pawn in his twisted race toward domination and ruination. He'd spent almost seven years putting the pieces in the right place on the board and it was up to me to make his final moves. Ruining the Sinclair dynasty was to be my life's greatest accomplishment, whether I wanted it or not.

I did want it. More than I wanted my next breath.

I fucking loathed Fletcher Sinclair and everything he stood for, including the lies he'd once let me believe. Taking him and his family down was the only thing my father and I would ever see eye to eye on.

It was with that in mind I found myself as Rose Hill University, incoming president of The Crimson Rose Society. Playing the part of an extremely selective fraternal organization, our true purpose had managed to fly under the radar for years. I had no doubt the school knew what we did and what we were about, but if they cared, they knew better than to say anything. It was our money and our success that kept the school and all its overpaid administrators afloat.

My reputation—thankfully—preceded me to campus, and most everyone had given me a wide berth upon my arrival. Everyone except Luca Mandeville, a relatively inconsequential wisp of a man, born to a prominent and long-serving senator father and a judge mother. He hadn't been scared off by my stature, which was closer to six and a half feet tall then; my nickname, The Beast, which I'd earned from aggressive personal records in the pool; or my actual name, which would always be Gideon North.

"Hey, B," Luca said, rapping his knuckles against the door of my bedroom.

I glanced up at him from where I sat on the edge of the bed, my stare previously focused outside toward the tree line. Rose Hill was a huge piece of property, with the society houses flanking each direction like the world's worst kind of compass. Roses to the west and Thorns to the east. My room as president was in the attic, far more sprawling than I'd expected, with enough space for all my books and a king-sized bed that faced a large bay window overlooking the valley.

"What do you want?" I growled.

Luca grinned at me, as undeterred by my moods as he ever was.

"Wanted to see if you were interested in getting dinner."

"I'm not," I told him.

The smile on his face grew. "Want to fuck?"

"I would tear you apart, Luca."

"I wouldn't mind." Luca's cheeks burned bright as if to prove how much he meant the offer.

"Try me on a good day."

"Do you have those? Rumors say no." Luca pushed his gold-frame glasses up the bridge of his nose.

"Rumors are correct." I climbed off the bed, straightening to my full height and leveling a tired look across the room at him. "I think we've used up all my good will for the day."

Luca put on like he was let down, but I didn't believe it for a second. I'd long ago learned people either loved or feared the men in the North family, and both of those feelings came with an unashamed sense of admiration and oftentimes attraction. Luca was only doing what a hundred men before him would have tried if given the chance. The isolation of my teenage years and early twenties left me unprepared to deal with the onslaught of attention after my enrollment at RHU, but my history with Fletcher Sinclair had been preparation enough.

I'd let someone get close to me once.

I was never going to do it again.

CHAPTER 13
FLETCHER

I didn't bother taking a flashlight when I left the house. The lights from the main floor washed down enough of the hillside I could almost see the trail that ran down the back of the slope to the edge of the property line. Normally, at night, I wandered onto Sinclair land, thinking of all the ways I'd burn it to the ground once I was finally in charge, but that night I found myself walking west, deciding to make a loop of the campus instead. It would be well over three miles, which I hoped would be enough time to clear my head. The fall air was still warm enough that my joints didn't ache, so the walk was an easy one, not a punishment.

Though, I would have taken either.

I was by no means isolated or alone, but I did enjoy my quiet interludes because it was the only time I didn't have to pretend. Being a Sinclair had been work since the day I was born, and the reminder of what happened when

I tried to walk away from that responsibility had been beaten into me my freshman year of high school. I'd toed the line ever since, even if there were always stray thoughts in the back of my mind that led me other places.

Halfway around campus, I stopped at a particularly tall tree, pressing my fingers against the rough and peeling bark. The trunk was sticky with sap, and I pushed my fingers together, enjoying the way they stuck before popping free. With a mess on my hand and my attention on it, I almost didn't notice the new light coming from Rose Hall.

It was in the attic. And I knew whose room was in the attic.

Gideon.

He'd been on campus at least two weeks, and though I hadn't seen him, I knew it was impossible to avoid him forever. There were rules and there were rituals because the competition between our families was not without a facade of civility. I had less than a week before we were due to come face to face for the first time since I crossed him at RHP and I definitely was not looking forward to it.

I was a different person, though, and it was a different time. It was ridiculous to think Gideon North would still have any power over me. He was my nemesis. The man I hated beyond all measure, all reason. He was the only man powerful enough to be my downfall.

We both knew it, and my father knew it as well.

Pressing my back against the tree until the bark cut into my spine, I forced myself to look up at the attic room, daring myself to not look away when a tall silhouette appeared in the window. It was dark at the tree line, and I was wearing all black. There wasn't any way for Gideon to see me out there...watching him...but the figure pulled the curtain aside just the same.

I remembered cum on my fingers, sticky like the tree sap, Gideon's slack-jawed, post-orgasm face still as fresh in my memory as if it had happened yesterday.

He hadn't been a beast back then. He'd been the softest thing, gentle and hopeful and all of the things that had no place in a world like ours. He wouldn't have survived. *We* wouldn't have survived. Almost a decade later, and I better understood the reality of our situations in a way he never had. There was too much power, too much money, too many lies wrapped up in the Sinclair and North families for us to pretend we could escape it. And we'd just been two boys who didn't know any better, pretending we were stronger than a generations-long legacy that would still exist after we were gone.

In the window, Gideon let the curtain fall back into place and I snuck out of the shadows, heading off campus and into town. An hour later, I made it to Thornhill Pub and Grub, ready for a drink.

Considering it was the Friday before classes were set to start, the place was packed, mostly with under-classmen who were still excited about all the ways the connections they'd make over the next four years would ruin their lives. Daren had apparently finished fucking because he was against the bar, a completely different man in front of him, ready to spread his legs to get close to the VP of The Black Thorns.

Daren saw me enter, laughing to himself when I rolled my eyes at his next conquest. I didn't judge him for the eager way he took new partners to bed. Sometimes, I envied it. The way he found release from it. Sex, to me, had felt like a responsibility for years, the only responsibility I had any power to ignore. I would often go days—weeks—without, testing my willpower and my resolve before I found myself on the brink of collapse. Then, and only then, would I find a partner.

Hardly.

I'd find a warm and willing body. And then I'd be done with it.

With initiation weekend just around the corner, I'd decided to hold out because...

Well...

There were many tools when it came to the games men like me had to play in life. Money being the most common currency, sex being the second. My self-imposed and short-lived vows of celibacy were one of the only chances I had to keep people from sticking to money when it came to me. Using sex to gain control had always felt like a coward's choice for me. Also too risky and too emotional. I couldn't touch my own cock without picturing Gideon North's shining green eyes and that was bad enough. I didn't want another man to come into my life and make things worse.

While Gideon's reputation as a quiet recluse had

come before him, I'd spent years on the ground making sure nobody had any doubt about the kind of man I was. Ruthless, rough, and unforgiving. I was Fletcher Sinclair, president of The Black Thorn Society, heir to the Sinclair dynasty, and whatever else I decided to make of myself... whatever my father decided to make of me.

I was not a lover. I was not a friend.

I was a threat.

I was the villain.

"Shit, sorry," a soft voice said behind me, a hard shoulder digging into the middle of my back.

I straightened my spine and groaned, grateful to find a distraction from my own tortured thoughts. Turning, I reached behind me, curling my fingers around the wrist of the man who'd knocked into me and effectively stopping him from making an escape.

"Shit, sorry?" I repeated his apology back to him as a question.

When he saw me, a series of things happened, nearly simultaneously.

He tilted his head back to look up at me, hazel eyes wide and scared.

My breath hitched in my throat, expanding until it was almost impossible to breathe.

"I didn't..." he trailed off, licking his lower lip with the tip of his short and oh-so-pink tongue.

"Didn't?"

"Didn't what?" I asked.

"Didn't know it was you."

I flexed my fingers around the delicate bones of his wrist. "And who am I?"

Before he could answer, I was jostled again. This time I knew from scent alone it was Daren behind me, pressing his cheek against the outside of my arm like an over-eager puppy.

"He's a teddy bear," Daren answered, and I elbowed him hard in the gut.

He keeled over, choking and laughing at the same time.

"Definitely not a teddy bear," he rasped, quickly righting himself and pushing his way in between me and the stranger who'd accidentally accosted me. "But he's no one you need to worry about."

"I..." The other man blinked quickly, stare darting from me to Daren and back again.

"He's right," I bit out, unwrapping my fingers from the man's wrist and handing him off to my second. "As far as you're concerned, I'm no one at all."

CHAPTER 14

BELLAMY

Fletcher Sinclair was prettier in person than a man had any right to be. From the broad swell of his shoulders to the punishing grip of his fingers around my wrist, I understood why people of every gender were so quick to throw themselves at him. His hair was dark as coal, but soft in the dim light of the club, his eyes blue as crystals, yet full of barely restrained rage.

"I'm no one at all," he said to me, voice dangerously low, causing an unexpected combination of feelings to churn in the pit of my stomach.

I looked from him to the man who'd swooped in to save me from him, a dashing-looking man, older than me and smaller than Fletcher, with a tangled mess of dark blond hair and curious brown eyes.

Fletcher let go of my wrist, pins and needles prickling beneath the skin as he all but shoved me straight into the stranger's waiting arms.

"You're all right," the second man whispered, breath hot against the top of my ear.

I was anything but all right, but I had no choice but to believe him.

Three days into school and I was already failing at the one thing my father had asked of me.

"He's all bark and no bite," my unexpected savior said next, giving me a turn so we were face to face. "I'm Daren, by the way. Daren Moore.

"I know who you are," I said softly, immediately regretting the slip.

"Everyone knows who I am," he said, looking proud. "But I have no idea who *you* are."

Licking my lips, I blinked up at him nervously. It took all my willpower to not look over my shoulder so I could see where Fletcher had gone off to. I'd see him again soon enough, assuming everything went as it was supposed to. I pulled my hands together in front of me, rubbing my thumb over the place Fletcher had just held me.

"Bellamy," I whispered. "Bellamy Marchant."

I watched the gears turn in Daren's head as he tried to place my name or my face, coming up short.

"Bellamy," he practically purred my name, stepping closer and taking my wrist into his hand, replacing the memory of Fletcher's fingers with his own.

The confusing feelings in my stomach quickly sorted themselves, arousal taking precedent over everything else. My skin burned—how did Daren not feel it—and heat pooled between my legs, causing my cock to make an embarrassing twitch for attention. Thankfully, we weren't close enough for him to feel my interest.

"I'm an initiate," I blurted, trying to pull my arm back.

His hold tightened, amusement coloring his features. "Good for you. I'm the deputy."

"I know," I said. "Doesn't it matter?"

I had a very limited understanding of what I was walking into as a first year initiate, an offering, for The Black Thorn Society at Rose Hill University, but I had a sneaking suspicion it was a less than calculating plan to fall into bed with the deputy when I'd been intended for the president.

I was the youngest of six siblings, all boys, and I'd grown up in a relatively middle class home. I didn't want for much, except attention, until my senior year of high school when I finally got it. I'd come home from school and my parents were sitting at the dining room table, my mother looking distraught, her eyes red-rimmed and her lips pulled into a frown. My father, though...my father looked victorious. A brand new watch sparked on his wrist and a signet ring on his pinky far larger than his wedding ring on the next finger.

"I know you wanted to go to California for college," my father said.

My heart sank as I lowered myself into my seat at the table at the far end, five seats away from my father.

"I do."

"You're going back east instead," he'd told me, "to Rose Hill."

"Why?"

"It's my alma mater," he said, and my mother covered her mouth to stifle a cry.

I glanced at her nervously, twisting my hands together under the table.

"Why me, though?" That was what I'd meant all along. I had five older brothers who'd been allowed to pursue the education they wanted. Why were my hopes being taken away from me at the last minute?

"You're being given a chance your brothers never had," he told me. "You can redeem my legacy. Build your own."

"I just want to be a journalist," I said, digging my nails into my palm. "I've been accepted to USC already."

"And you've been accepted to Rose Hill as well," my dad interrupted. "You have a full scholarship there and an automatic acceptance into The Black Thorn Society."

With that statement, my entire life changed. I had no say in it, no more goals of my own. My ability to pursue journalism at Rose Hill was directly tied to the success I had with the tasks from my father. He'd gotten me a golden ticket, he'd said, though it felt like anything but.

The society will keep you safe, keep us all safe.

My mother had left the table at that point, and my dad knocked his tarnished signet ring against the weathered oak surface.

"Fletcher Sinclair is the only ally you need," he said before standing up and leaving me alone at the table, my hopes and dreams shattered around me like glass. "So make him one."

Fletcher Sinclair wasn't the one touching me, though. It was Daren Moore, deputy of the society I was on the cusp of initiating into who held my wrist—my future—in his hands.

"I think tonight, I can decide what matters," Daren said, tongue licking slow lines up and down the corner of his mouth. "Assuming you find that agreeable."

Daren wasn't Fletcher, but he was close enough.

"I think I do," I told him.

Tightening his hold on my wrist, Daren let out a hum that reverberated up the bones of my arm and straight into the center of my chest. He sank his teeth into his bottom lip, fighting back a smile that looked far more predatory than I thought possible.

"Let's go someplace quiet, then," he said. "So we can get better acquainted with each other."

CHAPTER 15

DAREN

Bellamy was pretty.

Clark was pretty.

Jack was pretty.

The guy before Jack was pretty.

Everyone I'd fucked since coming back to campus for my senior year was pretty, but they were nowhere near as beautiful and perfect and *mine* as Luca Mandeville. They were playthings and distractions, a useless balm to soothe the ache of being torn away from the one person I wanted most in the world.

We'd agreed, and he knew I wasn't a saint. Neither was he.

We both had marching orders from our parents. Mine, to hold steady at the right hand of Fletcher Sinclair. His, to fuck Gideon North into submission. I imagined only one of us was going to have a successful year, but not for lack of trying on Luca's part. Gideon North hadn't earned his nickname out of nowhere. He was a beast of a competitor, a beast of a man.

He looked like he would tear you apart with his dick. Fuck you against a wall so hard the plaster would shatter. He looked like all of the things Luca wanted most in a man. All of the things I had spent the past year being for him.

We'd met in the way of most at RHU, sitting a little too close together in class thanks to a teacher who didn't care—or didn't know—about the hierarchy of the Thorns and the Roses. That didn't matter because he and I knew who the other was. We knew what we were walking into, but some things were stronger than the wills of our fathers. Luca and I were young and hopeful, knowing better while not caring. We were careful; we were skilled at keeping secrets, at lurking in the shadows. But as the summer before our last year wound down, and the rules and expectations that came with our roles ramped up...

We had one last chance to be together.

Luca smelled like sugar when he cried, and I had a sweet tooth that would never be satisfied. I'd dug my nails into his hips so hard he bled, our own kind of ritual meant to hold us together even though we had to remain apart. Things would be different once we were out of the constraints of RHU because, even though the Thorns and the Roses were a lifetime commitment, being past initiation came with enough freedom for us to return to the dark corners and the quiet spaces we'd found each other in to begin with.

I distracted myself with being the perfect deputy to Fletcher and a willing cock to anyone who wanted it. If the other initiates thought they could fuck their way to the top, I wasn't going to stop them from trying. They'd learn the hard way that what mattered wasn't whose bed you warmed, but whose table you occupied, whose whiskey you drank, whose secrets you kept.

Luca.

Luca and I kept the biggest secret of all.

It was his body in my mind when I ushered Bellamy up the stairs to my bedroom, Luca's hands and his mouth I thought of when I pushed the door closed and backed Bellamy against it. It was Luca's cries I remembered when Bellamy whimpered.

"I'm scared."

"Don't be," I whispered, burying my face into the crook of his neck and licking the salt from his skin. "I won't hurt you unless you want me to."

"I don't, but…"

Bellamy settled his hands on my waist, head thumping softly against the door as he arched to make more room for me. I reached between us and undid his fly, shoved his pants down to his ankles.

"But what?" I asked, nipping and kissing my way up to his ear.

I teased my hand behind the waistband of his boxers and felt the hard heat of his cock against my fingers.

"I need to get over it," he said.

He moaned, thrusting toward my hand.

"If I wanted it to hurt..." Bellamy trailed off, and I wrapped my fingers around the base of his shaft.

"I don't think you do." Using his cock as a leash, I walked him across the room toward the bed, easing him down onto his back. "Take your boxers off and spread your legs."

He scrambled out of his plaid underwear, leaving his faded gray t-shirt on.

At least he was a good listener.

Bellamy flattened his feet against my blankets and bent his knees, taking his cock and balls into his hand and lifting them to show me his hairless, pink asshole.

"Do you wax your asshole, Bellamy?" I asked, crawling onto the bed between his legs. I had lube in my pocket because I hadn't planned on taking anyone home, instead fucking in an alley or a bathroom somewhere.

He didn't answer me, but he blushed like a tulip in the spring.

I didn't bother taking my pants off, my shirt, I never got naked for any of these men. Pulling my jeans open enough to get my dick out, I rolled a condom down my length and slicked it with enough lube to make sure it didn't hurt...too much.

"A little pain then?" I asked, blood already thrumming for how much I wanted to give him so much more than a little.

He was too innocent to be half naked on my bed with his asshole on display like he was...like he was a prize to be won. Narrowing my eyes, I rocked back and gave him a slow onceover, really looking at him for the first time since he'd knocked into Fletcher at the pub.

Bellamy was short and slender, but not without muscle. His skin like gold and his hair much the same. His hazel eyes were nearly amber in the light of my bedroom, his lips parted and puffy, teeth marks still visible in the lower one from where he'd been biting it.

He wanted me to hurt him, but he was afraid of it.

He had enough hair on him for me to be certain he'd definitely waxed or at least shaved his ass recently, which struck me as an odd choice for someone who was as nervous to fuck as he was. I didn't know for certain, but I would have bet an hour alone with Luca that Bellamy Marchant was meant to be Fletcher's offering for the initiation this weekend and he had no idea what he was in for.

"A little hurt," he whispered.

I could give him that.

Lining my cock up with his hole, I braced myself with one hand beside his head, then I did my best to get him ready for initiation weekend.

For Fletcher Sinclair.

CHAPTER 16

GIDEON

Luca returned from dinner just before midnight with a fair amount of vodka in his bloodstream. I listened to him climb the stairs to my attic bedroom, and I knew what was coming before he even leaned his weight against the door frame.

"B," he said softly, a reduction of the nickname I'd never asked for and barely earned.

"Go to sleep, Luca," I warned.

He huffed, taking a step into my bedroom.

I'd been perched in front of the window since he left, alternating between staring across campus and reading a book I'd known by heart for four years. When he walked into my room, one unsure step after another, I closed the well-worn paperback, spine malleable against my palm.

There were a lot of problems with Luca. The first being he never walked away from a challenge. The second being he was too pretty for his own good, all long legs and graceful arms, with those big brown eyes behind the gold frames of his glasses.

The third...

As he closed the space between us, I forgot the third.

And the fourth.

And the fifth.

"How long has it been?" he asked.

"Since when?"

The corner of his mouth quirked up into a knowing grin. "Since you let someone get you off."

I huffed a long breath out my nose, clenching my jaw.

There was no way in hell I was going to tell Luca how long it had been since I'd been with another man. The timeline was for me, the name of the man...for me. While I knew I could trust Luca as much as anyone else, he was my VP after all, my most trusted second, there were limits to what he was meant to know.

He didn't know, for example, about the violence that had gotten me to where I was, and the lack of it that had gotten him to his current state. The things he knew were superficial at best. He knew I was Gideon North, but he didn't know my favorite books, my favorite songs. He didn't know it was hard for me to sleep most nights, didn't know how I took my coffee, or why I didn't open up to strangers. He assumed lots of things about me, though, letting the rumors do most of the heavy lifting so I didn't have to.

"I warned you earlier about this," I said, setting my book down.

Luca was pretty and his hair looked soft, and he was standing dangerously close to me, swaying gently as he steadied his weight on his feet.

"I don't listen well."

"That's going to be a problem."

"Maybe you should punish me," he suggested, reaching behind him and rucking up his shirt. It was over his head and on the floor before I could protest, revealing a dark rose tattoo spread across the center of his chest.

It was the Crimson Rose crest.

Luca was even prettier up close, his pale body dusted with light brown curls that ran down his stomach, disappearing behind the waistband of his dark jeans. He was far smaller than me, shorter and skinnier, but not without strength to his build. The tattoo over his heart was a combination of blacks and dark reds, a stark contrast to the lightness of his skin. Even though he couldn't have been more different from me, the tattoo was a reminder Luca and I were very much the same.

"I told you I would tear you apart, Luca," I warned him again, my self-control hurtling toward its limit.

It had been easy, since Fletcher, because my father had isolated me for so long by the time I returned to public life everyone was scared of me. I didn't have to push people away; they stayed back on their own. Luca was an anomaly, absolutely undeterred when I begged him off. If anything, my resistance was an allure, bringing him deeper into my orbit.

Every breath brought both of us one step closer to the

point of no return. Every time I told him no, he came closer.

"What if I do all the work?" he asked, popping open the button on his jeans.

"You're drunk."

"I'll recite you the alphabet backward," he offered, pushing his glasses up the bridge of his nose, bringing my attention to his wide black pupils and flushed cheeks.

I chuckled, dragging my tongue back and forth across my lower lip while I watched him. I was hard, grateful Luca hadn't bothered to call me out on it. He'd instead kept as much of his attention on my face as he could manage, like staring down a predator to let them know you weren't afraid. And it was with our stares connected that he pulled down his zipper and shoved his pants to his ankles. It was with eye contact that he reached into his underwear and stroked his cock, jaw quivering when he reached the tip.

It was too intimate.

Too familiar.

Too much of a memory.

"Get out," I said quietly, swallowing hard.

Luca gave another stroke down the length of his dick, and he didn't back away. He had the decency to look down, but it wasn't to do me any favors. He was trying to scope out the situation between my legs.

"B, come on."

His plea was breathy, needy...almost impossible to ignore.

"Get out, Luca." I stood from my seat, towering over him.

Luca was right. He wasn't that drunk because he didn't fall over. And he wasn't that drunk because he took the meaning of my stare to heart in less than five seconds.

"I'm sorry," he said, grabbing his clothes up off the floor. He stumbled into his pants, staggering backward toward the door with an apologetic smile on his face.

I'd never understand why Luca Mandeville wasn't afraid of me the same way everyone else was.

"It's not *you*, Luca," I said softly, palming the erection that the sight of him had grown between my legs.

He gave me a sad smile and a half shrug. "You told me earlier it wasn't a good day. No harm, no foul?"

"No harm," I assured him.

Luca pulled his shirt over his head and adjusted his glasses back onto his nose. "If you ever change your mind..."

I chuckled, his audacity maybe the sexiest thing about him. "I know where to find you."

CHAPTER 17

LUCA

It was fine that Gideon didn't want to fuck me yet. I wouldn't stop trying because I never stopped trying. There wasn't a single thing in my life that anyone simply handed me. I'd fought for all of it, my name included.

I was the bastard son of Charles Mandeville, born to a mistress out of wedlock. That wasn't so uncommon in circles men like Gideon and I grew up in, but being abandoned by your mother on a white marble doorstep at the age of six had to have been somewhat unusual. Being housed in servants' quarters until a paternity test came back to prove the truth of the handwritten letter clutched in your hand, not normal.

The letter was the last thing I had of my mother. Not that I remembered her in any way, but sometimes when I couldn't sleep, I would trace my fingers over the worn and tired cursive to remind myself of where I'd come from and where I was meant to go. I would never know what my mother was thinking the day she gave up and dropped me off at the Mandeville mansion, but I like to tell myself if she'd have known what was in store for me, she would have acted differently. Maybe she'd imagined getting a Mandeville into her bed would be enough to secure her the future she always dreamed about, but that would have been childish of her. Men like my father took mistress after mistress after mistress, his wife always turning a blind eye because she had already secured what everyone else wanted.

After confirming I was, in fact, my father's child, I found myself moved out of the servants' quarters and into a small room in an unused wing of the house, far away from my father and even farther away from my half-siblings. An older sister and a younger brother. They despised me as much as my step-mother did, which was fine. I didn't care for them much either.

I always assumed I'd attend the right schools and meet the right people as a courtesy, not a birthright. So when my father told me three years earlier I was going to RHU, I was shocked. When he'd called me up later to let me know I was expected to step in as second my senior year, I'd choked on my tongue. It was as much a recognition of my lineage that he'd ever given me, and it only made my younger brother hate me more.

"Get close to the Norths," my father had said. "Make me proud."

Gideon North represented nothing to me except

opportunity. If I could get him to trust me, I'd finally earn my father's respect. But my third year at school, things had gotten complicated.

I'd fallen in love, and not with Gideon North.

Duty had eventually required me to push my need for Daren aside and call up the things that had worked for me throughout my teenage and early adult years in an attempt to get close to Gideon after his arrival on campus. Unfortunately, it all fell flat when it came to him. I could tell he wanted me, or at least wanted to fuck me, but for some reason, he held himself back.

He'd been close this time, I told myself, slinking downstairs to my own private bedroom. My cock still ached and while I was definitely using sex to try and get to Gideon on behalf of my father, I really did just want him to fuck me. It had been weeks since I was with Daren, the bruises shaped like his fingers nearly gone from my skin.

Gideon talked about hurting me and tearing me apart, losing control, and that was exactly what I wanted from him. If I couldn't have the man I loved, at least I could get fucked until I forgot both of our names.

My favorite kind of sex was the kind that left me a little worried I'd gotten in over my head before getting on my back. It was the way most of my father's friends liked to fuck, and the power that came from that kind of thing was heady.

It was what I knew.

A sliver of fear mixed with dripping arousal was

enough to have my cock shooting off like a goddamn geyser, and when I made it back to my room and slammed the door closed, I tried to imagine how Gideon would fuck, if he ever did.

He was so much bigger than me, taller and broader, and there was no way his cock didn't match the rest of him. Maybe he would use lube, maybe he wouldn't. Maybe he would spit on his thick shaft and impale me on it, lifting my toes off the ground for how hard he forced his way into me. Most of my father's friends were small-cocked old men who preferred to use their hands to hurt me.

That was okay sometimes too.

I imagined Gideon could do both.

Licking my palm and taking my cock back into my hand, I closed my eyes and pretended Gideon's fingers curled around my throat, taking my breath away while he pounded himself into me. I didn't think Gideon would choke me until I passed out, but that had happened before and I didn't hate it. It was a little disconcerting, but the orgasms were worth it.

My father had a friend that liked to fuck that way too.

I imagined Gideon would rut into me like the beast he was, growling and grunting as he tried to saw me in half with his dick. In my fantasy, he'd come so much inside of me, it would drip down my thighs before he even pulled out, and he'd call me a loose whore for not being able to keep it all in.

Shivering, the thoughts brought a sharp and unexpected orgasm up from the base of my spine and I came with a stifled cry. Collapsing onto my knees, I painted the floor with spurts of sticky, white cum, then I cleaned it up with my tongue, sighing and closing my eyes.

Trying to forget that father had a lot of friends.

Trying to forget Daren too.

CHAPTER 18

FLETCHER

It was initiation weekend, and Daren stepped up close behind me, pressing his palm against the small of my back. We were alone in my third floor bedroom, muffled conversation drifting up from the basement.

"This is a barbaric tradition," he said.

"You're not wrong. But..."

"It's still a tradition," he finished for me.

I nodded, shivering when he dragged his fingers up my spine and back down again.

"I don't want to do it" he said, like he'd meant it as an offering even though neither of us was in a position to let him out of his responsibilities.

"This isn't a matter of want."

The initiation had been a standard for generations, my father and grandfather both bore the scars from it, and shortly I would as well. It was no small affair when a new Sinclair came to power, and the fact Gideon and I were both the same age, coming into our roles at the same time...

Almost unheard of.

Either way, whether both of us together or one of us alone, my father had done right by keeping the reality of initiation weekend a secret until it was too late for me to back out, because if I'd known the truth, I wasn't sure I'd have gone through with it. No, that was a lie. If I hadn't walked away from the Sinclair name yet, the initiation ritual wouldn't have been the thing to push me any closer to that outcome.

The incoming president—in this case presidents—had to go through an initiation ritual at the start of their senior year. Tradition was tradition and even though I'd been at Rose Hill for the first three years of school, the president's seat sat vacant until my final year. There was no real reason for it I could make sense of, save counting three more years to keep the heir in line. The initiation was meant to demonstrate a handful of things—the first of which being my loyalty to my family, the second being everyone else's loyalty to me. It was intended to demean us all, but under the guise of an outdated ritual hazing designed to keep everyone—including me—in line.

"What is the point of whipping you?" Daren asked, still positioned behind me, hand still steady on my back. "What's it meant to prove?"

"It's to demonstrate my self-control," I told him, swallowing. "My self-restraint."

"Chasing a first year through the woods with blood streaming down you back doesn't reek of either of those things."

"The chase is the reward." I turned halfway so I could see his face. "The restraint comes from not tearing *you* into pieces first."

"I don't want to do this," he repeated.

"Honestly, Daren." I needed to get his reluctant voice out of my head and get my shit together. I didn't need doubt. I needed focus. I needed to breathe. "What you want doesn't fucking matter in this house and it never will."

The initiation rituals had been guarded secrets until it was too late for any of us to try and back out. We'd learned Daren was meant to whip me with a leather strap until my skin was flayed open, all while I recited my promises and vows to him and everyone else in attendance. Then, as a reward for the dedication demonstrated by both of us, I was to chase an offering—an initiate—into the woods and claim them as my own. It was feral and primal, surely designed to beg submission from everyone around me. It was also designed as a reminder to me that sex was as much of a bargaining tool as money ever would be.

"You're right. Sorry, Fletcher." His answer was quiet and responsible. It was contained and it was archaic. It was what was expected of him. "Can I..."

He trailed off, jaw ticking just below his ear.

"Can you what?"

"Nothing."

"You can do whatever you have to," I told him. "Count out the five and make sure you draw blood before you're finished so you don't have to do any more than that."

Daren looked like he wanted to argue, the protest tangled around his pursed lips and the tense set of his shoulders. At his side, his fingers flexed, knuckles whitening.

"And then I'll clean you up when you make it back," he said.

"I won't need a nursemaid."

"You can't take one part of the ritual and not the other," Daren snapped. "What's the fucking point again? Teamwork?"

"There's no team here," I said.

Sure, the ritual had always been sold that way to people who weren't in charge, but my father told me a different story when we'd talked about the initiation expectations. The second was meant to draw first blood and clean up the mess because that was what was expected of them in the real world. It was as much a loyalty test for Daren as it would be for me. But while Daren viewed the process as a service, I saw it for what it really was.

Someone lesser than me obeying orders. Even uncomfortable ones.

It was his chance to prove himself to me, while I proved myself to everyone else.

"Do you have everything you need for the chase?" he

asked, clearing his throat and taking his hand away from my back.

"Yes," I rasped, grateful for the change in topic.

I had a bottle of lubricant in my pocket and a condom, even though I wasn't supposed to use the latter. My father would have been pissed if he knew, but he never would. I'd make sure whichever first year had been selected as the offering didn't ever know I used one, and my father would be none the wiser.

The chase was the part of the ritual I was worried about the most, not because I had concerns about being able to pursue a first year through the woods after getting whipped until I bled, but because I didn't *want* to. Of all the things I'd done because my father had told me, getting whipped on a dais for the entire Black Thorn Society to see was the least appalling of them. Racing after an initiate into the darkness just to pin him down and rut him into the ground in a display of dominance?

Just because it was the way I *chose* to fuck didn't mean it was the way I *wanted* to fuck.

Especially with someone who wasn't entirely willing.

"Do you know who was chosen for the offering?" I asked.

Time was ticking, and I tore myself away from Daren for one last check in the mirror. The one part of the ceremony I had control over was my outfit. I'd settled on a pair of black jeans and black leather boots. The boots were half laced, which would make running a little problematic, but I wasn't in a hurry to claim and conquer. And the wait would probably be good for all of us.

"I've heard rumors, but nothing for certain," Daren said.

"What are the rumors?"

"His name is Bellamy Marchant."

"The name isn't familiar," I murmured.

"You didn't stay long enough to ask it," he said.

I searched his reflection out in the mirror, one brow raised.

"He's the kid from earlier in the week, the tiny little thing who bumped into you at the pub."

One day I really was going to crack a molar for how much teeth grinding I did. Even though I hadn't known his name, I'd remember Bellamy Marchant and his ghostly hazel eyes for the rest of my life. He looked too much like the boy Gideon used to be for me to ever forget him.

"Why do you think it's him?" I asked, swallowing down any hint of interest—or resistance.

Daren grinned at me, the change in conversation washing away his concerns about walking me down to the basement and beating me until I bled. "Because he says all kinds of things when he wants a cock up his ass, Fletcher. Ask me how I know."

CHAPTER 19
DAREN

The basement was dark, nothing more than candlelight illuminating the temporary raised stage against the western-facing wall. The air was thick, nerves of the first year students almost tangible, excitement of everyone else much the same. Counting Fletcher and myself, there were fifty-four people in the basement, but only three of us really mattered.

Fletcher, myself, and the offering...Bellamy.

I'd been correct in my guess about his role in the Thorns, but the fact I hadn't been sure was enough of a reminder of just how deep secrets in this society ran. The offering was always the closest kept secret, proof to all of us that we had no control over our own lives. There were men older and far more powerful than us who pulled the strings in all things.

In all ways.

The leather strop creaked under my grip, the original

use of the tool-long forgotten when it came to its need between these four walls. There were no blades to sharpen here, only free will to dull. I swallowed, my wary stare shifting toward Fletcher in the middle of the stage, still shirtless but looking far more sure of himself than he had when we were together in his bedroom.

"Together tonight we stand on the precipice of our destiny," Fletcher said, voice steady and clear. He gestured broadly before curling his fingertips against his palms and letting his hands fall to his sides. "We find ourselves reminded that we are the guardians of knowledge, the keepers of secrets."

He paused, and I looked toward Bellamy, the secret that neither of us had kept. Bellamy swallowed thickly, his Adam's apple visibly bobbing in his throat, and he tangled his fingers together in front of him before giving up and shoving his hands into the pockets of his white linen pants.

"Outside these walls lurks chaos and discontent, the likes of which we must never succumb to. In pursuit of our highest good, we are stronger than all of the wants of the world combined," Fletcher said, turning his back and raising his voice to finish the recitation passed down by his father, "I'll take my vows before you now. My blood a promise. The offering a seal."

"Go," I said to Bellamy, who turned and ran so fast from the room, it was like he'd never been there at all.

Fletcher turned and flattened his palms against the brick

wall in front of him, fingers splayed, the spread of his arms drawing attention to how broad and strong his shoulders and back were. I stepped up behind him, knowing better than to wipe my sweaty palms before saying my piece of the vow.

"Five promises," I said loud enough for him and everyone behind me to hear. "One oath."

"My life belongs to the Thorns," he said.

I cracked the strop through the air, the thick leather landing hard and loud across his back. The spot immediately burned red, but no blood was drawn.

"Secrecy," I recited the first promise.

"I vow to guard the secrets of the Thorns with my life," Fletcher said with a grunt.

I raised the strop and hit him a second time.

"Tradition."

"I honor those who came before me."

I flexed my grip on the leather strap, delivering the third hit.

"Unity," I said, biting the inside of my cheek. I'd yet to break skin with the ancient leather implement. If only they'd let me use my hands...

"We are stronger together," Fletcher offered the return to me, and I could hear the anger in his voice. He knew I hadn't broken skin yet and we were running out of promises to make.

"Discretion," I called out next, landing the fourth strike. Blood pebbled just beneath his skin, but not enough to count.

"My secrets are solely my own and what's yours is mine."

We both knew that was a lie. *We* weren't allowed to have secrets, at least not for long. Even with Luca across the campus, it was only a matter of time until someone found out about the two of us. It was only a matter of time until our free will was fully stripped, either by promise of power or threat of loss.

Fighting back my knowledge of how untrue the vows of the Thorns truly were, I worked my jaw, doing everything I could to block out the labored breathing coming from the group assembled behind me. They were nobody of substance. Their secrets were Fletcher's and mine were his, and they wouldn't be anyone who mattered in their hopefully long and definitely insignificant lives. Being a Black Thorn didn't count for much, beyond ensuring you were beholden to the men who *ran* the Thorns.

Men like my father, like Fletcher's father.

Their fathers before them.

And soon, us.

Regardless of my own displeasure over the unfairness of the hands we'd all been dealt, the initiation ritual was clear. In my role as the deputy, I reminded Fletcher of the five tenets that had held The Black Thorns together for generations, that secured our place toward the top of politics, finance, society. He offered his oaths in return, a combination of the five promises making one whole, then he sealed his vow with the two most meaningful things a man possessed.

Blood and seed.

It was up to me to draw the blood, him to offer the rest.

Tightening my fingers around the strop, I raised my arm high and struck him for the fifth—and hopefully final—time. Fletcher's knuckles went white against the brick wall and two parallel lines of blood bloomed across his back, a clear stripe from his shoulder blade across his spine. Blood prickled up from the angle of the fourth strike as well, the skin finally pulled too taut to hold him together any longer.

"Loyalty," I demanded of him, watching the droplets roll down his back.

"Above all," he said, rolling his shoulders and straightening to his full height.

"Above all," the rest of the Thorns uttered the promise from their place below us.

Fletcher turned to face me, to face the room. With his shoulders pulled back and his chest puffed out, he truly looked like the powerful man he was meant to be. Dark hair fell across his bright eyes, and his lip curled up in a predatory and hungry way that had me stepping to the side.

"Bind yourself with the Thorns and go forth with purpose," I offered up the final piece of my promise to Fletcher, letting the strop fall at my feet.

As planned, Fletcher said nothing. He jumped off the stage and set off at a run.

The chase of the offering was on.

CHAPTER 20

BELLAMY

Everything hurt and I wanted to die.

I'd torn fingernails fighting Fletcher off of me, screamed until my throat ached, until he'd sealed his massive hand across my mouth and warned me in the most dangerous and low voice to shut the fuck up.

I'd listened.

With every thrust of his hips, *Fletcher Sinclair is the only ally you need* rang through my head like a bell, and I didn't know in what world this was what my father had intended. But he had to have known, right? This society was part of his legacy, and now it was mine. He must have understood what fate he'd signed me up for with the scholarship and the invitation to the Thorns.

Nothing my father had told me, nothing I'd done earlier in the week with Daren—or any man before him—had prepared me for the brutal onslaught of the way Fletcher

Sinclair fucked. He'd chased, he'd caught, and then he'd claimed. That was the expectation and those were the rules, but I didn't understand the why of it. Why had my father signed me up for this? What would I get from this?

What would *he* get from this?

I knew it was meant to be scary, meant to be rough, but this was beyond terrifying. Sobbing, I screwed my eyes closed while Fletcher finished, finally rocking back onto his heels with a frown. He tucked himself back into his pants before I opened my eyes.

"You really didn't want this," he said quietly, using the back of his hand to wipe sweat off his brow.

"Who would want this?" I scrambled away from him, tucking my knees against my chest. My shirt was torn, my ankle throbbed from when he'd taken me down to the ground and climbed on top of me.

"It's..." He frowned, scratching the bridge of his nose. "You really didn't..."

"I'm not from here," I said. "I...my father."

Recognition flashed across his face, and then regret, and then it was gone and he was Fletcher Sinclair again, the man I'd seen at the pub earlier in the week who'd warned me away from him and instead sent me home with Daren instead. I'd known then; I'd understood that I would have to give myself to him, but I hadn't been prepared. Not physically and not mentally.

"You knew I was meant to fuck you tonight, didn't you?"

"Yes, but..." I trailed off, and Fletcher had helped me to my feet, dusting me off as best he could.

"You knew it was a chase, a game for us to play."

I nodded, because I had known. But I hadn't *known*.

"I'm sorry," he said softly, reaching toward me and picking a stick out of my hair. "I...it's..."

He gave me a wary look, turning away from me and tugging his hair at the roots hard enough to make him grunt.

"You're bleeding," I said, reaching out and pressing my fingertips against the small of his back. Thick rivulets of blood ran down his shoulder and spine, some blood fresh and some already dried. At my touch, he startled and pulled away, spinning back to face me head on.

"I deserve it for..."

"For what?" I asked, taking another step toward him.

There was no doubt in my mind Fletcher Sinclair was one of the most dangerous men I'd ever meet, but he was also one of the most magnetic. Undeniably handsome, even as he came apart in front of me. With blood and dirt and sweat streaked across his skin, his hands trembling and unsure, I wanted to throw myself back onto the forest floor so he could finish what he started.

The fear was an aphrodisiac, and I was drunk on it. Scared and horny, all at the same time.

"You didn't want that," he said.

I gestured at the erection between my legs. "I didn't mind it."

"You fought me."

"I was scared."

"Because you didn't want it," he said again.

I palmed my cock, hips gently thrusting toward him this time, "I didn't mind it."

"But you didn't want it."

"I didn't expect it, but I want it very much, I think," I admitted, voice barely louder than a whisper. He shifted his weight, a twig snapping under the sole of his boot.

"You liked being chased," he said. "You liked being forced."

"I didn't." I gave him a crooked shrug. "Not when it was happening, but now...I'm sad it's over."

Fletcher exhaled and shook his head, blinking quickly at the ground before looking up at me. He caught my stare and it was like a tractor beam. Magnetic had been an understatement. Fletcher Sinclair was unavoidable.

"After this, I have to take you deeper into the woods," he said slowly. "I have to gift you to Gideon North."

"The Beast," I murmured.

Fletcher grimaced. "He's just a man."

"He has a reputation," I said.

"And don't I?" He held his hands out at his sides, mouth still twisted into an angry half-scowl.

"You do," I agreed.

"And what is it then?" Fletcher took a step toward me, bringing into focus how much taller and broader than me he truly was.

"Fletcher Sinclair, heir to the Thorns legacy, the Sinclair dynasty."

"What else?"

"You're ruthless." The twist in my back when I tried to straighten my spine was reminder enough of that. "You're a cruel villain."

Fletcher snorted, rolling his eyes. For the briefest moment, even in the dark of the woods, I saw the pain in his face, the lie of the whole thing, but the wind blew, the trees rustled... and it was gone.

Fletcher Sinclair is the only ally you need.

"I don't think you're so bad," I told him, taking a breath and reaching for him once more. He didn't shy away from my touch, but he went rigid and still beneath my fingers. His pants were still undone, and I slowly moved my fingers beneath the waistband of his underwear. His cock hadn't softened yet, throbbing against my palm when I wrapped my fingers around him.

"You don't know a thing about me..." He trailed off on a gasp as I stroked him from root to tip.

"I know you stopped when you thought I didn't really want it," I said.

Fletcher moved quickly, collaring his hand around my throat and slamming my back into a tree. He lifted me onto my toes, and I kept my hand around his cock, kept stroking as he tightened his fingers around my neck. His hand was so large I imagined his fingers almost touched in the back.

"You're right," I rasped. "You're right."

He came across my fingers with a look of agony on his face and he dropped me back onto my feet without so much as a warning. My next breath hurt my lungs, and my dick pulsed in response, leaking hot precum against my leg.

"I'm taking you to Gideon North," he said, shoving his flagging erection back into his pants.

"I understand."

"He has the same..." Fletcher trailed off again.

So much power and so often at a loss for words. He was no better than me, just a lost little boy playing dress up and I didn't think anyone knew it besides me and him.

"I understand now," I said again. "I know what you both expect."

"That's what the society expects," he corrected, brushing his hair away from his face, and then doing the same to mine with far more tenderness than he'd given himself. "What I expect is for you to find out all you can about him before he sends you back. I want to know everything you can learn about Gideon North."

CHAPTER 21
GIDEON

The initiation ritual was something I'd been dreading since I found out about it. The only consolation as I prepared myself to head into the woods was that I was sure whatever Fletcher had to go through was worse. Between the Thorns and the Roses, one society was known for being ruthless and it wasn't mine.

"A quick fuck to take the edge off?" Luca asked from behind me with a tight laugh.

I shook my head. "Today is definitely not the day," I told him.

"Tonight is," he reminded me.

He was wrong, but he didn't know it. To his understanding, we'd perform the first part of the ritual, then I'd pick an initiate to fuck, to trade. It was a childish power move, undoubtedly put into place generations ago by a weak man who had no choice but to coerce people into bed with him.

I would not.

There was a third option of the ritual Luca didn't know about, and I couldn't tell him.

It would be a test of the loyalty he had toward me... toward the Roses, and I intended to selfishly hold him to it so I wouldn't have to bed another man and to minimize the impact of my father's reach.

It was also a favor, but only I was supposed to know that.

"Are you ready?" I asked him, ignoring his assumption about how our nights would end.

He gestured weakly, lifting his left hand to pass me the soft, black cloth bag. I took it from him without another word, sliding it over his head and loosely knotting the strings at the base of his throat. Luca sucked in a breath, the fabric pulling against his mouth as he tried to get air.

"Small breaths," I reminded him.

He nodded, and I attached a thick leather collar around his neck.

Everything about this ritual was meant to injure and demean. From the veiled eyes to the collar and leash, Luca was to be reminded at all stages of the night that as my second, he was nothing without my guidance. He was on display as much as I was, a reminder to the rest of the initiates and members that they were only meant to do what they were told, go where they were taken.

Twisting the well-oiled leather leash around my hand, I gave a sharp tug against Luca's throat and pulled him out of the house. He only stumbled a handful of times before finding his footing, following after me as proud as a sightless man could. I led him through the dark and into the tree line, just off the property as to not run afoul of any campus safety rules.

As if they'd hold us to anything anyway.

In a large clearing, a bonfire crackled, flames shooting toward the sky. The other members of the Roses gathered around, speaking together in hushed tones. When Luca and I arrived, everyone immediately went silent, falling to their knees and bowing their heads. The power was heady, and I understood why so many men before me had fallen victim to chasing it. My father being no exception to the rule. Blind loyalty could be addicting, but I didn't want the loyalty of all these men. I wanted the one thing I wasn't allowed to have.

Even still.

Even now.

"I stand before you tonight to make you five promises," I said, loud enough for my voice to carry to the far edges of the clearing. I didn't speak often, and it was the first time many of the men around heard my voice. "I give you my discretion and my confidence. My loyalty and my union."

I bit the inside of my cheek, an unwanted memory from another life flashing against the backs of my eyelids like a firework.

Sub rosa.

"I honor the traditions of those that came before us by taking the mark of my forefathers on your behalf."

Beside me, Luca shifted.

"Head toward the fire," I demanded.

He hesitated for less than a second, stepping toward the flames before us. Luca took small but measured steps, awaiting my next instruction. He was dangerously close to the edge of the bonfire when I called out to him next.

"Stop."

He was quicker to obey that command. The fire sparked madly as it licked into the sky, and I imagined if not for the hood, his eyelashes might have found themselves singed on the tips.

"Two steps forward, Luca."

Again, small steps toward the inferno.

"One more."

He was close enough to do what I needed him to do, but this was meant to be a display of power.

"More, Luca," I said, voice booming across the field.

He rolled his neck and squared his shoulders, taking a step so big that his boots knocked into the logs built as a perimeter around the base of the fire.

"Stop there," I told him. "Two steps to the left and you'll find it."

He followed instruction well, reaching down and finding the heavy leather glove in the dirt.

"Put it on. Take up the brand."

If he had any nerves, his steadiness didn't betray him.

Blindly, Luca slipped the glove onto his right hand, then he felt around for the long iron poker, tip burning neon orange in the fire.

"Did you count your steps?" I asked.

Another lesson.

While men acted without thinking, that didn't mean they were mindless.

"Yes," he called out to me.

"Then return."

Luca took two steps back to the right and turned his back to the flames. I took a step back, as I was meant to, on account of the length of the poker. Luca, again with his small steps, like if he walked slow enough we could delay the inevitable. It was some comfort that he hated this part as much as I was about to, but it was a small price to pay for the promise of peace in the future. When he'd closed half the space, I made quick work of undoing the buttons on my shirt and letting it fall open.

"Raise it," I said.

Luca nearly startled, my voice closer maybe than he'd expected. He lifted the brand, the iron burning orange and red, the shape of a five-petaled rose easy enough for me to make out. Bracing his free hand around his gloved wrist, Luca continued to close the space toward me until he was near enough for me to smell the burning metal.

"This is my oath," I whispered, as Luca took the final step into me, searing the brand of The Crimson Rose directly over my heart.

CHAPTER 22

LUCA

The scent of burning flesh made me want to vomit, and if it wasn't for Gideon pressing himself *into* the brand, I don't think I would have gotten through it. I was thankful for the hood because it hid my tears and muffled my cries. Listening to the way Gideon grunted through the barbaric ritual was the straw that broke me, the absolute misery and unfairness of all of our lives crashing down on my shoulders all at once. There had to be another way.

"It's done," he said, the crisp words drawing me back into the present, back into the clearing.

I tried to drop the brand at our feet, but it stuck to his skin, hot iron still burning. I had to pull to get it off, and without the sizzle of his flesh, I had to bite my lips between my teeth to quiet my own noises of discontent.

"It's done," everyone around us repeated back.

"It's done," I muttered from behind the wet cloth, even though my heart wasn't in it.

Gideon closed the space between us, loosening the buckle on the collar before pulling it off entirely. He untied the cord around the opening of the bag, the cool fall air rushing into my nostrils as he pulled it off. I was so close to being sick, so close to throwing my entire life into the garbage. I looked away from him, choosing to stare at the ground instead of his face.

Instead of the brand.

I hated myself. I hated myself and I wanted to die.

Pressing my hand flat over my heart, checking to make sure I hadn't somehow taken the brand myself, I screwed my eyes shut, tears leaking out from the corners and racing down my cheeks.

"Walk with me," Gideon said, spinning on his heel and heading away from the bonfire. He didn't look back to check if I would follow—we both knew I would.

With thoughts racing through my head, I waited until we were well out of earshot to speak to him.

"Can I be candid, B?" I asked him, falling into step half a pace behind him to his left.

"I still don't want to fuck, Luca," he said, huffing out what sounded like a laugh.

The lightness in his voice and the pride in his gait was enough to tear a strangled sob out of my throat. It took all my strength to not double over and throw up on my shoes. I just needed a minute, needed the nausea to pass, needed to remind myself this mattered, even though I couldn't remember for what.

"I'm sorry," I choked out the apology that would never be enough for him…or for me.

"You need to get it together," he said, turning back and grabbing me by the biceps, giving me a shake. With him so close, it was even harder to breathe, impossible to not break down. His shirt fluttered open in the breeze, his skin still charred from where I'd pressed the rose into his chest.

"I'm sorry."

"This is what I signed up for. What you signed up for."

"I wasn't born for this," I whispered.

"You were," he said, "whether you want to admit that or not."

"I want to just…go."

"Enough of that fucking nonsense!" he roared, shoving me back. I stumbled over my own feet, falling flat on my ass in the dirt.

Gideon intimidated everyone, but he'd never intimidated me. I'd always been awed by the way he commanded a room, a society, even from his quiet isolation. He was more at home in the pool or in the library than he was anywhere else, and I was admittedly curious to know what had made him that way.

"This is the hand we've been dealt," he said, extending his to help me back to my feet.

And that was the way of him, wasn't it?

I slid my palm against his, and he helped me stand.

Brushing dirt off the backs of my thighs, I let out another sob when he spoke again.

"This is the hand we have to play."

He was right. He was so right, and I was so hopeless for this life.

Dusting off the dirt, I swiped the tears off my face and righted my glasses.

"You're right. I'm sorry, I—"

"Stop apologizing."

"I'm s—" I clacked my mouth closed, teeth rattling in my head.

"I owe you an apology, actually," he said.

"I don't believe you."

He inclined his head toward the path we'd been walking before my little meltdown, and we set off again with him in the lead where he belonged. He didn't elaborate, and I was too worn down from emotion for my curiosity to get the better of me to ask.

"There's three parts to the initiation," he said, hand flexing at his side.

"I thought it was two."

"I know." He glanced at me from the corner of his eye. "You're not going to like the third."

"You haven't even done the second yet," I reminded him, not having forgotten the sex element of the whole thing.

"And I'm not going to."

"I wasn't aware you had that kind of veto power."

Gideon huffed another laugh. "I'll deal with the repercussions of that one later. The third involves you, and I don't think you're going to like it."

"I can't imagine there's a single thing I'd like less than what we just did," I told him.

He hummed thoughtfully as the trail ahead of us spread into another small clearing, the Black Thorn house visible on a hill in the distance.

"I'm glad you think that, because tonight you're going home with Fletcher Sinclair."

CHAPTER 23

GIDEON

"You've got to be kidding."

Luca's shock was quick and expected, but he didn't stop walking. If anything, he closed the half-step between us into a quarter.

"I didn't think you'd mind a chance to see Daren again."

His next protest died sharply on his tongue, as I knew it would.

"Gideon," he said instead.

"There's not a single thing about you that I don't know, Luca. I may not like this life, but that doesn't mean I'm not living it."

Luca cleared his throat, averting his gaze. "I didn't... we..."

"Stop," I warned.

I knew enough, but not all of it. I knew he'd spent more than one night with Daren Moore and I knew the encounters had ended as soon as the two of them stepped into their respective roles alongside Fletcher and me. Whether it had been by choice or by need, their connection had been severed and their loyalties—at least Luca's—seemed to hold true.

"Every ritual has an offering," I explained, "and I've chosen to offer you."

"I didn't know…"

"That's the point, Luca. This night is as much a test of my command as of your loyalty. How much are we both willing to give?"

"Hasn't it been enough?" He raised his hand and covered his heart where the brand would be if it were his.

"It's not enough until they've sucked us dry," I said simply.

"What if I don't want to?" he asked,

I raised a brow, sincerely shocked at the request. I wondered if things with Daren had ended as badly as they had for me and Fletcher.

"We both know it doesn't matter." I sighed, letting out a breath until my chest was hollow enough it felt like my ribs would cave in. "And better you and me than someone new, someone who doesn't understand this life."

Luca made a sad noise in the back of this throat. "Do I have to fuck Sinclair?"

"You have to do whatever he wants," I said. "But take the moments you can and hold on to them, and never forget where you're going to end up when the night is through."

"You have my loyalty," he whispered, almost mechanically. "My place is at your side."

Across the clearing, three figures came into view, and I recognized Fletcher immediately. He was taller than I remembered and far broader across his chest. He didn't have on a shirt, his chest and knees covered in dirt. To his left was his deputy, Daren, and further still, a man I'd never seen before, smaller than both of them and dressed in clothes that looked like they'd once been white. His shirt was torn on the shoulder and his golden hair disheveled. It was reassuring to know Fletcher hadn't changed. Still ruining everyone who dared to come into his life.

"It's one night," I said softly, offering him more explanation than I was technically allowed to. "The exchange is meant to remind all of us that one cannot exist without the other."

"If you'd fucked someone else after the branding, would..." Luca's question died off.

"They would be offered instead of you."

"Is this a favor then?" he whispered. "These moments."

"It's an apology," I told him truthfully, "for all the things that are yet to come."

Luca cursed under his breath, steadying himself as we came to a stop in the center of the clearing. Fletcher and the other two stopped ten feet away from us, and I chose instead to focus on the way Daren's eyes widened for the briefest second when he saw Luca beside me and not a random first year initiate. The weight of Fletcher's stare was impossible to ignore for long though.

He always knew how to suck the air out of a room.

Or in this case, a forest.

"My oath is sworn," he said, voice deeper than I recalled.

"As is mine."

"I offer you the proof of my charge," he said, fixating his stare on me with such a weighted intent I worried I would collapse the way Luca had done on our walk out.

"I accept."

Daren pressed his palm against the middle of the third man's back, giving him a shove into the empty space between our delegations.

"I offer you the proof of my charge." I said the line expected of me, and Luca stepped forward without being told.

"I accept," Fletcher rumbled, his piercing blue stare still focused on me. Life had either been good to him, or not. I didn't know him enough anymore to tell the difference.

Luca and the other man changed places, and it was impossible to not see the aching and desperate love between Luca and Daren. Even though they couldn't touch, their bodies swayed close, almost like Daren could sense the guilt weighing Luca down and trying to bury him in the ground.

Had Fletcher ever felt that way about me?

No, it would have been impossible because instead of helping me stand, he'd chosen to dig the pit and throw me into it himself.

"Take him back to the house," Fletcher demanded. "I'll catch up."

Daren and Luca were quick to leave, and I hoped he'd taken me seriously when I told him to absorb the moments. I needed his discretion, but not for nothing.

"Come," I said to the man whose name I still didn't know.

I'd ask him later, but not in front of Fletcher or anyone from the Thorns.

Tearing myself away from Fletcher was like ripping off a Band-Aid, the way he'd dragged his stare from my toes to my hair, up my arms and down my neck, lingering on the insignia Luca had just seared over my heart. The pain from the brand had hurt so much for a split second and then...nothing. The brain was a miraculous thing, blocking my receptors from registering the temperature, the charred skin. On the other hand, Fletcher's body bore no visible scars or marks from his initiation, and I tried to imagine what could have been worse than talking your most trusted confidant into marking you for life.

The man came close to me, shorter than Luca, shorter than Fletcher. He blinked up at me with tired, angry eyes, took one step past me, one step away from Fletcher, then he came to a stop.

"Gideon," Fletcher said my name like an apology and it made me want to rip him limb from limb.

"You don't get to speak to me with that voice," I warned, pivoting away from him and giving his offering an urge toward the edge of the clearing.

"Gideon," he said again, tone less forgiving.

"The Gideon you knew is dead, Sinclair." I threw the barb over my shoulder as I headed home with the worn-down offering by my side. "And you should know that. After all, you're the one who turned me into The Beast."

CHAPTER 24

DAREN

The top of Luca's hand brushed against mine, warm and sure as I knew him to be.

"What are you doing here?" I asked under my breath.

"Gideon knows about us."

I grabbed his hand to pull him close, but quickly remembered myself and let go. Crossing my arms in front of my chest to stop from touching him, I kept walking back toward the house.

"How did he find out?"

"There's no secrets in this life, Daren," he reminded me.

"*You* are my secret," I hissed, glancing back over my shoulder to see if Fletcher was on his way after us. "This exchange..."

"Also a secret," he finished for me. Clearing his throat,

Luca was next to look behind us. "Is he going to fuck me, do you think?"

I sucked my tongue across the front of my teeth, unbridled jealousy rearing up as I thought about Fletcher even daring to lay a hand on Luca, let alone fuck him.

"Please don't ask me that," I whispered to him just as the sounds of crunching leaves grew louder in my ears.

"If he does…"

"You have to," I said.

The footsteps behind us grew louder and the dominating presence of Fletcher Sinclair pushed its way between us. I'd expected him to stop, but he didn't. He stormed through us, past us, without a word. I looked at Luca, my brows knit with worry, then picked up my pace to walk faster after Fletcher.

He hadn't spoken to me the whole way to the meeting place so I had no idea how the chase or the claiming had turned out. All I knew was he and Bellamy emerged from the woods with Fletcher covered in dirt and Bellamy with torn clothes and tear-stained cheeks. It was impossible to look at him like that, battered and beaten down, and not remember how willingly he'd spread himself open on my bed just days before.

Fucking Bellamy had felt better than it should have, the tight heat of his body like a glove around my cock every time I sank inside of him. I'd teased Fletcher later about missing out on it, but that was before I knew he'd be forced to find out for himself anyway. Bellamy had been so nervous with me, but steadfast and focused in his goals. After seeing him emerge from the woods on Fletcher's heels, I realized he'd used me just as much as I'd used him.

When Fletcher was out of earshot again, I let out a breath and spoke softly to Luca, who'd kept pace beside me when I slowed down again to give us more time to talk. "I haven't slept with Fletcher."

"I haven't slept with Gideon."

"Though not for lack of trying?"

He huffed out a tired laugh into the small space between us. "I've missed you," he said.

"It's been agony. I try to...try to distract myself so I don't have time to miss you."

Luca groaned, scrubbing a hand down his face. "Please don't tell me that."

"It's the truth."

The house was less than one hundred yards away.

"I have one night. These...they're just stolen fucking moments. I can't even stay with you. I have to go to him, and then..." Luca swiped angry hands across his face, lifting his glasses to press shaking fingers against his closed eyelids.

"I'm told he's rough," I said to him, swallowing down as much of the jealousy as I could manage. It didn't matter we'd agreed to fuck whoever we wanted during our forced separation, the thought of him and Fletcher together while I was one floor below felt like the grossest test of my loyalty yet.

"You know I like that."

"Maybe pretend it's me," I suggested.

Fletcher stomped up onto the back porch, slamming the door open and skulking inside. He didn't bother looking back to see if we were behind him. He knew we would be.

"No one is you," Luca said softly before sealing his lips and squaring his shoulders.

We'd reached the house, and I gave Luca one last look that I hoped told him how sorry I was, how much I hated this, how much our patience would reward us when all was said and done. We could have our secrets again—him and me.

"Both of you," Fletcher shouted from the stairs. "Up here, now."

"Look at me," Luca begged, hand coming out to stop me as I was quick to obey Fletcher's call. He stopped before he touched me, just like I had stopped in the clearing, but I couldn't give him what he asked.

"I can't. If I do, I'll..."

"It's okay, baby," he said, almost as much to himself as it was to me.

As I led Luca to the winding staircase what would carry us to Fletcher's third floor bedroom, I counted every sin I'd ever committed, wondering when I'd pay enough penance to be free of this place. It was so childish, I thought, curling my hand around the carved wood banister and pulling myself up the stairs. My legs didn't want to carry me, my body didn't want to be turned away from Luca, and yet...

And yet.

Men like Luca and me, we weren't meant to rule or lead. We were best played in the second seat, and I'd never cared about that until I found myself being called to sacrifice the only thing in my life that meant anything. It had been easy enough when we both knew what our roles would be, who we'd have to step back to serve. Whatever we were both walking into at the top of the stairs, though, it was far beyond anything either of us had expected. It was one year of active initiation, then graduation, then dissemination. After graduation there'd be more expectations but less oversight. It would have been manageable.

Livable.

I didn't dare say another thing to Luca, even though I found myself aware of the way his body vibrated behind me, the heat and nerves rolling off of him in trembling waves, crashing into my back like we were both diving into a high tide. Fletcher's bedroom door was cracked open and, with a steady hand on the brass knob, I pushed it wide and stepped aside for Luca to enter.

CHAPTER 25

FLETCHER

"Close it," I said.

Daren followed the command and locked it for good measure without being told.

"You're Luca Mandeville?" I asked, staring out the window instead of at either man unfortunate enough to find himself alone on initiation night in my room. I'd reluctantly pulled the curtains back, my gaze unsure of where to focus.

"Yes," he answered.

Daren cleared his throat. "Can I clean your back now?"

I reached behind me, picking dried blood off my spine with the tips of my fingers. Bringing my hand around to the front, I frowned down at the red and brown flakes beneath my nails. "Is it bad?"

"It's not good."

I rubbed some more grime off my skin, this time a

patch nearer my shoulder blade. It wasn't anything a hot shower wouldn't fix, and I was assuredly not going to let Daren tend my wounds in front of Gideon's deputy like I was some kind of helpless bitch.

"Bellamy put up a fight," I said, sitting down in an old leather armchair in front of the window. Dirt puffed off my clothes, particles floating in the air around me before settling or disappearing entirely. I'd never been so envious of something so insignificant. I would have given up nearly anything to be allowed to simply vanish in front of someone's eyes.

"You persevered," Daren said softly.

"Did he fight you?" I asked, crossing one leg and resting my ankle on top of my knee. My stare drifted between the two men in front of me who stood far closer than friends would, let alone rivals. "When you fucked him, I mean."

The only tell was a twitch in Luca's right eye I would have missed if not for the glare on the lens of his glasses.

"He didn't fight," Daren answered, swallowing hard.

"Will Luca fight?" I asked neither of them in particular.

"No," Luca answered me before Daren could.

"Good." I drummed my fingers against the outside of my knee, making sure the move I was about to make was the right one. It was a crapshoot based on a twitching eye and a lack of space between two people that I recognized from my past. "Prove it."

Luca stepped away from the wall and reached back to

pull his shirt over his head. He dropped it at his feet, revealing a massive tattoo in the middle of his chest. A mimic of the fresh brand I'd seen over Gideon's heart when we met up to trade in the clearing. I didn't think Luca's mark was mandated, and I wasn't sure if a willing scar was better or worse.

He dropped his hands to his belt and made quick work of his fly while kicking out of his boots and using his feet to shove them against the wall with the rest of his clothes. If Luca had any qualms about modesty, he did good at hiding them from me because his underwear was the last thing to go before he righted to his full height and turned his hands back, palms facing me.

"So quick to do what you're told," I murmured, admiring the thickness of the cock that had already started to swell between Luca's legs. "Handed off like cattle, stripped down like a whore."

Luca shivered, his dick twitching at the slander. "I'm here to serve," he said.

"I wonder if your counterpart is as keen to bend the knee," I said, stare flickering to Daren who looked like he either wanted to vanish into the wall or throw me out the window. When he realized I was watching him, he tore his stare away from Luca's ass, expression quickly settling into a mask of apathy.

"You know I am," Daren said.

"Prove it," I repeated the command to him.

With the same smooth efficiency, Daren stripped out of his clothes and moved them out of the way. He came to stand alongside Luca, and the sight of them together was enough to make the slightest inkling of my anger toward Gideon melt away. Luca was lanky where Daren was slightly more built. Almost the same height, but Luca was there with his glasses and his golden hair and Daren beside him with soft waves on his head and a delicate pink foreskin around his cock. Even with space between them, both of their fingers twitched outward, searching for something I wasn't supposed to know existed.

My anger surged forward again with such violence it took my breath away. Why was it the two of them had been allowed a life, even if it had been temporary, even if it had been short-lived, where they were allowed to know each other with such a perfect level of intimacy? They breathed in sync, chests heaving in time. I imagined if I closed the space between us and pressed my hands against their sternums, their hearts would thump the same way.

I should have made them both suck my cock. Choke them on it to wipe all that *want* from their faces.

Regardless, I was hard from the sight of them, the smell of them, precum and arousal thick in the air, but I didn't want either of them to taste the latex on my dick from the condom I'd worn with Bellamy. Rules were rules and condoms were never allowed as part of the initiation, but I'd never gone without and I had to be permitted at least *one* secret of my own.

The longer they stood together, the harder all three of our cocks became. Finally, I pulled mine out of my pants and gave a slow stroke from root to tip. Luca's eyes went wide, nostrils flaring as both of them turned their attention to the erection jutting up from between my legs. My cock was thick like the rest of me, hard to get my hand around, and hot to the touch. I spit in my hand and gave another stroke, spreading my legs to get more comfortable.

Luca's breathing stuttered, falling out of time with Daren's for the first time since I'd realized they were aligned. They might be hiding the fact they were in love with each other, but there was no denying Luca would have climbed onto my lap and rode me to completion while Daren stood in front of the door and watched.

That was what I should have done, what was expected of me. That would have been the display of power, of control.

But I was tired, and Bellamy's desperate fight to push me off was still too fresh in my mind, tangled with the cold shoulder from Gideon and the absolute lack of ownership I had of my own life, of the lives of the people I was meant to be responsible for. I couldn't claim another man who didn't want me.

Another man who wasn't Gideon North.

"Daren," I said.

I needed to bear witness to the outcome of this night.

I needed them to be aware I knew about them, to understand that the only secrets in this house were mine. Spitting again on the top of my dick, I used my fingers to smear saliva down the length of my cock, not bothering to hold back from the way I leered at them both. If it had been another night, I would have gladly taken the two of them at the same time, but having four men on my mind was three too many.

"Yes?" Daren asked, his voice pulled taut as his foreskin now was.

I grunted, hole clenching when I tightened my fingers around my dick.

"Fuck him until he comes, but don't let him come until he cries. I want to watch."

It was impossible to breathe, impossible to stand still.

I turned toward Daren, my nostrils flaring with every exhale, only to find his expression mirrored my own. Excitement, nerves, and an underlying current of concern that this was all too good to be true. Out of the corner of my eye, I could see Fletcher stroking his cock, his stare solely on Daren and me, and whatever we were about to do next.

"Get on your hands and knees," Daren said roughly.

Fletcher reached into his pocket and tossed Daren a small bottle of clear liquid as I went to the ground and steadied my weight. The floorboards creaked as I shifted around, and then Daren's hand landed a sharp and heavy strike against my right ass cheek.

"Make it easy for me," he warned.

Shivering, I arched my back until my chest was nearly

flat against the wood planks of Fletcher's bedroom floor. The stretch in my thighs didn't even hurt anymore because this was Daren's favorite way to fuck me. Maybe just a twinge in my hamstring for how long since I'd found myself prostrate for him.

His knees hit the floor behind me with two hard thumps, then a cold splash of wetness against my hole. Daren pressed his left hand against the small of my back to hold me down and speared his fingers into me with one quick twist of his wrist. I didn't have sheets to ball in my fist, my fingers instead scrabbling against the wood and the edge of the rug beneath me. He didn't give me long before adding a second finger, and even less for a third. Sweat beaded on my temple, the dip of my back. My arms trembled and I rolled my forehead across the floor, relieved to have this back, even if only for a night.

"He looks like he's about to come and he looks quite far from crying," Fletcher said from his seat in front of the window.

Daren fisted my hair and yanked my head up, forcing me to turn my gaze from the floor to Fletcher. To his strong, broad legs and the long, thick cock in his hand.

"He cries wh—" Daren snapped his mouth closed and twisted his hold in my hair until I grunted over the sound of him.

"Hmn?"

"He'll cry with a cock in his throat," Daren corrected himself, his initial statement far from being wrong. I'd cry with a cock in my throat and I'd come that way too. "But unfortunately I can't do both."

Fletcher hummed thoughtfully, tilting his head to the side and narrowing his bright blue eyes on the both of us.

"Please fuck me," I whined, thrusting back onto Daren's hand.

He didn't wait to see if Fletcher came to put his cock into my mouth or not. Daren pulled his fingers out of me and wiped them off on my flank, then he replaced them with his cock. One brutal thrust later and I found myself impaled, tears immediately springing to the corners of my eyes. Not because it hurt, but because it felt like coming home.

Daren—like always—gave me no time to adjust to him, no time to brace myself against the onslaught. He slammed into me with all his strength, over and over and over, and I cried for him the way I always did. Bitter and unrestrained sobs as he sawed me in half with his perfect cock. At some point, he'd let go of my hair, only realized when he grabbed it in his hand again, pulling my back into a deeper arch so he could get every inch of his cock into me.

Tears slid down my face, pooling against my nostrils and the bow of my upper lip, and I'd never felt better in my entire life. Fletcher had gotten up from the chair at some point, and he stood in front of me so all I could see was his knees. Even though his cock and arms were above me, the sound of his quick jerking motions was unmistakable. A shiver tore through my entire body and Daren growled behind me, his shaft thickening inside of me.

"Open," Fletcher said. His tone was low and gravelly, and I opened my mouth for him, sticking out my tongue and feeling far too desperate for him to put his dick into my throat like Daren had suggested.

Daren and I had never been with another person at the same time, but I could tell by the way his pace quickened and his palms slicked against my already sweaty skin that he liked it. Even though our fuck was meant to be for show, a scene on demand, the reality of who we were was right there beneath the surface and he *liked* the idea of Fletcher joining us just as much as I did.

"Please," I begged, knowing that with a dick in my throat, cutting off my air supply, I'd come on the spot and Fletcher would have exactly what he wanted from us.

Slowly, Fletcher lowered himself to his knees, Daren fucking into me like a machine from behind the whole time. I couldn't stop myself from moaning, from sighing, from begging, and the wet squelch of Daren's cock pumping into me wasn't even loud enough to drown the sound of me out.

"Open him more," Fletcher said.

His cock was dark and swollen, precum shiny against the entire head of his cock, the sides of his fingers. Daren shifted behind me so he could reach all the way up and hook his fingers into my mouth, curling into my cheeks and pulling my mouth open in what had to be the most demeaning position I'd ever been fucked in. Another shot of precum leaked from my dick at the humiliation of it all.

Fletcher's dick was so close to my face that I could smell him, and then a burst of his hot, white spend splattered against my cheek. Another against the side of my nose, one onto my waiting tongue, and one onto my eyelid. Fletcher restrained himself through his release, every muscle in my line of sight rippling and tensing as he shot his load across my face.

Licking a bead of cum from my upper lip, my own release slammed into me just as hard as Daren had been. I cried out, not concerned with trying to maintain any sort of appearances. Gideon had sent me as an offering, as a favor, and I was happy to be both of them. The force of my own end was enough to bring Daren over the edge, and he slapped his hips into mine once more, hard enough to bruise—I hoped—then he went still.

His cock throbbed and pulsed inside of me, and I screamed out again...because I didn't know what else do to. The pleasure, the arousal, the embarrassment—it was all too much, but I never wanted it to end.

Fletcher made a disgusted sound, using my face as leverage to get back onto his feet. His fingers smeared his cum across my face and into my eye as he stood and tucked himself back into his pants.

"Clean him up and make sure he's comfortable until tomorrow," he said.

"I will," Daren rasped, fingers sliding out of my mouth

and working their way down my neck and my back, around my waist again to haul me backward onto him.

"And hide yourselves better," Fletcher warned.

My blood ran cold, and I was immediately aware of the sweat, and the cum, and the tears that painted my skin. I bit my lip, relying on Daren to hold my weight up for whatever blow Fletcher was going to deliver next. But he offered us nothing, stepping over our spent bodies and walking out of the room without another word.

CHAPTER 27

BELLAMY

Gideon walked me back to the house in silence. He almost seemed out of place without his right hand, but he was far harder to read than Fletcher so I couldn't be sure. When we reached the house, he climbed the steps to the porch in front of me, his back bowed as he slipped through the door. Still not a word, still not even a look. I followed him up a creaking and winding staircase to the second floor of the massive house.

It was much the same as Thorn Hill, but dissimilar enough that it was easy to see the differences between the two societies. Rose Hall was cavernous and quiet. Thorn Hill was filled with conversation, laughter, and often-times sex. Not to imply people didn't live in fear—or awe—of Fletcher Sinclair. I hadn't been lying to him in the woods when I'd told him what I knew of him, but even the air in Rose Hall was different. I got the impression

Gideon commanded respect in a way Fletcher didn't care to.

Lost in my own thoughts, I stumbled and slammed into Gideon's back after he came to a stop in front of a door on the second floor. He grunted at the force of the impact, but still remained unspeaking. He opened the door, and I peeked around him, finding a well-appointed bedroom with what looked like a bathroom attached against the opposite wall.

Nothing that night had gone how I'd planned. After the chase with Fletcher and the way he'd warned me about Gideon, I'd expected to be taken with as much force and power as soon as we arrived back at the house, but that was yet to happen.

"Did you want me to clean up?" I asked, assuming that the state of me was too disheveled for him to take interest. "Fletcher didn't...I'm..."

Gideon shot me a scathing look, and I snapped my mouth shut before I said anything else.

The fear-laced arousal from the woods hadn't faded, and even after the long and silent trek through the woods, my erection hadn't even thought about giving up. My middle finger burned with a sharp pain where my nail had torn below the quick, and every time I poked at it, another burst of arousal exploded out from the base of my spine.

I realized, standing there in the hallway, I wanted to tempt The Beast.

I needed to. I was meant to make an ally of Fletcher

and if I was going to get any information about Gideon to take back to him, I had to work fast. My time at Rose Hall was beyond limited.

While the thoughts raced through my brain, Gideon let go of the door handle and spun on his heel. He was halfway down the hall before I realized he was leaving me and I chased after him, fingers curling around his wrist and drawing him to a halt.

"Where are you going?" I asked.

"Don't touch me," he growled.

He didn't even need to shake me off, I let go on my own.

"It's just...where are you going?"

"My room."

"I thought—"

"You thought wrong," he snapped, glaring at me over his shoulder with so much force I wished the forest floor had swallowed me up beneath the weight of Fletcher's thrusts.

"I'm...I'm here of my own accord," I said softly, wringing my hands together in front of me, aware of how dirty and tattered my clothes looked, at how much of a lie the words must have sounded to him.

"Did Fletcher force himself on you?" Gideon asked, squaring his shoulders but still keeping his back turned to me.

"Technically," I said, "but I did want it."

Gideon turned his face toward the wall, giving me the soft angles of his profile and the tight purse of his lips. His dark-blond hair fell in soft waves toward his shoulders, strands escaped from the knot at the base of his neck.

"I want *you*, too," I said.

"You don't know what you're saying."

If he'd look at me, he'd see how untrue his assumption was. He'd see clearly, with his own eyes, how much the fear and the adrenaline turned me on.

"What, then?" I asked.

"What, nothing," he said. "Do whatever you want, but do it in your room."

It was playing with fire, but I hadn't gotten off with Fletcher and my body was electrified. The adrenaline was a drug and I never wanted to come down. I couldn't stop the words from coming out of my mouth, but I knew if Gideon left me alone to jerk off in the shower of one of Rose Hall's many guest rooms, I would claw my way through the lathe and plaster walls until I could escape.

"I didn't come here to twiddle my thumbs."

He ignored me, instead saying, "I'll bring you up something to eat shortly."

Before I could argue further, Gideon was gone, down the stairs and somewhere into the heart of the house that was too far removed for me to see. Resigned, I stepped into the guest room and closed the door behind me. It latched closed louder than I expected, and all it took was one quick test of the knob to figure out it had a self-locking mechanism and I was trapped inside.

"Son of a fucking bitch," I cursed Gideon North *and* Fletcher Sinclair under my breath before stalking through the room toward the bathroom. Any malice I had toward my host died on my next breath.

The bathroom was bigger than the bedroom itself, a palatial landscape of black marble with gold fixtures. A clawfoot tub sat comfortably under a window, a shower with the biggest rainfall head I'd ever seen tucked into the far corner. The vanity had two gold sinks situated beneath the most ornate gold-framed mirror I'd ever seen.

I left the bathroom and tried the bedroom door one more time, confirming I was going to be stuck inside for the long haul. A different sort of fear laced up my spine, but there was no point in letting it overwhelm me. The only escape was through the window, and I knew without looking it would be locked and barred. Without anything better to do, I stripped out of my clothes and left them in front of the door. I was going to appreciate that bathtub for as long as I could.

CHAPTER 28
GIDEON

I knew what was expected of me, and I knew it was bad enough I'd given Luca up to Sinclair instead of following the traditional expectations about the offering and offering exchange. I'd done Luca a service, while only causing myself more hardship. If Luca were here, I could pawn Bellamy off on him and pretend to care while they fucked. But Luca was at Thorn Hill, and I was trapped with a man who reminded me so much of the boy I used to love that I wanted to scratch his face off with my bare hands.

Bellamy didn't look anything like Fletcher, didn't walk like him or talk like him, sure as hell didn't own a room like him, but he had this quiet and speculative way of peeling back my layers without even trying that made him just as dangerous as the boy I'd loved before. Of course, he was probably just trying to do what was expected of him.

He was an offering from the Thorns, an irrelevant member of an inconsequential family, using the same tools we were all born with to try and level the playing field.

He would have done anything I wanted, anything I asked.

I could have asked him to let me choke him unconscious during sex and he probably would have let me. Even if he hadn't agreed, I would have been within my rights to take it from him anyway. Not morally or ethically, but there were things my name and rank allowed me that other men would never have. I wouldn't take what wasn't freely given, though. But I could have...if I wanted to.

Instead of taking *anything*, I went to the kitchen and made Bellamy a sandwich with sourdough and roast beef. Piled high with cheese and fresh lettuce and tomatoes, I chopped up an apple and grabbed him a bag of chips from the pantry. I didn't know what he wanted to eat, I hadn't asked, and I didn't care. He was a burden for me for one night only. All I had to do was keep him alive and keep him away.

I needed time before going back after him. The adrenaline from the initiation ceremony was finally wearing off and every bone in my body ached from the weight of holding me up. Not to mention the agonizingly fresh scar in the middle of my chest. I had no idea how to treat a burn of this caliber, but I'd have to pay it some attention sooner rather than later. I didn't want it to get infected, though maybe if it did, I wouldn't have to spend the rest of my life looking at it.

Leaving the tray on the counter, I made my way to the first floor bathroom and flipped on the light. It was bright white, which was bad enough, but the shadows it cast beneath my eyes and around the corners of my mouth couldn't have all been artificial. The five-petaled rose in the center of my chest was a bloody mess, as crimson as the image on the society crest, but very real and emblazoned in my flesh instead.

"A reminder," my father had told me over the summer, "that it's the blood of men like us that make this real."

I didn't feel real.

As if the brand itself wasn't enough, tonight in the clearing was the first time I'd talked to Fletcher since he'd failed me out of our first year English class at Rose Hill Prep. I'd always found him to be larger than life, in the way he carried himself, in the way he'd made me want him, but he'd actually finally grown into it. Fletcher was so muscular, I had no doubt in my mind what it would feel like for him to put his hands on me again, the way he had so many years ago. I imagined his palms would carry more calluses now. Lord knew I carried my own scars, but still...

Fuck, I hated him.

Flipping off the light, I retrieved the tray, cursing him —and his offering—under my breath as I made my way back up the stairs. I'd put Bellamy in a room that had an

automatically-engaged lock, which woul⸢
gered open from turning the outside han⸢.
carried a special FOB tag, so I wasn't worried a⸢
being anywhere besides where I'd left him whe⸢.
back because I was the only one with the FOB.

I knocked my shoulder into the door to announce myself, then twisted the handle and stepped inside...right onto the pile of Bellamy's discarded and dirty clothes. The door swung closed behind me and latched shut, casting the room back into darkness. The only light on was the one in the bathroom, spilling out onto the carpet. Wet footfalls echoed from the black marble floor, then it was two bare feet, two wet legs, one very hard and very pink cock, and then...

"Thanks for knocking," Bellamy said, corner of his mouth twitching in amusement.

"I did."

"Not loud enough."

I huffed a frustrated breath, setting the tray of food down on the nightstand and turning to go. There was no way I was going to be verbally berated by a fucking nobody. Not with my flesh seared raw by the brand and my heart torn open by Fletcher Sinclair, and not by a nameless initiate who didn't have the common sense to stay dressed.

"Can I have some clean clothes?" Bellamy asked, undeterred by my intent to leave.

"You have clothes. I stepped on them on my way in."

"Great," he said. "Can't wait to put those dirty pants back on and crawl into these nice clean sheets."

"Sleep naked," I told him, stepping on his pile of clothes again. The clothes he'd worn when Fletcher fucked him.

"Does it ever get exhausting?" he asked when I reached the door.

"Does what get exhausting?"

"Being such a prick."

"What gets exhausting," I explained, yanking open the door and stepping into the hallway, "is all the time I spend trying to convince people who don't believe the rumors about me that it's the truth. Have the night you deserve, Bellamy."

CHAPTER 29
FLETCHER

The night air did nothing to calm my nerves. The walk across campus didn't either. I'd thrown five rocks up at the attic window of Rose Hall before the light turned on, and three more before Gideon yanked open the window.

Somehow, he knew exactly where to look. He knew right where to find me.

I gestured for him to come down, and he slammed the window closed. The light stayed on, but less than five minutes later his angry footfalls over the fallen leaves and grass grew louder, and then his hands were in my shirt, my back was against a tree, and there was no air in my lungs. Steadying my hands on his trim waist, I closed my eyes and let my exhale tremble against his chin as I breathed. He adjusted his grip on my shirt, giving me another rough shove against the trunk of the oak tree. It hurt, the bark digging into the still open wounds from the whipping Daren had given me earlier, but the pain was the least of what I deserved when it came to Gideon North.

"Why are you here?" he asked.

"I go to school here."

"You know what I meant." Another press against the tree and a fresh trickle of blood ran down my back, pooling in the dips above my ass.

"I don't know," I admitted, slowly blinking my eyes open. Gideon had gotten so tall, so mean. "I never know what I'm doing when it comes to you."

He didn't like that, letting out a dismissive sound and pushing me away from him. But instead of heading back to the house, he went deeper into the woods. Of course, I went after him...just like I'd gone after him before.

"Fuck off," Gideon said when I closed the space between us.

"Gideon, please."

" Please, what?" He stopped, chest heaving.

"I don't know." I dragged my tongue across the front of my teeth and walked a few paces past him. "I don't know, Gideon."

"I promised myself next time I saw you, I'd..."

I didn't need to prompt him, we both knew what he'd promised himself when it came to me. The two of us made a slow circle around each other, both predators at the same level on the food chain, trying to see which one of us was going to be made into prey. The longer we kept up the charade, the more aroused I found myself, which was admittedly ill-timed, but it was his fault. I couldn't help myself.

He was Gideon North, and I wanted him as much as I ever had. Maybe more, because one time in another life, he'd shown me another way out. He'd given me a taste of what our futures could be like if we were strong enough to fight for them, but I hadn't been strong. He was better than me in all ways, even if he didn't realize it. Even if his father tried to tell him otherwise. When I looked at Gideon, I was reminded of what every promise I'd ever made anyone in my life meant...because they were nothing compared to the promise he would have made me if I hadn't been so fucking scared of my father.

But I was still scared of him, and I worried I would be forever.

"He tried to kill me," Gideon finally said, voice hardly louder than the rustle of the leaves around us. "I'm all of the things I am because of you, because of him."

The accusation drove all the breath from my lungs. "What do you mean he tried to kill you?"

"Our first year of high school, after you lied to the teacher and got me expelled."

My palms were sweating, fingers shaking.

"How?" I asked.

"It doesn't matter."

"It matters to me," I protested, needing to know the true repercussions of my actions—of my father's actions. "I didn't mean for it to happen. I did what I had to, Gideon. I wish you'd understand."

Gideon came to a quick stop, rounding on me again with all the anger I deserved. He rocked me back against another tree, but my feet tangled beneath me and I fell, taking us both down to the ground with a thud. Fire exploded from the lash marks on my back, but the weight of Gideon on top of me was the only thing I'd ever wanted in my life and I'd bear the pain a thousand times over if this was the end result.

"Fuck you." He spat the words into my face, knee pushing up between my spread legs for balance. "You don't deserve to know what I've been through. You ruined me. You fucking ruined me."

"I ruined myself," I said, daring to slide my arms around his waist, up the length of his long and muscular back. He was pulled taut like a bowstring, tension vibrating out of him, the restraint palpable.

He gave a rough jerk of his knee, right up into my balls, and I grunted from the pain of it, spreading my legs wider.

"Does it make you feel better?" I asked. "Hurting me? Because I'll let you. I'll let you tear open these scars on my back if it makes you feel better."

"A small consolation prize for what you turned my life into," he said softly, words deathly steady and his mouth only inches above mine.

"Kiss me, Gideon," I begged, curling my fingers around his shoulders, trying to pull him down to close the space between us.

"You are all of my firsts and all of my lasts, Sin." The

resolve in his voice was growing unsteady, the syllables quaking.

"I've wanted you my whole life," I promised. He was so close, so close after so long and it might be my only chance to feel him this way. "You're my biggest regret. No, *I'm* my biggest regret."

"I fucking hate you for what you did to us," he admitted, burying his face into the crook of my neck. He made a ragged sound that might have been a cry, might have been a scream, but he didn't wrestle himself out of my arms.

"I hate me too," I told him. "Every day."

He shifted his weight above me, hips pressing down until the burning hot thickness of his cock seared me through the layers of clothes and fabric between us.

"Gideon," I whispered his name, arching up against him and hooking a leg around the back of his thigh.

He cursed me, grunted, then thrust his hips, rutting against me and pushing me deeper and harder into the dirt. The whole while his lips moved, soft and wet against the side of my neck. I let myself tangle my fingers into his hair, coaxing him on and praising him for how he took what he wanted from me.

"Use me," I pleaded. "I deserve it."

He humped me faster, harder, more frantic, then Gideon sank his teeth into my neck hard enough to draw blood and a wet heat soaked through his pants as he went still. I wanted him to stay, tried to hold us together, but with his orgasm, the moment passed. He extricated himself from my arms and sat up, that soft gorgeous hair falling loose and tangled over his face.

"You deserve nothing from me," he said, climbing to his feet and leaving me alone on my back, leaves in my hair, blood and cum smeared across the rest of me.

I closed my eyes, scrubbing my hand down my face and trying to pretend it wasn't tears I wiped from the bottom of my lash line. The cruel truth was, if I could go back in time, I wouldn't change a single thing about the course of our lives. Hurting Gideon then was the only thing that allowed him to be alive now, his cum hot and sticky against my hip.

And that...

That was worth everything.

CHAPTER 30

DAREN

Luca lay on my bed, wearing my shirt, and it was almost like we'd time-traveled back to the year before when everything was so much less serious than it felt now.

"I missed this," I said softly, tracing a swirl across the jut of his hip bone. His cock lay spent against his thigh, freshly cleaned from the shower we'd taken together after Fletcher took off.

"I don't want to get used to it again," he said, scrunching his nose. "Not yet."

I sighed, desperate to lay down beside him but not trusting the house to alert me to Fletcher's eventual return.

"Tell me about him," Luca said, rolling onto his side and propping his head in his hand. "Tell me about this place."

Never once did it cross my mind that Luca would be

asking for underhanded reasons. For as much double-crossing as there had been and would continue to be in our lives, I didn't doubt the sincerity of him, the truth of us.

"Fletcher isn't as bad as everyone thinks he is," I said with a half-shrug. "He's cold, but he's not cruel."

"Have you fucked him?"

I shook my head. "I tried a few times, but he's not interested in me. The first time he ever paid attention to me naked was when you were beside me."

Luca's cheeks turned pink. "Why didn't he fuck me tonight?"

"Are you jealous?" I asked, pinching his hip. "Are you left wanting? He came on your face, remember?"

Luca's eye was still tinged red around the corners, in case he'd forgotten.

"He does look like he fucks rough," Luca said softly.

"You saw the state of Bellamy when we met up for the trade."

"I've been trying to sleep with Gideon since I got to the house," Luca confessed, rolling onto his back.

This conversation was one we'd had before, but only in hypotheticals and long before either of us had truly understood the depths of the rivalry between the Thorns and the Roses.

"That feels useful."

"Useful and selfish," he said, giving me a coy grin. "He's hot."

I arched a brow, not jealous in the slightest, just glaringly aroused at the thought of someone else fucking Luca while I watched, or better, with me.

"Aren't I hot?"

The laughter in Luca's face died off, and he darted a glance at the closed door to my bedroom before snaking his hand around the back of my neck and pulling our faces closer together.

"You're beautiful," he whispered, kissing the corner of my mouth. "You're everything I've ever wanted."

I hummed, licking my way into his mouth and finally giving in. Flinging a leg over Luca's waist, I shifted my weight on top of him and pressed him down into the sheets. I wanted my bed to smell like him for the rest of the term.

"Do you think Gideon is fucking Bellamy right now?" I asked, kissing my way from Luca's mouth to the curve of his neck.

"Gideon doesn't fuck anyone." Luca arched up against me, his cock twitching back to life. "But you do."

"We talked about this."

"Tell me how you fucked Bellamy." Luca dug his fingernails into the small of my back. "Was he the last person you fucked?"

"You're the last person I fucked."

I reached up and shoved my fingers into his mouth, partly to silence him and partly so I didn't hurt him too bad when I shoved them into him. Luca gagged around the intrusion, jaw going wide as he choked. I flattened his tongue, tutting mine against the roof of my mouth.

"There's no way you're this out of practice," I taunted, reaching for the back of his throat.

Tears ran from the corners of Luca's eyes and he slowly relaxed. My knuckles dusted across his teeth and his cock spasmed against my hip.

"Bellamy wanted to be prepared for Fletcher," I said, using my hand to angle Luca's head back at a sharper angle. "I fucked him as hard as he could take it, which you'd have probably considered soft."

Luca sputtered a laugh around my hand, and I yanked it out of his mouth. Trails of spit connected the back of his throat and my fingertips, splattering across his chest as I reached down blindly between his legs. I forced two spit-slick fingers into his still-stretched ass, covering his mouth with my other hand to stop his cry from echoing through the house.

He sounded so perfect, so *mine*, that I didn't hear the door open.

I heard it close.

I heard Fletcher's heavy footfalls, and then beside me, the mattress depressed as he sat down.

I froze.

Luca froze, except for the muscles of his asshole contracting around my fingers.

Fletcher knew about Luca and me. It wasn't a secret to him, but what was happening right now wasn't necessarily allowed either. In fact, he'd warned us both when he told us to hide better. A task I'd immediately failed.

"You should have locked your door," he said quietly,

reaching over and brushing Luca's damp hair back from his forehead.

"I didn't think I was allowed."

"Fair point." Fletcher swallowed, and a twig fell out of his hair, landing in the small space between his knee and Luca's ribcage. "How many fingers do you have inside of him right now?"

"Two," I rasped.

"Give him a third."

I was well on my way to that point anyway, so I did.

Luca loosed another cry against my palm, and Fletcher pressed his palm down against Luca's forehead, stilling his desperate thrashing.

"Have you fisted him before?" Fletcher asked me, like Luca wasn't even there.

"Yes."

"Were you going to?" he asked next, like Luca wasn't half naked beneath me with most of my hand already up his ass. "Fist him tonight, I mean."

"I hadn't planned it out."

Luca grunted his approval for fisting, and I shot him a death glare.

For what felt like a lifetime, none of us moved until Fletcher finally asked me, "How long has this been going on?"

I knew he didn't mean the current sex act, but our relationship in general. It was bad enough I'd lied, because the last thing I wanted was for him to doubt my loyalty.

"Over a year," I admitted.

"Have you been underhanded with me about every-thing, Daren? Or just this?"

"I'm loyal," I promised, and it was the truth. I might not always understand the hows or the whys, but I was loyal. "To you and to the Thorns..."

He sensed my hesitation.

"But?"

"But I love him," I said.

Luca whined against my palm, teeth gnashing against my skin.

"How innocent," Fletcher said with a frown. "To think any of that matters."

CHAPTER 31
LUCA

Daren's slick fingers and Fletcher's cruel words were almost enough to make me come untouched. I groaned, relaxing and letting Daren's fingers get as deep inside of me as they could reach, focusing on the wet press of his palm on my mouth and the callused grip of Fletcher's hand against my face.

I wanted him.

I wanted *him*.

I wanted them both.

"Love is a liability, Daren," Fletcher said, climbing off of the bed.

I winced, immediately missing the proximity of his body heat, but Daren was quick to fill the absence, stretching his three fingers inside of me until I screamed against his hand.

"I don't care," Daren told him, gorgeous and sincere eyes locked on me.

"Does he?" Fletcher asked, acknowledging me for the first time.

Daren dragged his palm away from my mouth, resting it on my throat.

"Not as much as I should," I answered, giving Daren a knowing look before my stare darted up toward Fletcher. "I love him, but...I want *you*."

"Sex is just as bad, Luca," Fletcher said, lips angled into an almost frown.

"Is that why you won't fuck him?"

He huffed. "I think the question you're meaning to ask is that why Gideon North won't fuck *you*?"

Daren pulled his fingers halfway out of me and spit on his knuckles before pushing back inside. I twisted beneath him, arching off the bed with a groan.

"Gideon doesn't fuck anybody," I said, "but I do."

"Does it bother you?" Fletcher looked to Daren, eyes narrowed. "That you sit there and say you love him, and in the next breath he's begging me to fuck?"

Daren shifted his hand so it was palm up, the heel of his hand cradling my balls. The way they talked to each other like I wasn't even there was fucking *doing* things to me, and if one of them didn't get it together and fuck me soon, I was going to throw myself off the roof.

"He's asking you to get in his asshole, Fletcher, not his heart."

Fletcher's mouth quirked up into the first honest smile I'd ever seen, and he let out a quiet laugh, hand resting on his belt. "Is that what you want? You want me in your asshole, Luca?"

I shivered, and Daren wiggled a fourth finger into me. Spreading my legs wider, I planted my feet on the mattress and closed my eyes.

"That's why I'm here, isn't it? As an offering?"

"Don't demean yourself like that."

Daren chuckled. "He likes it."

"I want you both," I admitted, reaching down and wrapping my fingers around Daren's wrist. He smiled, nostrils flaring as I tried to drag him deeper. "I don't know how to explain it and I don't think I need to. I'm here and I'm..."

The words left me when Daren moved to get the lube, squirting a more than generous amount onto his already spit-slick knuckles. He twisted around my rim, trying to press the rest of the way inside of me and meeting resistance.

"Say it," Fletcher prompted, resting his knee again on the edge of the bed.

"I'm here and I'm asking for both of you. Not because of any obligation." Daren's chin tipped toward the tattoo on his chest. "But because I find you both attractive, because I love Daren and I love fucking, and they're not mutually exclusive."

"Show me, then," Fletcher said. "Show me again how you take his cock and prove there's room for me in there."

Daren flipped our positions before I had time to fully

process what Fletcher had just agreed to. He shoved his pants down as his ass hit the bed, and he promptly fitted me on his lap, my still gaping hole sucking close around his shaft as he fucked up into me with one quick thrust.

Fingers gripping my waist, Daren set a hard and steady pace, the sound of our skin slapping together the loudest noise in the room. I fell forward, burying my face into the crook of his neck. Tears again wet my face, but not because I was in pain and not because I was scared. I was just so happy. Happy to be with him, even if under watch and even if under false pretenses. My entire relationship with Daren was stolen moments, so I would be a thief and steal some more.

"I love you too," I whispered into his ear, a promise meant just for him. "No matter what happens."

Daren kissed the side of my head, slowing his thrusts at the same time the mattress depressed at the foot of the bed. Resting my weight on Daren's chest, I reached behind me and spread my ass cheeks apart, giving Fletcher a view like he'd asked for.

"Do you hate sharing me?" I asked softly in the damp skin of Daren's neck.

"I love everything about you."

Slippery and thick fingers traced the outline of my hole, pressing hard against the places where Daren and I were joined. Beneath me, Daren grunted, hips snapping up of their own accord as Fletcher slowly teased us both.

"Hold still," Fletcher said absently, the thick swell of his cock pushing into my hole against the top of Daren's shaft. Daren went entirely still, both of us holding our breaths as Fletcher forced his cock into my body.

"This doesn't feel like there's room for two," Fletcher said, a hint of amusement now lacing through his tone. He made no move to stop, feeding inch after inch of his erection into me until I cried into the pillow with relief. "Oh, there it is."

Daren stroked his hands down my back, soothing me like a skittish horse as I adjusted to the feel of both of their cocks inside of me, laughing gently as I mumbled nonsense into his ear. Promises, and secrets, and hopes, and nightmares, all of them ours and his and mine. Fletcher let out a low groan, the last inch of his cock sliding into me, and his fingers grazing over Daren's around my waist as they both found room for themselves in and around me.

I'd never felt so full, not even with half of Daren's arm up my ass. Never felt so vulnerable, shaking between two men who had the power to make or break the rest of my life. Fletcher could ruin me with a word, Daren with a look, and between the two of them with their pleasure on the line, I'd never had more control over my life.

"This is a mistake," Fletcher said under his breath, the words not meant for either of us, maybe not even for himself.

"Then make it count," Daren said, sinking into the bed and thrusting up into me. He had limited movement with Fletcher and me on top of him, but as with all things, he made it worth it. His cock jerked Fletcher out of whatever preemptive outcome he'd built in his mind, and then the two of them delivered me the most ruthless fucking of my very short life, not stopping until I was covered in cum and blood, on the brink of consciousness and silently begging for more.

CHAPTER 32

BELLAMY

Gideon stormed back into the bedroom as soon as I'd finished picking at the crust of the sandwich he'd left for me. Startled, and still naked, I dropped the plate onto the bed and reeled back. The sheets over my lap pooled low around my waist, and Gideon's stare fell to the place against my leg where the sheet hadn't managed to cover my thigh.

"You remind me of him," Gideon murmured, kicking the door closed behind him. He stalked across the room and crawled onto the bed, swiping the plate onto the floor with one fast swing of his arm. It shattered, and then Gideon was on top of me, his weight bearing down oppressively against my chest as I tried to breathe beneath him.

The already familiar spike of fear shot up my spine, and my traitorous dick responded by pushing hard and insistent against Gideon's muscular thigh. I tilted my head back against the pillow and closed my eyes, not sure what he wanted or what he planned to do, but knowing well enough I couldn't—or didn't want to—get away from it.

"Does this turn you on?" he asked, breath hot against my cheek.

I nodded.

"Touch yourself," he said.

Swallowing, I reached between our bodies and curled my hand around my dick. Gideon was fully dressed, but the front of his pants burned hot against my knuckles as I gave the first stroke up my shaft. He grunted, upper lip contorting into a scowl as I accidentally—on purpose—touched him through his pants as I touched myself.

I tried to hold my pleasure off, waiting for him to take himself in hand or have me take us both, but he kept himself balanced above me, the only real pleasure I offered him being my fingers against his zipper while I brought myself off. The whole time, Gideon snarled at me, breath hot against my neck, but the longer it went on, the closer he came, until his nose was tucked securely against the patch of skin behind my ear.

"Can I touch you?" I asked.

"No."

"Are you going to touch yourself?"

Another snarl instead of an answer.

Licking my lips, I adjusted myself beneath him until his weight scared me, until his obvious *hatred* for me was close enough to bleed into my skin. I was terrified, and on the brink of coming, when another question popped into my head and before I could stop myself, it was in the space between us.

"Are you a virgin, Gideon?" I whispered, lifting my hips and pressing up against him.

He cursed, moving above me and grabbing me by the throat. Like a rag doll, Gideon shook me and hauled me up until I was half sitting, half sprawled beneath him. Completely naked with my cock still in my hand, I kept stroking myself because the rough handling and the nerves only made me more turned on. With anger in his eyes and his fingers tightening around my throat, I came with a shudder violent enough to make the bed creak.

Spurts of cum lashed out of my cock, splattering against his stomach and my fingers. Gideon's expression turned from hatred to confusion, then something that felt very similar to disgust. He flexed his hand around my throat, which only drew another burst of cum out of my balls, then he shoved me into the sheets.

Glowering down at me from above, Gideon's body heat still radiated against me and, lacking sense, I hooked my cum-slick finger around the waistband of his pants, trying to pull him back down against me.

"Gideon," I whispered his name, chest still heaving with the tremors from my orgasm.

"Who are you?" Saliva swirled around his mouth before he swallowed loud enough for me to hear over the ringing in my ears from the force of my release.

"Bellamy Marchant," I told him simply. "I'm an offering."

"From *him*."

"From Fletcher," I confirmed, even though Gideon knew the rules of initiation night far better than I did.

"Why you?" he asked, "You're no one."

Gideon looked at me for what felt like the first time. His moss green eyes searched my face for an answer I didn't think either of us had. My finger pulled gently against his belt, and Gideon sighed, rocking back onto his heels.

I missed the warmth of his hand around my throat.

Scrambling out from the tangled mess of sheets, I mirrored Gideon's pose, not caring that he saw me naked, saw my half-hard cock, sticky and wet against my thigh. I committed everything about Gideon that I could to memory, not just to tell Fletcher, but for my own memories. His hulking presence and the terrified way he touched me, like his anger got the better of him and he didn't know how—or didn't care—to stop it. I knew without being told that Gideon was a virgin, which was the biggest secret I'd ever held.

"I don't know," I told him honestly. "I was supposed to go to college in California. I didn't know about...I didn't want any part of this."

"So, you're here against your will?"

"No." I shook my head, carefully reaching a finger out and pressing it against Gideon's knee. "This wasn't the plan I had for myself, but I'm where I want to be, all things considered."

"That's achingly hopeful," he said.

"It's the best I can do."

"You're resilient."

I huffed a laugh. "I'm the youngest of six brothers, I have to be."

Gideon tilted his head to the side and regarded me thoughtfully, then ever so slowly, like I was the caged predator, not him, he reached for me. His fingertips ghosted across my jawline, and my lashes fluttered, falling closed. A shiver raced from my toes to my throat, and I was helpless to stop the quiet moan that fell out of my mouth at his touch. Even slower than he'd moved for my jaw, Gideon curled his fingers, nails digging into my cheek. He pressed hard, moving them to my mouth, hooking them around my teeth and pulling my jaw open.

My dick expanded back to life and I groaned, back arching as Gideon painstakingly manipulated my mouth with his fingers. Behind my teeth, against my tongue, hooked into my cheek, Gideon molded my mouth against his palm and I was happy to let him.

"Keep your eyes closed," he warned, fingers pressing against my molars to pry my lips farther apart.

When he unzipped his pants, my jaw twinged with the stretch. The sound of skin against skin had me all the way hard again in seconds, and I ached to touch myself, but I knew better. There was no way I was going to break whatever spell had fallen over us. Just as quickly as it had begun, it was over. Gideon sighed and groaned as he finished, a shot of cum landing against my thigh. His other hand was still in my mouth, fingers pinched against my tongue, pulling it out like a display platter.

I wished he would have come there instead of my leg. Instead of his hand.

Without a word, he zipped up his pants, yanked his hand out of my mouth, and stormed out of the room, leaving me hard, alone, and confused.

Again.

CHAPTER 33

FLETCHER

Much to my surprise, I woke up in Daren's bed, a warm body flattened against my chest and a tangle of someone else's hair in my face. Fighting my first instinct to recoil, I took a steadying breath and settled deeper into the sheets. I inhaled an unfamiliar scent, opening my eyes enough to recognize the man in front of me was Luca and not Daren. He was either a light sleeper, or a horny one, because he must have sensed me waking up. Luca made a sleepy noise and pushed his ass against my sleep-hard erection, reaching back and digging his fingers into my thigh.

I was still half-dressed, my pants from the night before absolutely beyond repair, and I'd probably owe Daren a new set of sheets for what a mess I'd made of his bed the night before. Reaching behind me, I felt around the bed for my deputy, finding Luca and I the only two bodies tangled in the sheets. I did, however, find the lube, casually discarded half under a pillow. Closing my eyes, I groaned in warning, Luca starting a slow and steady grind against my dick, arching his back to search out a better angle.

"I can take it," he said sleepily, letting his hand slide from my thigh to my fly, which was still undone. He worked his fingers into my underwear, grazing against my cock before pulling me free of my pants.

"I don't care what you can take," I told him.

He hummed. "I like that about you. You're so much like him."

"Like who?" I opened the lube and shot a glob of it onto my cock and Luca's talented, manipulative fingers.

"Like Daren," he murmured, notching my tip against his asshole. After the way I'd fucked him the night before, the way Daren and I had fucked him, I was impressed he had another round in him. Even more impressed that I had to fight to get inside of him. One inch and then another, and then Luca said, "Like Gideon."

I went still as a statue, and Luca worked his hips back to take me down to the root, content to do the work on his own if I wasn't going to help out. He started fucking himself on my cock while I fought back a thousand questions I wanted to ask about what the fuck exactly he'd meant by that comment.

Deciding against any of them, I rolled Luca onto his stomach and slammed my entire length into him so hard I wondered if I was going to end up buying Daren a new bed to go with his new sheets.

"Oh, fuck," Luca moaned, turning his face to the side against the pillow. He didn't have his glasses on, and his golden brown eyes rolled back as I thrust into him, hard and long strokes meant to bring the both of us pleasure.

"You're a minx," I accused, pressing my palm against the flat of his back for leverage.

Luca laughed, a sleepy and all too seductive sound, then squeezed his muscles around my shaft.

"My downfall," I murmured, dragging my hand from his back to his face. I meant to press him into the bed, hide his face, but he had other plans.

Luca took one of my fingers into his mouth, sucking it like it was a cock, moaning and writhing beneath me like he'd never been fucked this well in his life. I wanted it to be the truth, but I'd watched Daren fuck him twice and I'd seen Daren fuck plenty of other times too.

I knew he was endowed and talented, but so was I.

There was something intoxicating about the way Luca spread himself open for me, the way he took my cock like he was a starving man and I was the only sustenance he'd ever been offered. His expressions, his sounds, it was enough to drive anyone mad, and I understood how Daren had fallen prey to the enticing other man.

Falling forward, I sank my teeth into the back of his neck, almost hard enough to draw blood. Instead of pulling away, Luca spread his legs wider, moaning like the perfect little cock slut he was. No wonder Daren loved him; he was a gem in a pile of shit.

"This ass could ruin empires," I whispered, laving my tongue over the divots shaped like my teeth.

"I don't..don't care about all that," he panted.

"I believe you," I told him. "You wouldn't be here if you did."

Luca was attractive enough to be calculating and dangerous, but he didn't have designs on any of that. He just wanted to love Daren, get fucked, and get out alive. Admirable goals across the board, though I worried if he'd find success with the first and the latter. The second one... he'd never struggle to fill that void. Physically and otherwise.

"I don't want to leave here," he said on a moan, clamping his teeth down on the finger he'd been sucking on earlier.

I pulled back enough to lift one of his legs over my shoulder so I could flip him onto his back. With his leg up, I could get even deeper inside of him, every thrust of my cock punching the air out of his lungs.

"Don't. Say. Shit. Like. That," I grit out, a snap of my hips against his pelvis punctuating every word. I wanted to tell him dreams were worthless here. They had no place and would only bring everyone misery, but I was interrupted by the sound of Daren's voice behind us.

"He's addicting, isn't he?" Daren asked, not sounding anything besides amused and aroused.

One last pump of my hips and I stilled, cock spilling a fountain of cum into Luca's tight and hot asshole. I bowed forward, pressing my forehead against the back of his neck, lungs expanding on every breath but nowhere near large enough for me to actually breathe. I hadn't meant to come inside of him, not just now, and not the night before.

It was this house, that stupid ritual from the night before. Doing things to my head, to my heart.

I reached down and pressed two fingers around my shaft, pulling out of Luca with a wet pop. My body ached from exertion, and I was desperate to flop down on my back beside him, invite Daren between us, and find the strength for another round.

I wanted to *let* Luca stay. For Daren, and for myself.

"He is," I agreed, tucking my dick back into my pants and climbing off the bed.

"Hope you had your fill of him, because we have a problem."

I finished looping my belt, and Luca grabbed his glasses off the nightstand, looking from me to Daren with concern knit loosely through his sex-drunk brows.

"What's wrong?" I asked, years of obligation and expectation taking precedence over anything else I was feeling.

Daren grimaced, running a nervous hand through his hair. "Gideon North is downstairs."

PART THREE
THE UPRISING

CHAPTER 34
GIDEON

When Daren opened the door to Thorn Hill Manor, a hundred lives flashed across his face. Fondness when he saw Bellamy standing in front of me, oversized hoodie hanging down to the middle of his thighs, to bitter contempt, then resignation when he looked up and saw me behind him.

"Can we come in?" I asked.

He shifted his attention over my shoulder. "Did anyone see you?"

"We came around the long way," I said.

He ushered us in, reaching for Bellamy as soon as the door closed.

"I'm fine," Bellamy said with a small laugh as Daren shoved up the sleeves of the hoodie to inspect his wrists.

"He's better than fine," I grumbled.

Daren opened his mouth like he had something smart

to say, but Bellamy pressed his hand against Daren's chest and he snapped his mouth closed.

"I'm fine," he said again. "Thanks to you."

Color flooded Daren's cheeks, and he covered the place Bellamy's hand rested over his heart.

"What do you want?" Daren asked, staring at me over Bellamy's messy, golden hair. "The return isn't until noon."

"What if I was here to check on Luca?" I asked, raising a brow. "If I was worried about his welfare."

Daren narrowed his eyes. "You know he's safe with me."

"I do," I confirmed. "And that's just one of the *many* reasons I'm here."

Bellamy stood between us, the fingers of his left hand still entwined with Daren's, and I found myself drowning in jealousy. Bellamy was so perfect and pure and so absolutely unaware of the shit show he'd been thrown into with his initiation into the Thorns. He'd gotten me so twisted up in my own head the night before, the demanding way he asked for what he wanted, even through his fear, reminded me so much of the Fletcher I used to know. It hurt to look at Bellamy because he so clearly exemplified the best parts of the man I'd loved for my entire life. A man who put family and loyalty over all else, even to his own detriment, and I was ready to put a stop to it.

Once and for all.

"Fletcher is still in bed," Daren said. "With Luca."

"Does that bother you?" I asked, bothered myself with the knowledge Fletcher had another man with him, and bothered that Bellamy stood between Daren and me, swaying toward Daren and back to me then to Daren again, wanting us both, even after how I'd treated him.

The boy had no sense of self-preservation.

"I love it." Daren lifted Bellamy's hand to his mouth and dusted a kiss across his knuckles. "I'll go let him know you're here."

Daren climbed the stairs and disappeared down a long, dark hallway, leaving Bellamy and me unattended in the living room. Decorated with rich, overstuffed black leather couches and dark wood furniture, the house reeked of money and power. There was no escape unless we were willing to make one.

"I owe you an apology," I said, taking Bellamy's hand and raising it to my mouth. I pressed a kiss against the place Daren had just done the same. Bellamy's knuckles were warm, and after I kissed him, I held his fingers against my cheek.

"For what?"

He looked so helpless in the middle of that massive room, wearing a hoodie that was easily four sizes too big for him. But he also looked like he could be at home—if he wanted to be.

"Leaving you last night."

"I don't think spending the whole night together was ever meant to be part of the plan," he said simply.

"I think I'm done with the plan."

"Why now?" Bellamy asked, blinking up at me.

"I—"

The thought was interrupted by three sets of footsteps coming down the hallway, down the stairs. Daren in front with Luca close behind, Fletcher a few paces back. Luca looked like he'd just been fucked, skin glistening with sweat and fresh hickeys peppering his neck. His glasses sat lopsided on his face, but he fixed them before reaching the bottom of the stairs. Fletcher was in the same clothes as the night before, except he was barefoot now and his belt hung undone and loose, the button of his pants open.

The urge to grab Luca by the throat and put him through a wall for whatever he'd just done wrapped around me like a weight, and suddenly I was back at the bottom of my father's pool, lungs burning with the need to breathe. But I was stuck, trapped and unable to get back to the surface, to get the one thing I needed the most. Violent tears welled in my eyes as my chest fought to find a breath, and then Bellamy slipped his hand into mine, giving my fingers a gentle squeeze. His touch cut the ropes, and I kicked to the surface, sucking in the most beautiful breath I'd ever had.

Fletcher's stare darted quickly down to our joined hands, and the only sign he gave over having any feelings about it at all was the way his jaw ticked just below his ear.

"Last I checked, it's not anywhere near noon," he drawled.

"I think I'm done with doing what I'm told," I said,

tightening my grip on Bellamy's hand. I didn't know why he'd reached for me, why he'd chosen to stand beside me. I'd been nothing but rude to him.

Fletcher licked his lips, his bright and thoughtful eyes taking a quick appraisal of everyone and everything in the room. Then, he sighed.

"Daren, take Luca and Bellamy upstairs to your room. Stay there until I come and get you. Do you understand?" Fletcher cocked his head back and to the side, staring down the sharp line of his nose at me, even though I was taller than him by inches. Another tick in his jaw, a twitch of his fingers.

Daren extended his hand and I didn't realize how hard I'd been holding onto Bellamy until he fought his way out of my death grip. It wasn't choosing sides, but it felt that way. Luca would be loyal to me, but his heart was with Daren, and Daren stood with the Thorns. Bellamy had no investment either way, and I searched his face for some hint of feeling before he went. He lifted my hand and kissed my palm, the heel of my hand, then he let Daren and Luca take him upstairs.

And once again, I was alone with Fletcher Sinclair.

CHAPTER 35

DAREN

Luca and Bellamy followed behind me like obedient little cats, wandering up the stairs like we had nothing better to do and no place better to be. I brought them both back into my room and closed the door behind me, my fingers hesitating on the lock before deciding to leave it undone. There was a very real chance whatever was going on between Gideon and Fletcher would end in bloodshed, and that second to flip the lock could be the difference between life and death.

"It smells like sex in here," Bellamy said to no one in particular.

"Probably because there's been a lot of it since we got home," Luca said, face contorting in a grimace. "Since we got *back*."

I hummed, plucking mindlessly at Luca's t-shirt. "Our time is running out. Take this off."

He took his shirt off, then his pants, without being

told. Crooking my finger, I beckoned him closer, and as soon as he was close enough to touch, I snaked my arm around his waist and brought us chest to chest, slanting our mouths together. He moaned and parted his lips for me readily, giving me the space to sink into him entirely. To lose myself.

"You were so hot last night," I whispered, tearing myself away long enough to breathe. "So hot this morning."

Behind me, Bellamy let out a slow breath.

"He's pretty, now that I get a good look at him," Luca said, smiling against my mouth. "Does he taste good?"

"He's right here," Bellamy said.

Luca opened his eyes and stared Bellamy down over my shoulder. "Do you taste good?"

"I...I don't know."

"You didn't let him taste it when you fucked him?" Luca asked me, mouthing kisses against my neck with his lips and his tongue.

"He came all over the sheets," I murmured. "It felt cruel to make him lap it up from there."

"You've made me do worse."

"You like it," I reminded him, pinching his ribs until he untangled himself from my arms. Luca was naked and hard, hickeys bruising his neck and throat from where Fletcher and I had our way with him last night. He looked debauched and used, which was good...because he was. "Go get in the shower, Luca."

I reached behind me and caught the cuff of Bellamy's

hoodie between my fingers, pulling him close. He stumbled, maybe, and reached for Luca, sliding an arm around his waist to stop himself from falling over. It gave Luca a small shove off-balance, then he circled his arms around Bellamy and pulled at the bottom of the massive hoodie,

"Whose sweater is this?" he asked.

"Gideon's," Bellamy whispered.

"Save it for Fletcher," Luca teased, stripping it over Bellamy's head and discarding it onto my bed.

Beneath the hoodie, Bellamy wasn't wearing anything besides the disheveled white pants he'd worn the night before at the offering. The shirt had to have been ruined, and how gracious of Gideon to not parade him through the woods half-naked. Maybe he wasn't such a beast after all.

Reaching out, I pulled Bellamy away from Luca's wandering hands, making sure there was enough breathing room between all of our overheated bodies.

"Bellamy," I said softly, spinning him around to face me. He was a sight, as he always was, but now with messy hair and flushed cheeks, blown pupils and a dangerously hungry mouth. "Do you want to be here?"

"Why does everyone keep asking me that?"

"Because it's important," I said. "Because you went from asking me to fuck you rough so you were *prepared*, to letting Luca manhandle you into the shower without so much as a hello."

"I was under the impression we're all past small talk." His mouth quirked into a smile before falling flat.

"No." I shook my head. "Small talk is all *we* have sometimes."

Bellamy sighed, fidgeting his hands in front of him again like some kind of nervous habit. I remembered him kissing Gideon's palm after I'd kissed Bellamy's knuckles. The five of us were so close and so tangled, but so treacherously far away from each other.

"I told Gideon last night, I didn't want anything to do with this life, but it's mine now and I have to make the best of it," Bellamy explained.

"And is this making the best of it?"

"Isn't it?" he countered, shrugging his shoulders up toward his ears.

"I think it is," Luca said, taking a step toward Bellamy and closing some of the space I'd put between us. "We're only allowed what we have, and we only have what we can take."

"The two of you are together?" Bellamy asked.

Luca walked his fingers across the top of Bellamy's shoulder, and Bellamy inclined his head to the side so Luca could move further up his neck.

"I love him," I answered, "but you cannot tell a soul, Bellamy. I'll burn both of these houses down before I lose him."

"You're a romantic," Luca murmured, propping his chin on Bellamy's shoulder. His lips were still slick with spit from our kiss, and I knew without asking his hole was just as wet, thanks to Fletcher's early morning fuck.

Which I only missed out on because I'd gone downstairs to make some coffee.

"Fletcher knows, though. Doesn't he?"

"Fletcher has his own secrets," I said.

"I think Gideon does too," Bellamy whispered.

"Yeah." Luca brushed his lips across Bellamy's jaw. "Fletcher Sinclair is the biggest secret of them all."

CHAPTER 36

LUCA

"I don't know how long any of this is going to last," Bellamy said, giving me more room to kiss his jaw, his throat. "I don't even know what any of this is, but I like it."

I was beyond spent from initiation night and the rough fuck Fletcher had given me earlier in the morning. I couldn't have forced another orgasm out of myself if Daren had demanded it of me, but that didn't mean Daren and Bellamy had to suffer alone. Bellamy was irresistibly beautiful, no wonder Daren had bedded him the week before, and I would be more than happy for him to do it again.

"Fletcher said to shower," I reminded the two men in front of me, grabbing Bellamy around the waist and hauling him toward the en suite in the corner of Daren's room. "We should do what we're told."

"You're a horrible listener." Daren rolled his eyes and

shoved his sweats down to his ankles, pulled his shirt over his head. I made quick work of Bellamy's pants, and then all three of us were in the bathroom, the shower was on, and there was more skin beneath my fingertips than I knew what to do with.

My cock didn't know what to do either.

"I don't think I have another one in me," I said with a pretend frown, dipping under the spray of the massive shower head and slicking my hair back.

"That sounds like a challenge and you know it," Daren teased.

He pressed me against the wall, his other hand wrapped tightly around Bellamy's wrist. His erection against my ass, Daren circled his hips against me, pushing my chest into the cold tile wall, but there were no signs of viable life between my legs. With a twist of my shoulder, I turned so my back was against the wall. My breath caught in my throat, Daren and Bellamy together a sight to behold.

Both of them were gorgeous in different ways. Daren with his broad shoulders and strong hands, Bellamy with his slight frame and golden curls that led down to a delicate and hard cock. He had scratches around his shoulders, a couple abrasions on his thighs, and I wondered how hard Fletcher had gone on him the night before.

"Let me suck you," I whispered, reaching down and taking Daren's cock into my hand. I glanced at Bellamy before stretching my fingers toward him as well. He was quiet, but brave...so unsuited for this way of life. "You too."

"I love it," Daren said, pushing me to my knees.

"Yes," Bellamy breathed his consent out like a prayer.

I pushed Daren's cock against his stomach and sucked the spot where his shaft turned into his balls into my mouth, making a fist around Bellamy's cock with my other hand. Both of them were burning hot, hard, and leaking. I wanted them both in my mouth, needed it, blood pooling between my own legs even as my cock begged off from exhaustion.

"Closer," I pleaded, using their cocks to move them into a place where I could take turns putting each of them into my mouth.

"Oh, Godddd." Bellamy's voice raised at least an entire octave when I sucked him into the back of my throat on the first go. His back bowed, and Daren was quick to steady him, leaning in and slanting their mouths together before Bellamy was able to make another sound.

I angled my head to the other side, licking my way up Daren's shaft, relishing the ways he groaned his pleasure into Bellamy's mouth. Back and forth I went, from one to the other, until Daren and Bellamy both had their hands in my hair, fighting for my mouth.

Sex was the most powerful weapon a person could have, but it was important to wield it carefully...with discretion. Sometimes that discretion meant you gave your body away so no one took you seriously as a threat. They assumed it meant you didn't understand the power you held, and they would assume wrong. But unlike most of the men in my world, I'd never had aspirations of power beyond the power I found on my back.

Falling in love with Daren wasn't enough to make me forget I was supposed to get close to Gideon, that I was supposed to earn his trust. Earning his trust would mean I earned my father's respect, but for what end? What did he matter to me anymore? He was small and old and nothing compared to Daren, compared to me, compared to any other person currently inside the four walls of Thorn Hill.

My father meant for me to be calculating and conniving. He meant for me to make myself invaluable, gather secrets, and betray the man I'd become confidant to. But the more I got to know Gideon, the more I understood him, the less I wanted to do that. The only problem was, I didn't know how to not. I didn't know how to have Daren.

I didn't know how to *keep* any of this.

"I'm close," Bellamy whimpered, snapping me back into the present, into the burning of my knees and the stretch of my jaw.

I doubled my efforts around his thickening shaft, pulling him out a few inches when I felt the first burst of cum shoot against the roof of my mouth. He spilled his release onto my waiting tongue, and then I tipped my head back and showed it to both of them.

"Taste yourself," Daren urged. "Take it back from him."

I moved off my knees halfway, but Bellamy was on the

floor with me before I could get there. He crashed our mouths together, our teeth cracking as he used his tongue to scoop his cum out of my mouth. He was ravenous and wild, and I was at his mercy. With Daren's hand in my hair and Bellamy's tongue in my mouth, I stroked Daren until he came with a growl, his load splashing against the side of my face, my mouth, Bellamy's cheeks.

I broke the kiss long enough to drag his cum onto Bellamy's kiss-swollen bottom lip, then I sucked it into my mouth, groaning at the way the two of them tasted together. I kissed Bellamy until I couldn't keep my eyes open anymore, at which point I collapsed onto my ass with a happy sigh.

"This doesn't feel very clean," Bellamy teased, climbing back to his feet.

I didn't have enough energy to laugh, so I gave him a huff of breath that turned into a whine when Daren hauled me back up onto shaking legs.

"You're everything that matters," he whispered into my ear, stroking his hands down my arms to the tips of my fingers. "Let's get cleaned up and make sure the house is still standing."

CHAPTER 37
BELLAMY

It was jealousy, I realized. Sitting on the edge of Daren's bed—again in borrowed clothes—watching the way he and Luca moved around each other like they were in a shared orbit. I'd never met two people more destined to be together, more meant to be, than the two of them.

Sighing, I fidgeted with the cuff of Gideon's hoodie, which I'd put back on after the shower, even though Daren and Luca had teased me about the necessity to leave it behind for Fletcher. The history between Fletcher Sinclair and Gideon North was simultaneously the best and worst kept secret between the two houses. There was no doubt the two men hated each other beyond reason, but the hate was too present and violent for it to be based solely on their names. It was a personal kind of invest-ment, one I knew too well because it was how my father felt about the Sinclair family as a whole.

"Respectfully, Bellamy," Daren said, leaning against the wall opposite the bed and folding his arms in front of his chest. "Why are you here?"

"Why am I..."

"How did you get chosen for this?" Luca clarified. He sat on the floor between the bed and the wall, but to the side. Our bodies formed a triangle, easy for all of us to see the other two at all times, which felt important.

"My dad," I explained, a story I didn't know the whole of that would never make sense. "I was supposed to go to school in California. But that changed and now I'm here. My mom was..."

"Was what?" Daren pressed.

I remembered her tears, her anxiety the night they'd sat me down and told me about my pending enrollment at RHU, about my involvement with the Thorns. I wonder if either of them knew what it had meant at the time. If they knew I'd be a human offering, a sacrifice to seal generations of secrets between a handful of families who had more money than most countries. Maybe that was why my mom had been so distraught over the whole thing.

"Not happy about it," I said. "She cried when I found out."

Luca shot Daren a concerned look, eyes crinkled around the corners behind the crystal clear lenses of his glasses.

"Why?" I asked. "What was that look for?"

"I don't know," Luca said, features clear once again. "It's just weird."

"Why is it weird?"

"Because you're nobody," Daren said simply, mouth twisted. "That's not—"

"I know how you meant it," I said simply.

"I don't think I've ever even heard the name Marchant before you." Luca stretched his legs out in front of him, flexing his toes toward the ceiling and stretching his arms back behind him.

"We aren't anyone. I have five older brothers and at home I shared a room with two of them. We don't have money; we don't have anything."

"Quite the offering," Luca mused under his breath.

I wanted to be offended, but it was the truth. I'd learned little about the organization of the Thorns and the Roses in the lead-up to initiation night, but I knew they had money and power and everything they did was an exchange of those things. There was no reason for me to be part of it at all. No reason for my dad to be a part of it either.

"My dad told me to make Fletcher Sinclair an ally."

"Fletcher has no allies. That's why he's"— Daren pointed to the upstairs—"up there and we're down here."

"Aren't you an ally?"

"I'm a deputy," he said. "Luca is a deputy. Right hand. Advisor. Whatever you want to call it, but ally? I think you have to trust an ally, don't you?"

"Gideon doesn't trust anyone," Luca said.

I remembered Gideon coming back into the room at Rose Hall, remembered him crawling on top of me and rutting me into the bed like the beast he wanted everyone to believe him to be. I'd seen the cracks in his façade, though, just like I had when Fletcher had me by the throat in the woods. The two of them were so much the same, but blind to see how much stronger they could be together instead of apart.

"Who do you trust?" I asked Luca.

"I trust Daren," he said quickly, "and most of the time I trust Gideon."

"And you?"

"Luca and Fletcher."

"Blindly?" I asked.

"They've given me no reason to doubt them."

I swallowed, shoving my hands into the front pocket of the hoodie and staring down at my feet.

"Who should I trust?" I whispered.

Luca climbed to his feet, and he and Daren together closed the center of our little triangle into a point.

"Yourself," he said, brushing his fingers down my cheek until I tipped my head back to, once again, look at them both.

"Not either of you?" I asked. "Not Fletcher? Not Gideon?"

"Not until you understand why you're here," Daren answered.

"We're pawns." Luca sniffed, the scrunch of his nose lifting his glasses. "Even Daren and I. We're just pawns in someone else's game, and until you know who's moving the pieces, you shouldn't trust anyone but yourself."

"What happens after today?" I dared to ask, but barely above a whisper. Luca ruffled his fingers through my hair and I closed my eyes, letting myself lean into the warm cradle of Daren's hand.

"I don't want to think about it," Luca murmured.

"That's up to us," Daren answered. "Either everything's the same, or everything's different."

"Who decides?"

Before he could reply, a deafening crash rang out from downstairs and then everything went silent.

CHAPTER 38

FLETCHER

For a moment, I was sixteen again, the same height as Gideon, all knobby limbs and too big hands...too big hearts. And we stood in the middle of his bedroom at Rose Hill Prep, mouths pressed together like we had any right.

Like we deserved it.

Daren's bedroom door slamming closed upstairs brought me back to the present, back the man in front of me who was so far removed from the boy I'd known. The boy I'd fallen in love with.

"You're not supposed to be here," I said.

Gideon licked his lips, stare raking down my chest and stomach, lingering a little longer than he should have at my waistline. "Did I interrupt?"

"I'd just finished."

He exhaled loudly out of his nose, lip curling up in disgust.

"Don't be a prude."

"I'm not."

"That's why you brought Luca to the exchange instead of a first year?" I arched a brow and took one step toward him, clasping my hands together behind my back.

"I was doing him a favor," Gideon said, which just confirmed to me that he also knew about Luca's relationship with Daren.

"We don't do favors for people, Gideon," I said. "They do things *for* us to *earn* favors."

"That's the way it's always been," he said with a shrug. "Maybe I'm tired of it."

"I've heard this from you before."

He laughed, the sound catching in the back of his throat like it hadn't been meant for me. The noise was so aborted, so bitter, there was no way it could have come from any iteration of the boy I'd fallen in love with at sixteen.

"Don't worry, Sin. Those kinds of dreams haven't been mine for years."

His use of the old nickname landed like a knife in my chest. I was glad I'd spent so much time apart from Gideon because I don't think I would have survived having to see him, having to watch him grow up and change into whatever he was now.

"Why?" I asked.

"Why ask me that if you don't care about the answer?"

"If I didn't care, I wouldn't have asked." I took another step toward him, and he stepped back.

That wasn't going to stop me.

"After you failed me out of freshman year English, my father took me out of school," he explained, which was already common knowledge, at least to me. I'd noticed his absence immediately. "He...punished me."

"How?" I closed the space between us until Gideon's back was against the wall. He'd grown so tall, so muscular, but up close I could see the same flecks in his green eyes that had been there before. Maybe he wasn't lost for good.

Maybe *I* wasn't lost for good.

"It doesn't matter."

"Tell me," I whispered.

"It's not your business."

"Tell me," I demanded again.

"He isolated me," Gideon rasped, eyes narrowed as his earlier look of appreciation had turned to barely constrained hatred. "I'd go days without seeing another soul, without talking..."

He exhaled quietly, dropping his head against the wall. He wasn't scared of me anymore, and I didn't know why.

"Just when I thought I couldn't take it anymore, he showed up in my room. It had been a couple of weeks by then, maybe a month. I don't know." He smiled sadly. "He grabbed me by the hair and pulled me through the house."

"Where?" I asked.

He pressed his fingers against a spot on his scalp and I touched him there. I didn't ask and he didn't flinch. He didn't push me away when I pressed my fingertips into the softness of his skin until I felt the raised ridges of a scar.

"He dragged me to the pool and threw me in. When I tried to climb out, he bent over the edge and wouldn't let me out." Gideon held my stare for the first time since that night in his bedroom. "I tried to fight him and he kept pushing me under, holding me down. He tried to drown me, Sin. He *did* drown me."

"I'll kill him."

Gideon ignored me. "After that, after he pulled me out of the pool by my hair and I threw up all over his shoes, he brought in a tutor and started acting like everything was normal again."

"He's insane." I pushed against the scar on Gideon's scalp, feeling the way it was inconsistent in its shape, as if multiple chunks of hair had been torn out of his head at the same time.

"It was the last time he had the upper hand on me in the water," Gideon said.

"The Beast, indeed," I murmured, letting my hand fall away from his hair to the side of his neck.

"But what he did to me then, all the things he did, I'd bear them a thousand times over rather than relive what it felt like when *you* hurt me." Gideon stabbed his finger into the middle of my chest, using enough force that it knocked me back. He pushed off the wall, shoving me again. I stumbled over the low coffee table, catching myself on the couch. Even if he hadn't touched me, his words would have been enough to throw me off balance, and he still hadn't answered my question.

I had no idea why Gideon was here.

"I don't expect you to believe me," I explained, righting myself, only for him to give me another shove back down onto the couch. "But I did you a service."

The things my father had threatened the night he found out about my *friendship* with Gideon North went far beyond a little isolation and play drowning. My father was on the brink of ruining empires over the affair. He had so much dirt on Gideon's father and his business dealings, he was going to try and take down the North empire, and the boy I loved with it. The things he'd promised to do if I didn't do it first still haunted me.

"You did me a service," he repeated.

He mocked.

He didn't sound like himself, barely looked like himself. Fingers flexed into fists at his sides, body posed like a predator ready to pounce. I climbed back to my feet, and for the first time, found myself face to face with not Gideon North, but The Beast himself.

CHAPTER 39

GIDEON

I had my hand around his throat before I even realized it, his back against the wall before I'd taken a single step. I squeezed, the delicate bones and cartilage of Fletcher's neck like putty in my hands. He sputtered and gasped, blue eyes going wide, but far from scared. And he didn't fight me.

He did me a *service*.

I would wring the breath from his throat and then spit that declaration right back onto his grave.

"I used to wish I was dead," I said, tightening my fingers around his throat until his face turned red as a strawberry. Spit gathered in the corners of his mouth, he lifted his hands between us. Instead of grabbing for my wrist like I expected, he shoved the heel of his palm forward, connecting hard against the fresh brand in the middle of my chest.

I dropped him back on the floor and fell onto the

coffee table, which somehow held my weight. Fletcher bent over at the waist, hands braced against his knees as he sucked in breath after breath after breath.

"That was rude, Gideon."

I stood from the table. "I should have killed you when I had the chance."

"I'd rather we just fuck and get it over with," he said, closing the space between us, fisting my shirt into his hands and crashing our mouths together.

It had been years since I'd been caught off-guard, since I'd underestimated someone. The treatment from my father had long ago ensured I was at least a step ahead of most people in most things. Bellamy had been a surprise, with his daring advances that felt far too bold for someone as soft-spoken as he was. Daren and Luca's secret relationship, another unexpected turn of events, but not entirely a shock.

This, though?

Fletcher's mouth against mine, his tongue begging permission to slide past my lips?

I hadn't seen this one coming.

"I hate you," I said, grabbing his cheeks and puckering his mouth away from me like a fish on a line.

"I deserve it," he muttered, yanking his face out of my grip. "I fucking deserve it and you can kill me later if you still want to, but not before you fuck me."

"Sin."

He reached under my shirt, fingers teasing their way over my ribs to the center of my chest. He went for the brand again, hooking the edge of his fingernail over a sunken piece of flesh in the shape of a rose petal.

"Do I have to make you angry again? Because I can."

"I'm always angry at you," I warned.

He pushed against the petal and twisted his finger, bringing our mouths back together, licking his tongue across my lip in a long and sinfully decadent slide.

"I think everything is going to go wrong," he said, almost like he was thinking out loud, but he was closer to the truth than I think either of us wanted to admit. "I just want this one thing first."

"This one thing," I repeated.

"It's everything." Fletcher's mouth fell open and he breathed heavily against my chin, chest heaving with every inhale. His attention flickered up toward the stairs and then back to me. "Why can they have it, but not us?"

"We could have," I reminded him. "We did."

"Why are you here?" he asked again, dragging his nails down my chest hard enough to draw four lines of fresh blood from my sternum to my navel. It took all my strength to not cry out in pain, but my father had taught me years ago about the importance of suffering in silence. "Why are you here? What do you want? If you're not here for this, Gideon, why are you *here*?"

He was nearly frantic, eyes wide with my skin and blood beneath his fingernails. And I realized, he was right. There was one thing we both wanted from each other, one thing we'd never been allowed to have. Maybe it was seeing Daren and Luca together that had brought our lives into such sharp focus for the first time, but Fletcher was far from wrong in his assumption. Even if I hadn't realized it when it happened, my need for him was the one thing that had always kept me going.

"When I thought I was dying," I said to him, freeing my cock from my pants and giving it a tight stroke. "I saw you."

"What?" He swallowed and shoved his pants down to his knees, spitting onto his fingers and reaching between his legs.

I pushed him down onto the couch and settled my weight on top of him, between his legs. He was practically bent in half, fingers up his ass like he had any right to put anything up there besides my cock. I swatted his hand away, wondering if I'd always felt this sense of propriety over him and how I'd managed to ignore it for so long.

Spitting into my own hand, I slicked my cock and notched myself against his barely-prepped hole. "In the pool that day, right before I lost consciousness, I saw you. You held out your hand and I took it, and I thought that was the end of everything."

I pushed my hips forward, easing my cock into him, one agonizingly slow inch at a time. Fletcher whimpered, clenching his jaw and throwing back his head. He reached between his legs and started to stroke himself like mad, far faster than the pace I set on his ass.

"Holy shit, Gideon."

He whispered my name and I stole it from his mouth with my tongue. I kissed him, pushing him down into the corner of the couch until I felt like I could move without shooting my load into him on the next thrust.

"Hmn?" I hummed into his mouth, deepening the kiss and finding a pace that delivered all of the punishment I knew he deserved. It was, after all, his fault that we hadn't been doing this for the last six and a half years. His judgement, his decisions, his selfishness.

"You feel so good," he said, burying his face into the crook of my neck. He sank his teeth into my skin and it hurt more than the brand ever had. It was a different kind of mark, one that I'd wear forever, even after the scar itself faded. "Sin, I've…"

"Tell me." Fletcher took my face into his hands, cradling me while I fucked him. His palm smeared precum across my cheek and I turned to the side, licking him clean.

"I've never been with another man before," I admitted. "I haven't…haven't done anything else with anyone that I haven't done with you."

His blue eyes went wide, clear as the sky and innocent as they used to be back when we thought we were bigger than we were. He cursed under his breath and grunted, a hot burst of cum streaming out of his cock and splattering against the underside of his chin. Another across his bare chest, his stomach. His hands were still against my face, digging in deeper than before, and I wondered if he'd drawn my blood a second time.

Knowing that he'd just come—untouched—based off my confession alone, unfurled a complicated tangle of emotions in the middle of my chest. It was overwhelming, enough to send my brain to the place it went when I felt like my life was out of my control. Leveraging my weight onto the couch, I pumped into Fletcher so hard, he finally cried out. The couch dragged across the room, and I fucked into him again, again, chasing after the pleasure I'd been deprived of my entire life.

"I'm still..." he trailed off, head thrown back in pleasure as the couch slammed into a cabinet against the wall. Books and vases and trophies all fell out of the case, raining down onto us as my orgasm barreled through us both.

"I'm still coming," he gasped, and I filled him to leaking. Using my back to shield him from the debris, I dropped my forehead against his when the violent aftershocks of my orgasm finally quieted down.

"Well," Daren said from somewhere behind us. "That's quite the development."

CHAPTER 40

DAREN

I was one to talk, considering my cum was still deposited in two of the four men sitting across the table from me, but walking in on Fletcher taking Gideon North's cock up his ass was the last thing I expected to happen that day.

Sitting a bottle of red wine in the middle of the table and collapsing into a chair beside Luca, I scrubbed a hand down my face and waited for either Gideon or Fletcher to explain themselves. After the three of us walked in on them, Fletcher had told us all to fuck off, then had taken Gideon to his room. They'd emerged half an hour later, both freshly showered and both in Fletcher's clothes.

"Isn't it early for wine?" Fletcher asked, stretching his legs out and crossing them at the ankle. He was still barefoot, a sharp contrast from the way he normally carried himself around the house, the way he held himself when he talked about Gideon.

"Isn't it early to get bent over a couch and fucked by your sworn enemy?" I shot back.

"He was hardly bent over," Luca said, reaching for the wine and pouring himself and Bellamy a glass. He raised it toward me, and I slid my glass in his direction. After he'd poured, he set the bottle on the center of the table again, and the three of us turned our attention to our leaders.

"Let's talk about the two of you first," Fletcher said, brow raised.

"All our secrets are already on the table, it seems," I said.

"How can I trust you knowing you're involved with him?"

"I could ask you the same, President," I shot back, words quiet and calculated. "But let me remind you that I'm not a Sinclair and I'm not a North. I'm here because it's what's expected of me until I graduate."

"This isn't something you just walk away from after school is finished." Gideon grazed his fingers across the center of his chest and, beside me, Luca winced. I'd known, but somehow I hadn't realized there was no way that brand had made it to the center of Gideon's chest without Luca's assistance.

"No," I agreed, "but the oversight drops dramatically once that diploma is handed over."

"That's when the work begins," Luca whispered, bottom lip pushed into a frown that I wanted to kiss right off his face.

"And what's your work?" Fletcher asked.

"Proving to my father that I'm trustworthy."

"Are you?"

"You said you can only trust yourself," Bellamy said from his seat between me and Fletcher. He was so quiet and so small, I almost forgot he was there, except I could never really forget him...not with a mouth like that.

"I trust Fletcher a lot more now than I did an hour ago," I said, which earned me an eye roll from the man in question. But it was the truth. We all had leverage over the other now, and it was leverage that made alliances. Leverage was what made people dangerous to each other.

"We're all at an impasse," Luca said, sipping carefully at his wine. "I'm of the impression that neither of us will move against the other now."

"Don't be so sure," Gideon murmured, not quite under his breath.

"That was almost a decade ago," Fletcher protested.

"And I'm just supposed to believe you've somehow gotten better and not worse?"

"You're both insufferable," I said, drawing sharp and scathing looks from across the table. "It's tentative enough that we can make it out of this weekend alive, but we do need to address the elephant in the room."

Fletcher raised a brow again, and I threw a sidelong glance at Bellamy.

Fletcher and Gideon were in their positions because of their names, much the way Luca and I had drawn short straws and landed in our deputy roles. Our families had grasped at power and money for generations, cementing our places in the upper echelons of not just society and politics, but also the Thorns and the Roses.

Bellamy was a Marchant and the Marchant family didn't matter. Marchant was a name I didn't even remember hearing before he'd shown up at school, before he'd landed in my bed. I'd fucked him anyway because I was far from discerning and sex to me was the same as power. But then he'd shown up as the offering and everything had changed. Unfortunately, I was a sucker for a pretty man with a nice whimper, and Bellamy, much like Luca, ticked all of my boxes.

Fucking Luca alongside Fletcher the night before was a complication because I knew Luca's responses and noises well enough to know just how much Fletcher did it for him. How much both our cocks up his ass got him off. And then there was this morning, watching Luca with Bellamy had only given me permission to lean into my attraction to the newcomer...and for the first time I worried I'd fucked my way into a corner I couldn't get out of.

The five of us were playing a complicated game of chess, moving pieces around to keep the game running long enough to get the upper hand over the other, but the appearance of Bellamy Marchant on our doorsteps and in our beds gave me the terrifying feeling there were more hands in the game than any of us had realized.

Maybe we weren't as untouchable as we'd always imagined.

Maybe our secrets weren't ours to keep anymore.

Four sets of eyes settled on Bellamy, with his golden hair and innocent eyes, the hickeys peppered across the back of his neck and the cum of three men mixed inside of him.

"Who the fuck is he and why is he here?"

CHAPTER 41

BELLAMY

It was one thing when Daren, Luca, Fletcher, and Gideon looked at me with hunger in their eyes; it was another when they looked at me with doubt. Daren and Luca's words from our time upstairs were sharp in my ears. These men barely trusted each other, and they surely didn't trust *me*.

I didn't trust me either.

"My father..." I trailed off, licking my lips nervously.

"That's hardly news," Luca said dismissively, gesturing at our tablemates. "All of our fathers."

I was supposed to make an ally out of Fletcher Sinclair, and while I hadn't yet succeeded, I hadn't quite failed either. A shifty sort of alliance hovered in the air, something the four men in front of me desperately wanted but were too scared to reach for. I didn't know how I played into the creation—or the destruction—of that.

223

It wasn't uncommon for my dad to make demands of me or my siblings, but it was unusual for my mom to react the way she had the day they sat me down and told me about my future at Rose Hill. She'd been distraught, nearly inconsolable, and by the time I left for school, her mood hadn't gotten any better. Deep in my bones, I knew there was something more pervasive at play. I hadn't simply been gifted a scholarship and an opportunity...that I'd never even asked for. There were stronger powers involved, my dad being one of them, even though I hadn't thought much of him up to the day he changed all of our lives.

"Tell us again how you came to be here," Fletcher said.

"My dad just told me I was going to Rose Hill. I was going to be in the Thorns." I swallowed, the spit lodging in the back of my throat and choking me. "He told me to get close to Fletcher. He said he'd be an ally."

"An ally." Fletcher scoffed, and my cheeks burned.

I turned my attention toward my lap, toward the oversized cuffs of Gideon's hoodie, frayed around the edges even before my nails had started to pick at the seams. Luca reached over and grabbed my hand, fighting it out from beneath the thick material and threading our fingers together. It wasn't a romantic gesture, more in solidarity as he gave me a reassuring squeeze.

"You're obviously planted here," Luca said, the accusation landing counter to the comfort of his hand.

"The question is who planted you and why," Daren added.

"It's obviously *your* father," Fletcher said to Gideon, tone barely laced with a tired and old accusation. "Why else would he have said to get close to me?"

"He said to make you an ally," Gideon countered.

"Then he must not know me at all," Fletcher murmured.

Daren huffed an affronted noise out of his nose. "I'm right here."

Fletcher glanced up, stare flickering from Daren to Luca and back again. "I know, Daren. I see you."

That shut him up, and I wanted to reach for him on my other side, to take his hand the way Luca had taken mine, but the thought of having my arms spread open with Fletcher and Gideon across the table felt more like an execution than anything else. I didn't have the heart for it, so instead I stretched my leg and wrapped my foot around the back of Daren's ankle.

"We all agree that Bellamy is here because someone above us wants him here," Fletcher summarized. "But we don't know who that person is yet."

The other three men nodded.

"I think the most likely suspect is yours." He pointed at Gideon, who seemingly bristled at the accusation, but didn't deny it.

"Maybe it was yours," Gideon suggested. "To make sure you stay away from me."

Fletcher's face paled, and he opened his mouth

quickly before closing it again. He reached for the empty wine glass in front of him, poured a healthy helping from the bottle, and swallowed it down in one go, cursing under his breath as he settled back into his seat.

"No one has asked me to report anything," I said quietly.

"Not yet," Luca interjected.

"It's still the weekend of the offering," Fletcher said, cracking his neck. "There won't be anything to report until tomorrow at best."

"I'd say there's plenty." Daren chuckled.

"What do I do?" I asked, palm sweating against Luca's hand. "What do I say? I don't know what was supposed to happen this weekend, but I certainly don't think it was supposed to end like this."

"I did what I was supposed to," Fletcher said sharply, which had Gideon frowning beside him. "Did you?"

"Not entirely," he answered, pointing at Luca. "Obviously."

"This is a mess." Fletcher poured himself another glass of wine, poured one for Gideon as well.

"I hate to interrupt." Luca carefully untangled our fingers, giving me a reassuring look as he took back his hand. "But there's another matter at play here that no one has brought up."

"What now?" Fletcher asked.

"You two, obviously." Daren said it so Luca wouldn't have to.

"What is going on with the two of *you?*"

"Nothing any of you need to worry about," Gideon said, almost growling.

I shivered, leaning back in my chair, but there was nowhere for me to go.

"It's something we very much need to worry about," Daren said, and to my other side Luca nodded in agreement. "*Our* plan was to survive the year and find a way to be together again, but whatever's happening here has made that excessively more complicated."

"I won't let anything jeopardize that plan," Luca said quietly, pushing his glasses up the bridge of his nose. He leveled Gideon and Fletcher with the most serious look I'd ever seen him wear, and for the first time, I was scared of Luca. As scared of him as I was of Fletcher and Gideon.

And as scared I was of my dad, and whatever he'd done to get me here.

CHAPTER 42
LUCA

By noon, the five of us had gone our separate ways.

We had a loose plan at best, a bad idea at worst. I was looking forward to crawling back into my bed and sleeping until classes started on Monday, but the anxiety rolling off of Gideon was something new that probably needed my attention.

"You good, B?" I asked as we climbed the stairs to the house.

The night before, the place had been packed with initiates and members, but much like Thorn Hill, their numbers had been quick to disperse. The houses were meant to be a home for its leaders at all times, a gathering place some of the time, and an external residence only in case of emergencies. This meant with the ceremonies completed, Gideon and I had the place back to ourselves again...for the time being.

"Far from it," he said.

The door was unlocked since that was how we'd left it, because people knew better than to come into the house without permission. Closing it behind me, I suddenly found the whole thing exhausting, the weight of our names and our fathers bearing down on me like a truckload of anvils. I pressed my back against the door and slid down until my ass hit the ground, then I kicked my legs out in front of me and closed my eyes.

"Are you?" he asked the question back to me, sneakers hitting the floor, one thump after another.

"What's the point of all this? I don't even want to be rich. I don't want to control and manipulate people."

"No." Gideon sat down beside me and stretched his long legs. My toes barely came to the middle of his calf. "But you want to impress your father."

"I don't even know why anymore."

"It's unavoidable, I think."

"Remind me again," I pleaded, knocking my head against the heavy wood door.

"They'll die eventually."

I snorted a laugh that died in the back of my throat.

"It's the order of things," he said, far more somber. "And it's easier to dismantle things from the inside out."

I scrubbed a hand down my face.

"Does it bother you?" Gideon asked me next, out of nowhere and out of context.

"Does what bother me?" I rolled my head to the side so I could see his profile in my periphery. "All of this?"

"Well..." He scoffed. "I meant about Daren."

I gently bit the inside of my lower lip, the pain of losing him again was still fresh, and even though I knew I'd see him sooner rather than later, the distance was already a wound I hadn't asked for.

"Are you asking me if I care he fucked Bellamy? Or if I care he fucked Fletcher?" I frowned. "Actually, he didn't fuck Fletcher. They both fucked me."

"Yes," Gideon said sharply, left eye twitching in the corner. "All of that."

"We don't live a normal life, B. I don't expect a normal love."

"But you do...love him?" He turned toward me, eyes dark and expression unreadable.

"You knew that when you took me over there in lieu of another offering," I whispered.

"I suspected you were sleeping together," he corrected.

"And you were right. But it is more than that. I love him and I want him to be happy. We agreed that sleeping with other people wouldn't change the way we felt about each other."

If anything, fucking other people made it hotter. Made it better.

In our short separation since moving into the houses, I'd chased down other men like it was sport. Mostly to distract myself from the loss, but partly because I really did enjoy getting off. It was a point of contention that I'd failed to get Gideon in bed, but after walking in on him balls deep in Fletcher Sinclair, I understood why. And suddenly, in less than twelve hours, everything had changed.

My goal had never been to topple empires.

I wanted to get out alive and then find a way to be with Daren again.

But being in bed with Daren and Fletcher, then the shower with Daren and Bellamy...it had been some of the hottest sex I'd ever had. Resting comfortably in the understanding Daren was so steadfast in my love we could share each other like that? We could be together, drowning in so much pleasure? It was hard to not feel grateful for the stupid rivalry between Gideon and Fletcher's families because their posturing had opened up doors for my future that had previously been camouflaged into the walls.

I no longer only wanted to get out of this with Daren by my side. I wanted more of them, and still...

"Why don't you want to fuck me, Gideon?" I asked, apparently out of nowhere because he choked on his spit before pushing up to his feet." Everyone else does."

"I'm not like you," he said.

"No kidding."

"I see no value in sharing."

I scrunched my nose, letting the pad of my glasses slide up and down an itch above my right nostril.

"No one ever made you share your toys as a kid?" I asked.

"I learned very early on to keep the things I wanted to myself."

The statement felt loaded, and before I could ask him another question, he stalked away from me and climbed the stairs. The door to his attic bedroom slammed shut and I closed my eyes with a sigh. He might not see the value in sharing, but Daren wasn't the only man I had my sights set on now, so he was going to have to learn.

CHAPTER 43

FLETCHER

My father's ostentatious black Maybach pulling up in front of the house Sunday afternoon was the absolute last thing I ever wanted to see. My body still ached from fucking Luca and being fucked by Gideon, and there had to be a day when my ability to keep myself composed in front of the man would give out. The angry lashes across my back hurt far more than they had in the morning, and all I wanted to do was take a shower and go to bed for a week.

Maybe with company.

The thought was beyond unsettling, because while I'd spent so long dreaming about what it would be like to finally be taken by Gideon North, those dreams had been nothing compared to reality. I'd built the idea of him up in my head for so long, maybe as punishment for my teenage betrayal, maybe because I was a fool after all. But having sex with him wasn't much different from sex with other people. The mechanics were the same, though the way Gideon's body covered mine was entirely unique, the way my nails gouged his flesh was explicitly ours, but overall it had been the emotion that made it different.

I'd never stopped loving him, though I honestly hadn't ever realized I'd started.

Until our bodies crashed together in the middle of the living room, I'd loved Gideon as a hypothetical, a broad idea, a vague term. Now, I loved him consumingly and dangerously, and I didn't have time to make heads or tails of that revelation because my father was on the porch, hand on the door knob. He didn't knock because he never had to. Thorn Hill was just as much his as it was mine, an honor—or a curse—bestowed upon all past presidents. Not that my father ever knocked on any door whether he was welcome or not.

"Take Bellamy to your room," I said to Daren, but it was too late. They were on the stairs and my father was inside. He was slower than he used to be, but still quick enough to have appraised the entire room and all the people in it. He undoubtedly noticed the way Bellamy's pointer finger was crooked around Daren's pinky.

"That won't be necessary," my father said, locking the door behind him.

The air left the room, left my lungs. I still had dirt under my nails from the night before, cum in my ass from when Gideon had just fucked me on the couch my father was very likely about to make himself comfortable on.

The house could have exploded and collapsed to the ground, and I wouldn't have been surprised.

"What can I get you to drink, Mr. Sinclair?" Daren asked, clearing his throat and coming back down to the first floor.

"Glad someone in this house remembers their manners," my father said, sitting on the couch and bending one leg over the other. His pants hiked up toward his calf revealing navy blue monogrammed silk socks, a swirl of roses up the ankle.

Our earlier established plan disintegrated in my head. I was sixteen again, standing in the middle of my dorm room at Rose Hill Prep, phone pressed to my ear while I listened to his detailed instructions about what would happen to Gideon, what would happen to me, if I didn't break the tie between us for good.

I swayed on my feet, hopefully not enough for him to notice, and then Daren was at my back, literally, with his shoulder digging into the lash marks across my spine to keep me upright. The pain was all I needed to draw me back to the present, like getting tossed out of a black hole where everything goes from quiet and cold to loud and hot. I drew in a sharp breath and answered for my father.

"Scotch on the rocks for both of us," I said to Daren.

My father almost smiled, tracing his tongue across his thin lower lip. He looked from me to Daren, to me, to Bellamy, still on the stairs, still in Gideon's fucking hoodie.

"Bellamy Marchant, I presume?" my father said, not bothering to stand, not offering his hand.

"Yes, sir," Bellamy whispered.

I jerked my head toward the couch, and Bellamy finally slinked off the stairs and headed to the middle of the room, stopping a pace behind me to the right.

"I'm Mr. Sinclair," he said, as if he didn't have a first name, as if he had no identity outside of being the piece of shit who ran my family.

"I know."

"I imagine you do."

Daren returned with two crystal tumblers of scotch. He set them both on the table and backed up alongside Bellamy.

"Did you share, Fletcher?" my father asked, his gaze falling to the long sleeves of Bellamy's borrowed hoodie.

"When I was finished."

He nodded like he was almost proud of me. "Generous to share your leftovers."

That had to have hurt, but there was no way I could turn around to read either of their expressions. Even in our societies, to most people, my father was more of a presence than a person. Seeing him in the wild, pouring him drinks, conversing with him...that was not a common experience for people outside of his bloodline. They didn't know how to deal with him the way I did, how to say the right things.

"I would have preferred a woman," I lied.

His eyes narrowed, a quiet breath huffed out of his nostrils. "Is that so?"

"I've..." I licked my lips, swallowing bile. "Developed a taste for it."

"It's fine to dabble, Fletcher," he said, reaching for his drink. He swirled the ice, sniffed the liquor, raised it to his mouth. "As long as you know the difference between top shelf and well."

I took a breath, forcing my mouth to find the obedient smile he expected, forcing my legs to carry me toward the couch so I could sit beside him and pick up my drink.

"Of course, Father," I agreed, chasing bile down with thousand dollar scotch. "Now, to what do I owe this visit?"

CHAPTER 44

DAREN

Upon the arrival of the elder Sinclair, I decided it was best to take Bellamy back to his apartment off campus. Not to stay, of course. We'd agreed around the kitchen table to move him into the house because what better way to convey his success. No one would be allowed to make Thorn Hill their home without Fletcher's consent. Without his ally-ship. But the rules of the initiation were explicit that he come with nothing more than the clothes on his back. No phone, no identification, no keys.

Step one, we had to collect Bellamy's things.

The walk off campus and into downtown was a quiet one, Bellamy's fingers sometimes brushing against the top of my hand when we came too close to each other on the sidewalk, but he didn't reach for more and neither did I. We'd talked about a lot over two bottles of wine, but never once did we discuss...everything that had happened.

"My roommate is kind of weird," he said when we stopped in front of his third floor apartment. "My father picked him."

I licked my lips, gears turning in the back of my mind. It was entirely possible Bellamy wasn't the only unidentified player on the table and we all had to proceed with extreme caution.

"What's his name?" I asked.

"Vince."

"Did you know him before you came to school?"

Bellamy knocked on the door. "No."

The door opened so quickly, it was almost like the man on the other side had been waiting for our arrival, which had all of my guard raised from the gate. Bellamy's roommate Vince was his polar opposite, tall where Bellamy was short, dark in all the places Bellamy was light. Thick black waves floated around his head like a halo, and his eyes sparkled like there were galaxies inside of them.

"You're back," Vince said, palpable relief washing over him. "I was worried."

"I told you I'd be gone overnight," he said.

Vincent barely offered me a passing glance, which was also suspicious. "And that's fine, I was just worried about when you would make it back."

"He's back," I announced, gesturing vaguely in the air. "And we're leaving, so...Bellamy, go get your shit."

Bellamy dipped his chin against his chest and scampered into the apartment past Vincent, who did everything he could to make himself look taller when it was just the two of us in the entryway.

"Who are you?" he asked.

"You know who I am." I brushed past him, following Bellamy into the decently sized two-bedroom apartment. It looked like they had a shared living space with short hallways off either side leading to matching bedroom suites. The TV was on, muted as a baking competition played on; a paper plate with a half-eaten slice of pizza sat on the table beside a bottle of water and the remote. The scene was entirely too unsuspecting.

"What are you doing with him?" Vince asked.

"Right now? Waiting for him to get his phone and some clothes."

"And then?"

Vince's line of questioning was far from welcome and I was already tired of it. After the events of the night before, I was ready to sleep until Monday, ideally with Luca beside me, but I knew that was far from possible. Bellamy would be a soft and supple replacement in his absence.

Until we could all be together again.

Shit.

How had he wiggled so quickly and efficiently into our lives? He was an outsider, and worse than that, he was dangerous. We had all agreed there were some ulterior motives around his selection, even if we hadn't been able to figure out what they were yet. A tie to Gideon's family was the most likely, but Vince's inquisition had me wondering if there was more to the story than we realized.

"I'm going to let him sleep to recover from how much he got fucked last night," I said, sneering down at the person who represented another unanswered question, another threat. "And then I'm going to fuck him again."

Vincent swiped the side of his finger across his bottom lip, but said nothing.

"Bellamy!" I hollered, not breaking Vince's stare. "Are you ready?"

He was, thankfully. His warmth behind me, careful fingertips pressed against the curve of my spine. I spun around, giving my back to Vince even though I was unsure which of them was the bigger threat. Bellamy had changed into jeans and a RHU t-shirt that looked like it was fresh from the campus shop. He had Gideon's hoodie hanging over his arm and a backpack slung over his shoulder. He blinked up at me, golden eyes framed by brown brows, and I bit the inside of my cheek to fight off the directional change of my blood flow.

"I'm ready," he said quietly, affecting that same nervous demeanor he'd had the night I met him. Maybe he was nervous. He should have been.

I was.

"Let's go, then," I said, ignoring Vince as I went back for the door.

"Are you good?" Vince asked Bellamy, tone hushed like the question wasn't meant for my ears.

"You said you knew who I was," I said, twisting open the door and waiting for Bellamy to follow. "So you know that's a stupid question."

"It's exactly why I'm asking," Vince snapped. "Your reputation precedes you."

I smirked, raising a brow. "Which part of it?"

"The part where you indiscriminately fuck anyone who will spread their legs for you."

That was far from the worst part of my reputation.

I'd been destined for my role with the Thorns for my entire life, and the past three years of schooling had been designed to get me ready for the role of deputy to Fletcher's president, to ensure I acted in the ways the puppet masters intended.

"That's a rumor," I said to him, smiling as Bellamy stepped into the hallway. "I also take them on their hands and knees."

CHAPTER 45
BELLAMY

Daren all but slammed the door in Vince's face, stalking down the hallway until we were outside of the building. Instead of heading back the way we'd come, he made a sharp left into the alley and I chased after him. Once we were out of sight, his hand was around my throat and my back was against the wall. My backpack slipped off my arm as he lifted me up, my toes barely scraping the gravel beneath our feet.

"Who are you?" he hissed.

Daren's face had morphed into a mask I'd never seen before, eyes narrowed and lip curled in a scowl. His eyes were dark, shuttered, and a vein that ran across his temple throbbed in time with his heartbeat.

"Bellamy Marchant," I rasped.

Stars prickled the corners of my vision.

"But *who*?"

I blinked slowly, finding it hard to pry my lids open.

Daren showed no signs of releasing me, and the stars turned brighter, taking up more space in my periphery. I'd listened to his conversation with Vince while I packed a bag, and I didn't have an explanation as to why Vince had taken on such an annoying line of questioning. In the weeks we'd lived together, he'd basically spent the whole time ignoring me, coming and going at different hours than me, giving vague answers when I asked him questions about his day.

"I'm nobody," I croaked, the words harder to get out than I'd expected. My lungs rattled as I tried to catch a breath, and Daren tightened his fingers around my throat, pressed me harder against the bricks.

"You're far from that," he whispered, tilting his head to the side.

I grabbed his arm because I didn't know what else to do. My head throbbed, vision now more black than anything else, narrowed down to his terrifyingly dark and untrusting eyes. I dug my nails into the skin of his wrist and kicked my feet out, trying to get footing to take the pressure off my throat, but Daren was stronger than me, taller, broader, in all ways.

"Daren," I managed his name, which turned out to be the right answer. In a swift motion, he crashed our mouths together, spearing his tongue past my teeth and kissing me so hard it hurt. I kept my nails pressed into his wrist until he let go, and the next breath hit my lungs with so much force I was helpless to stop myself from coughing.

Tearing my head to the side, I sputtered and spit all over myself, body taking breath after breath to make up for the air I'd been deprived. My throat tingled, my dick *throbbed*. Daren grabbed my face and turned me back toward him before I could catch my breath, taking my mouth in another blistering kiss. My feet landed flat on the gravel and I hated it, so I hitched one leg over his waist instead. Daren groaned, curling his fingers around the underside of my thigh and hiking my leg higher.

I jumped, wrapping both legs around his waist, groaning when he rutted me against the bricks and dipped his head away from my mouth and into the crook of my neck. He peppered my throat and my jaw with kisses, using his teeth with enough force that I leaked in my underwear, already soiling the fresh pair I'd just put on.

And as fast as it started, it was finished. With a growl, Daren shook his head and lowered me back to the ground, stepping back and running a frustrated hand through his hair. He braced both hands against his waist. He licked his lips. He shook his head.

"What's Vince's surname?" he asked.

It was the last thing I'd expected him to say.

"I—"

I was interrupted by my cell phone vibrating a call in my pocket. Daren's eyes flashed and we both looked down at my leg. He saw my hard cock, pressing against my fly. We both did.

"Who's calling?"

I pulled my phone out and turned the screen toward him. It was my dad.

"Answer it," he said. "Put it on speaker."

He still fidgeted his hand through his hair and I accepted the call, clearing my throat.

"Hi, Dad," I said weakly.

He breathed into the phone. "Bellamy. How are you?"

"I'm fine."

"How is your weekend?" he asked, clarifying, "How was last night?"

The knowing in his voice was enough to confirm he knew *exactly* what had happened to me the night before. Not the details, but he knew what he'd signed me up for when he changed my entire life and moved me to Rose Hill University. Was that why my mom had been so upset over the whole thing? She'd known I was meant to be chattel?

"It was..." I swallowed, looking up at Daren, who studied me with curious eyes.

"Scary," he mouthed.

"Scary," I repeated diligently into the phone.

"How is the Sinclair boy?"

"Hardly a boy," I said, choking on the words. "We aren't boys, Dad."

"Compared to his father he is."

Daren's jaw ticked, but he said nothing.

"How do you know his father?" I asked.

"Doesn't matter." On the other end of the call, there

was a commotion, rustling of clothes, and then my mom, voice still tear-stained.

"Bellamy," she said my name.

"Hi, Mom."

I felt numb, fingers tingling, and I gestured with my phone until Daren reached his hand out for it. With mine free, I tried to shake out the pins and needles, close to punching into the wall to change the way my body felt. Like it wasn't my own. Instead, I wrapped both of my hands around my own throat, chasing after the terrifying press of Daren's hold. I found it quickly, and I closed my eyes to lean into it, relief washing over me.

"Did they hurt you?" she asked.

Another fight on the other end of the line, and my father was back.

"I'll call you soon, Bellamy," he warned. "We'll have plenty to discuss as the year goes on."

My eyes flew open in time to see Daren's go wide. He stabbed his finger into the hang-up button and offered the phone back to me. He didn't acknowledge anything my dad had said, and he definitely ignored my mother's desperate question. I didn't know what to say because I had more questions than answers.

"Put your phone away," Daren finally said.

Reluctantly, I took one of my hands away from my throat, hating how cold it felt, so I could put my phone back into my pocket. Daren studied me quietly, expression unreadable. His cool detachment left me feeling scared again, and not in the way that made me hard. And as quick as it appeared, it was gone. He bent down and picked up my bag, shrugging it up his own arm instead of mine. He picked up Gideon's hoodie like he didn't know what to do with it, then he handed it off to me.

"Who am I?" I asked, grabbing his hand, repeating his question back to him.

"The death of us all," he muttered, squeezing his fingers hard around mine.

CHAPTER 46

GIDEON

Four minutes and nineteen seconds.

It was a new personal best, but if I would have known my father would be sitting in the bleachers waiting for me to surface, I would have weighted myself down to the bottom of the pool and stayed longer.

"Chlorine can't be good for healing that scar on your chest," he said, mouth pulled into a smirk.

"It's been two weeks," I told him, toweling off as much of the water as I could with the small towel I'd grabbed out of my locker on the way in.

Two weeks.

Two weeks since the initiation weekend and two weeks since all of our lives had turned upside down. It had been two weeks since I'd seen Fletcher, even though I knew Luca and Daren were sneaking around together more than they should have. Bellamy spent most nights at Thorn Hill, and I would have been lying if I said I wasn't jealous of the fact. Even though I didn't know whose bed he warmed, the thought of it being Fletcher's was enough to make me see red. But the return to "normal" was part of our plan.

We'd agreed to lay low, a task Daren and Luca were failing miserably at. Fletcher and I had done better. We didn't even have classes in the same building at the same time, as if years ago someone had learned that lesson the hard way and the story had spread like wildfire. I had seen Bellamy in passing, but beyond a small smile, he didn't offer me much.

Fletcher had wanted to strike against our fathers quickly, but I'd begged for patience. We'd all started the year with the plan to lay low and make it out alive, but the revelations of the initiation made that harder to abide. Staying away from Fletcher, now that I'd finally had him, was the hardest thing I'd ever done. And it was foolish of me to want him, to maybe even still love him. I loved him once before, and he'd betrayed me.

We still hadn't talked about the why of it. But we would.

We just hadn't found the time.

"What do you want?" I asked, tossing the towel in the community hamper against the wall.

My father looked so out of place in the pool, sitting on damp metal bleachers in his three thousand dollar suit and his alligator leather shoes. One day, I would tie *his* arms behind *his* back. Bind *his* ankles together so *he* couldn't kick. I would put a cloth gag in *his* mouth, the knot digging into the base of *his* skull, and I would shove him over the edge into the deep end. If he managed to break the surface, it would be my fingers tangled in his hair, my hand pressing him back beneath the water.

"You're not even listening." His annoyed drawl snapped me out of my recurring daydream, and I made a show of tipping my head to the side to shake water out of my ear.

"I'm always listening," I said.

"How did you handle things with the offering exchange?" he asked.

"As expected."

"I mean with Sinclair."

I frowned, scratching an invisible itch at the corner of my mouth.

"As expected," I repeated, even though he didn't understand I meant in the "our fates are inevitably inter-twined" kind of way, and not the "I hate him the way you hate his father" kind of way.

"Glad to hear you're over that old dalliance of yours."

I remembered waking up at home, screaming for my father, screaming for my mother, for Fletcher, for anyone. Screaming until my throat bled, only to wake up another morning alone and ignored.

"You ensured that years ago," I reminded him. "That can't possibly be why you drove all the way out here."

"No," he said, standing up and smoothing out the creases in the lap of his slacks.

He was older than I remembered him, shorter, less muscular. Maybe I didn't even need rope to drown him. I could just wrap my arms and legs around his body and take him to the bottom with me. Maybe I'd kill myself in the process...

No.

Not that.

Not anymore.

"I just wanted to check in, son," my father said, buttoning his jacket. He came to stand next to me beside the pool, and it took all my willpower to not throw him in, to not worry he was going to throw *me* in. "Make sure all was well. That you remember everything expected of you."

He poked the brand in the middle of my chest, twisting his fingernail until he'd cut into the scab and drawn a trickle of blood out. It raced toward my stomach, diluted pink from the water I'd yet to wipe dry. If he expected a reaction, a grimace or a groan, he wasn't going to get it.

Fletcher had done far worse.

"I remember."

"The longevity of our family relies on you," he said. "Everything I've built will soon be yours to carry."

"I know."

"And it doesn't matter if you don't want it." He spit at my feet, wiping his bottom lip with the side of his thumb. I wanted to tear out his tongue. "There's things bigger than you, bigger than me, than all of this."

"I know," I said again, staring down at him.

He was such a small man.

"You're not capable of changing any of it, Gideon. I know you used to think you were, that you wished you could."

"You made sure to take those ideas away, Father," I told him. "When you tried to kill me."

He scoffed, rolling his eyes. "I did no such thing, Gideon."

He reached up and ruffled my hair, giving my head a rough shove. I held my footing, heels against the curved edge of the pool deck. "I knew you needed to be convinced to see it my way. I persuaded you."

"Of course, Father," I agreed.

His expression changed from a sneer to as much of a plea as I'd ever seen or heard from him. "There are lives on the line."

I nodded my concession, my submission. "I understand, Father."

And I did.

But it was his life in question now, not mine.

CHAPTER 47

LUCA

The weirdest thing about my senior year at Rose Hill had been going back to class after everything that happened over the initiation. Pretending that I hadn't just permanently seared the crest of the Roses into Gideon's flesh, that Fletcher didn't chase Bellamy through the woods and fuck him into the dirt, that we didn't walk in on Fletcher taking Gideon up his ass in the middle of his living room.

Like things between Daren and I would ever be the same.

It was easy for me to admit I was jealous.

Gideon had always been frosty with me, socially and sexually. The events of the initiation didn't change any of that. Even though I'd snuck out to see Daren a handful of times, I was still mostly alone and he was the opposite. He was tucked up safe and sound in that house with Bellamy *and* Fletcher, and on more than one occasion I'd jerked myself off thinking about the two of them splitting Bellamy wide open with their cocks.

I wanted to be split open. I wanted to be fucked.

And Gideon wanted to be left alone.

I headed back toward Rose Hall and was halfway there when I decided—fuck that. I flipped my hood up and changed course, taking the long way around campus until I reached the property line of Thorn Hill. Bellamy and Daren were sitting on the porch, both of their heads snapping up toward the tree line when I deliberately stepped on a branch. It shattered under my feet and Daren was off the porch like a rocket, gesturing for Bellamy to go inside.

I waited until he was close enough to see me, then I walked deeper into the woods. Behind me, his footfalls grew closer, louder. Then I could hear his breath, and the side of his forearm slammed into my back, rocking my chest and face into the closest tree.

"What are you doing here?" he whispered, free hand already working quickly at my pants, then his.

"I missed you," I said.

He spit in his hand and rubbed it on his cock, then forced the blunt head into my hole. I reached down and covered my own erection with my hand before Daren fucked me right into the tree, thankful for my quick reflexes. I liked it rough, but my masochism had limits.

"We're supposed to be careful," he grunted, thrusting his cock inside of me with one sharp snap of his hips.

Pushing back, I shoved him out of me and turned, flattening my back against the tree and hooking one of my legs around his hip. I spit in my hand and added it to his cock, drawing him closer to me.

"I'm all alone there," I whispered. "Gideon won't touch me."

Daren grunted, flipping his ball cap backward and shoving his shirt up underneath his chin. He lined himself back up between my legs and fucked up into me again. I brought my other leg around his waist and threw my head back, so grateful for the feel of his body once again inside mine.

I knew I was desperate and needy, and I wasn't ever going to change.

"I love you," I said, even though it sounded like a plea.

"I won't lose you." He pushed me into the tree and I closed my eyes, letting the feel of him and the pleasure of his cock wipe away all of my jealousy and my fear. I took my dick into my hand and jacked off while he thrust into me, the friction of our skin well past the point of painful. I had four frantic minutes before I shot my load all over my hoodie, and another two minutes before Daren spilled inside of me. He breathed ragged and hard into my ear, cock still throbbing.

"Try again with Gideon," he whispered. "I don't want you to be alone. And if he won't, then go find someone else like before."

I bit back a protest, not wanting to argue with him and ruin the moment. But trying to break through Gideon's walls was the equivalent of trying to get into

Fort Knox. There was no breaching his perimeter unless your name was Fletcher Sinclair.

Footsteps storming into the tree line had Daren easing me back down to the ground. I tucked my sticky cock back into my underwear while Daren righted himself, but I stopped him when he tried to turn his hat back forward.

"This is hotter," I said, dropping my forehead against the outside of his shoulder.

"Are you decent?" Fletcher asked from a few yards away.

"Rarely," Daren answered.

I looked down and tried to wipe the cum off my black hoodie, but my trembling fingers only made it worse. I was on the most dangerous kind of adrenaline high, and the crash was coming fast.

"Did anybody see you come up the road?" he asked me.

"No."

"The two of you are getting careless."

"It's been four times," Daren protested.

"How many times have I seen Gideon?" he snapped.

That was it.

I brushed past Daren and chased after the sound of Fletcher's voice. He leaned against a tree and I picked up speed as I approached, shoving him hard enough back that he lost balance and stumbled over a broken log. I went down with him, fists balled tight in his t-shirt as I pushed him harder down into the dirt.

"This is all your doing," I yelled at him, shrugging

Daren off when he reached the place we'd gone down. "You're the one who made the stupid plan."

"I wanted to move now," he hissed. "Your president was the one who wanted to wait it out."

"And you agreed! I'm tired of waiting. I want my fucking life back."

Fletcher glared up at me, bucking off the ground and flipping our weight around so quickly I was on my back before I even registered he'd lifted us up. He curled his hand around my throat, immediately tightening his fingers hard enough for the corners of my vision to go blurry.

"We may be allies, Mandeville, but you watch your fucking tone with me."

"Fuck you."

I would have spit in his face if I could.

"Fletcher." That was Daren, from a place far away I couldn't see. "Fletcher, let him up."

"It's not fair," I rasped. "None of this is fucking fair."

Above me, Fletcher grunted, and everything went black.

CHAPTER 48
BELLAMY

The front door to the house crashed open like someone had been thrown through the thick wood. Loud voices and the door slamming closed, and it was Daren I heard first, screaming at Fletcher with a rage I'd never known from him before. Quickly, I closed the book I was reading and headed for the stairs, shocked to find Luca half-unconscious in Daren's arms and Fletcher behind them, a mottling purple bruise around his eye and blood trickling from the corner of his lip. Daren had a matching black eye and sticks in his hair, his hat backward on his head and dirt on his knees.

"Bellamy, can you help?" Daren set Luca down on the couch, then he immediately rounded on Fletcher again. Fletcher grabbed him before Daren could land another hit, hauling him upstairs to Fletcher's bedroom without another word.

I ran down the stairs, skidding to a stop on my knees in front of the couch. Luca was conscious, mumbling something under his breath I couldn't quite make sense of. Gently, I pulled his glasses off his face and brushed his hair off his forehead. It didn't appear he had any black eyes like the other two, but he had red and purple marks around his throat that looked a lot like a hand.

"Are you all right?" I whispered, tracing my fingertips over the bruises. He had dirt and leaves in his hair, and I wondered what I must have looked like after Fletcher had his way with me the first night.

"Bell," he rasped, voice catching on the single syllable. "You're an angel."

"Daren doesn't think so."

Luca snorted, slowly blinking his eyes open. I gave him back his glasses and helped him prop up against the arm of the couch.

"What does Daren know?" he asked.

"More than me but less than Fletcher." I sighed and turned, situating my back against the couch. Luca mindlessly plopped his hand onto the top of my head and I closed my eyes, relieved he was quickly recovering from whatever had Daren and Fletcher in such an uproar. "What happened?"

"I swung on Fletcher."

I tried to turn around to face him, shocked that the scrawny, glasses-wearing member of the group was the one who'd had the balls to try and deliver the first blow.

"Why?"

"I was mad. I...I want my life back. I'm tired of waiting."

I pulled my thighs up against my chest and turned to the side, resting my cheek on my knees so I could keep my eyes on Luca, who looked beyond tired. I felt the same way, worn down to my bones from all the unknowns and the secrets. Exasperated by the confusion over whatever this relationship between the five of us was turning out to be. That might have been the most complicated part. Fletcher loved Gideon, but he fucked me and he fucked Luca, and Luca loved Daren, but he fucked everyone, and Gideon was obsessed with Fletcher, but he'd come so close with me...

So close.

"I don't know anything about your way of life. Don't know what it's been like to live the way the four of you had, but it all seems very calculating and slow-going. It doesn't seem like people move fast."

"Another thing worth changing," Luca muttered, reaching into his pocket and pulling out his phone. He read a series of messages on his screen, then cursed under his breath and slid down until he was flat on his back and dropped his phone onto the floor.

"Who was it?" I asked.

"Gideon. His father is on campus."

My heart rate immediately spiked, the confused organ battering against my ribs. Meeting Fletcher's father two weeks earlier had been bad enough. I had no idea what Gideon's father would be like, but I imagined it must take one hell of a man to create the beast that Gideon had turned into.

"What does he want?"

"Just throwing threats around, I think." Luca pushed himself up into a seated position with a wince, adjusting his glasses on the bridge of his nose. "I need to get back to the house."

"Daren is going to be pissed if you leave."

Luca groaned a laugh, slowly getting to his feet. He swayed a little, and I still didn't know whose handprint was darkening around his throat. I jumped to my feet to support him while his head settled, and he smiled, pressing a soft kiss against the corner of my mouth.

"Daren knows I'll always come back for him. Even if it kills us both."

I grabbed Luca's shirt, yanking him into me. "I don't like the sound of that. I'm getting rather fond of you both."

"It just might kill you too." He took my face into his hands, dark eyes scanning my face for any signs of fear. Little did he know that fear would have only transformed into arousal anyway. If it were present, which it wasn't. I wasn't scared of these men, of their lives anymore. I was invested.

What did scare me was not understanding my place among them. Not knowing how I'd come to find myself in their web...or how I'd get out.

Not knowing if I wanted to.

"Something has to give," I said, letting go of his shirt and smoothing the fabric out with a surprisingly steady hand.

"I know," he said with a slow nod. "I just hope it's not any of us."

CHAPTER 49
FLETCHER

I slammed Daren against the wall as soon as he closed the door to my bedroom, and he swung on me again with surprising accuracy. His fist connected with my left cheekbone sending a shower of sparks into my field of vision. I stumbled backward enough for him to shove off the wall, but instead of hitting me again, Daren lunged. He jumped onto me like a fucking possessed spider monkey, the weight of his body sending us both backward onto my bed. He raised his arm to hit me again, and I bucked off the bed, flipping him onto his back and grabbing both of his wrists. I pinned Daren against the bed, my lip curling up in a victorious sneer.

"You forget your fucking place, *deputy*," I warned, shoving him harder down into the sheets. My bed smelled like him, smelled like Luca, smelled like Bellamy. Like sex and sweat and a reminder that Gideon was the one I wanted most and I'd barely gotten a taste of him.

"If I wasn't your second, I'd have put you in the fucking ground by now." He made a vile noise in the back of his throat and then he spit into my face. A glob of his hot saliva landed against my cheek, and I shifted my weight to keep him pressed down into the bed with one hand so I could swipe my face clean with the other.

He glared up at me like he wanted to kill me, and I imagined if we were anyone besides who we were, he would have tried. Sighing heavily, I gave him one last shove down into the mattress, then climbed off of him. He stayed put, giving me a moment to pace the room, hands braced against my hips while I counted my steps from one wall to the other.

It had been two weeks since my father visited, two weeks since he planted the seeds I was determined to not let grow. I tried so hard to think about Gideon, to think about Luca and Daren, even Bellamy, but old habits died hard, and it was a rough battle to fight on my own. Behind me, the bed creaked as Daren sat up, and I turned in time to find him gently pressing his fingertips against his cheekbones and the side of his nose.

"I'm tired of waiting around," he said softly.

"So am I," I agreed.

"Then what are we waiting for?"

"I think while we've talked about staging a coup, my father already has one in the works," I admitted.

"Why?"

"Just some of the things he said." I worried my tongue against the corner of my lower lip. Instinct and years of knowing better told me not to reveal the truth of my father's message to anyone else, but a desire to break those old habits wanted me to scream it out for all of them to hear.

"Are you going to share with the class?" Daren asked, standing up from my bed and shaking out his right hand before balling his fingers back into a fist. "Or are we going to backtrack to how things were before?"

"I'll break your fucking fingers before I let you hit me again," I warned, "and I'd like to see you try and get a cast-covered wrist into your boyfriend's tight little asshole."

"I'm not scared of you," Daren said, cocking his head to the side.

The jarring ring of my phone snapped us both out of the fight we were about to lapse back into, and I knew by the tone it was my father and not anyone I wanted to talk to.

"Keep your mouth fucking closed," I told him, throwing myself down into the chair by the window and accepting the video call. "Hello?"

"Fletcher," my father drawled, the sound of my name in his voice making my skin crawl. "You look like you've had quite a tussle."

"Just some rough sex," I lied, switching off the camera.

He made a disgusted noise on the other end of the line. "Stay out of the well, Fletcher."

"To what do I owe your unplanned call?" I asked before he could decide to harp on me about my sex life.

"I need your help with that thing we spoke about after initiation."

"What thing?" I asked. "You said a lot."

"I have suspicions that Francis North is in serious debt."

My gaze flickered up to Daren, who stared at me with wide and unreadable eyes.

"You mentioned you thought there was something going on when you were here."

"Yes, and I'm working on a paper trail, but I need some first-hand information."

"And what do you want me to do about that, Father?" I rubbed the bridge of my nose gently, wincing when I pushed too hard against a bruise Daren had left behind. "You made sure I understood what happens if I get too close to the North family."

"I'm glad it's a lesson you remember," he said. "But what do you think Bellamy is for?"

Daren made a choking sound, which I covered with a cough. He slapped his hand over his mouth, eyes much more readable than they'd been before.

"What do you mean?" I asked.

"He's not there of his own accord, Fletcher," my father said, like it should have been common knowledge. "I bought him for just this purpose."

"You *bought* him?"

"Fletcher." My father sighed. "What are the two biggest motivators in this life?"

"Money and power," I answered without even having to think about it.

"And people do silly things sometimes for both of those. Bellamy's father was desperate for both and I brokered a deal to give him one of them."

"You aren't seriously telling me you bought him. Human trafficking is below you."

"Not in the sense that you're thinking, Fletcher, no. But Bellamy has a purpose and if he doesn't deliver on it, then I don't see a point in keeping him around."

It was high school all over again. I was sixteen and my father was detailing all of the ways he would ruin Gideon's life if I didn't break things off in a way that ensured they'd never piece back together.

"Bold of you to assume I care what happens to Bellamy." I forced the lie out, words barbed in my throat.

"But do you care about Daren?"

I glanced up again, finding Daren's stare focused on the phone in my hand and thankfully not my face.

"Why would I care about him?"

"Because you've always had a bleeding heart, Fletcher. It's your biggest weakness. If you don't send Bellamy over to Rose Hall to get information about the North family financials, I'll remove him from the equation entirely, and then I'll call Daren's parents and let them know that he suffers from the same sexual deviances as you."

"I don't..."

"Please tell me you know he used to fuck that Mandeville boy," he interrupted.

Daren sighed heavily, covering his face with both of his hands. I recognized the panic he must have been feeling, but I took it as a good sign my father thought Daren and Luca's relationship was past tense and not present. Even better that he didn't know of my involvement with either of them, or Bellamy...or Gideon.

"I heard rumors," I said.

"Luca is a bastard trying to earn favor with a father who never wanted him. Being second to Gideon North is the only way for him to do that. Are you really trying to tell me that you would ruin all of their lives instead of sending in a spy whom *I fucking paid for* to get information that will only serve you and your family when all is said and done?"

My father sounded so arrogant, so fucking proud of all the chess pieces he'd moved into place without any of us even realizing we'd been played. I tossed my cell phone onto the bed, a better option than throwing it out of the window and I gestured for Daren to go downstairs and round up Bellamy and Luca. He hesitated, like he wasn't ready to leave me alone with the kind of phone call that would give me nightmares for weeks.

"You're right, Father," I agreed. I lied. I swallowed down bile. "I just wanted to understand the mechanics of the next move so I can be prepared for whatever happens after."

My father huffed a laugh against the receiver. "I'm relieved to hear that, Fletcher," he said slowly. "It would have been horrible for everyone you know if you wanted to fight me on this."

"I know better, Father."

"See that you don't forget that you do," he said. "Send Bellamy into Rose Hall. He has one week to get you the information you need and you have far less time than that to get it back to me."

"Yes, Father."

"And Fletcher?"

"Yes," I whispered.

"Stay away from Gideon North," he warned. "Or every promise I made you at sixteen will finally come true."

CHAPTER 50
DAREN

Fletcher didn't have to tell me what to do after he disconnected the call with his father. He threw his phone against the wall and cursed under his breath, dropping his head into his hands.

"I'll go find Bellamy," I said.

"Send him back with Luca," he grumbled. "You stay here."

"Fletcher."

"Say your fucking goodbyes to your little boyfriends, Moore," he warned, standing and stalking past me toward the door. "Tell Bellamy what he needs to know, but under no circumstance is he to mention it to Luca or Gideon. And neither are you."

There was no way he meant that. After everything the five of us had already been through, there was no possible scenario I could imagine where any of us would have kept a secret that large from the rest of us.

"You can't be serious."

Fletcher spun on his heel, wrapping his hand around my throat and slamming me against the wall. "Do I look like I'm joking?"

I kneed him in the stomach and he stumbled back with a grunt.

"There's a reason you're not the one in charge here," he said.

"The only difference between the two of us is that my father has fucking morals," I snapped.

"Your father has bent over his fair share of desks, and you're a fool if you think otherwise."

I rubbed my hand across my throat, the press of Fletcher's fingers still uncomfortably warm around my windpipe. Watching Fletcher's wide and frenzied eyes, I wondered if there was any way for us to make it out of this whole game alive. The rivalry between the Thorns and the Roses had existed for generations. There were intricacies to the networking between the most powerful families in the country that I would never understand, that Fletcher and Gideon might never even understand. But still, we were expected to be dutiful sons and diligent soldiers. We were meant to do what we were told and do it without question.

Everything the five of us had done since the initiation weekend had been so far off the script...so far out of the realm of anything expected of us, there was no real worry yet about being caught. The level of subversion and disrespect was unheard of, and it was only some kind of divine timing that had put all of us on the same page together, opposite that of our fathers.

"I'm better than him," I said.

"I know."

"You're better."

Fletcher let out a shaky breath, running his hand through his hair and brushing it back from his face. "If you say so."

"This was all your idea," I reminded him, cracking my knuckles and shaking out my fists. My knuckles ached from where I'd hit him. "We have a chance at living on our own terms because of you."

"It's Gideon," Fletcher said quietly, frowning toward the window. "Once upon a time, he'd convinced me that maybe someday we could write our own future."

Something twisted uncomfortably in the center of my chest. How many nights had Luca and I shared the same kind of conversation together, tangled up in sweaty sheets pretending there was an escape from the lives that had been carved out for us since before we were born.

"That's why I don't understand keeping this from him? From the rest of them."

"Because Gideon has always thought with his heart over his head. Because Luca would burn the entire world down for you. They're too biased, too impractical." Fletcher held his hands out, palms up. Helpless. "Emotion isn't going to win this war. Strategy will."

"You're not thinking clearly about this."

"It's not your place to tell me what to do," he growled.

"Isn't it?"

Fletcher inhaled a deep breath, letting it out before speaking again. "Not about things like this."

I could tell no matter how much I disagreed with him, there wasn't going to be any getting through to him. I either had to do as he asked and keep Luca and Gideon in the dark about Bellamy's mission and the phone call from Fletcher's father, or I had to go behind his back and tell them all the truth. One course would jeopardize their trust in me, the other Fletcher's.

There was no clear solution, and I found myself between a rock and a hard place. If I lied to Luca especially, I stood to tear down everything we'd built. But if I lied to Fletcher...I had no doubt he would take all of us down with him...assuming his father didn't do the job first.

Luca and I had been so careful before...

I had no idea how we'd been found out, but Fletcher was right about one thing. I needed to say goodbye to Luca until we were able to get ahead of the game. And with that understanding, my next steps became painfully clear. I was going to have to lie to one of the men I loved most in the world, and in the next breath, send the other into the beast's lair, hoping he truly understood how much was on the line if he didn't deliver the information Fletcher's father was asking for.

The only way to save *our* future was to risk Gideon's.

I sure as fuck hoped Fletcher knew what he was getting us into.

"Are we clear, deputy?" Fletcher asked, voice low and measured.

"Crystal," I replied. "I'll go talk to Bellamy, then say goodbye to Luca. Do you want to see either of them before they go?"

Fletcher's jaw ticked just below his ear.

"Why would I want to see them?" he asked.

I cleared my throat and slowly raised my hand to the dark purple bruise developing just beneath his eye.

"Forgive me," I whispered. "It was a stupid question."

"I know," he agreed. "So, what are you waiting for?"

PART FOUR
THE FALL

CHAPTER 51
LUCA

Bellamy was beyond diligent about tending my bruises, about picking leaves and branches out of my hair. He nestled against me, tucked into the crook of my arm and I petted my fingers through his hair.

"I don't understand any of this," he murmured against my chest.

I made a thoughtful sound in the back of my throat, pulling him closer. "I've grown up in it, and there's a lot I don't understand either."

"Will you try to explain it?" he asked. "Don't I deserve to know?"

Kissing the top of his head, I inhaled the smell of his shampoo. It was Daren's shampoo, and jealousy tangled tight and thorned in my chest.

"It's like the one-percent of the one-percent," I said. It hurt to keep my eyes open, so I closed them. "Between

Fletcher's and Gideon's families, there isn't a politician or world leader who isn't somehow ensnared in their web. It's been that way for generations."

"But what does that have to do with us?"

"That sort of loyalty and power doesn't come from nowhere. We're sort of in the entry levels of it. Even though the rest of us have known what we're meant for, what the roles and expectations are."

"The initiation," he whispered.

"It's like the knots at the beginning of a bracelet. The foundation. Whatever you want to call it. Everything happening this year is meant to remind us of our place. To make sure we're ready to step into the real world and do what is required."

"What's required?" Bellamy's breath was hot, his lips smashed against my sternum.

"There's no way of knowing," I told him, "not entirely. At least, not at this point."

"Are you and Daren ever—"

I interrupted him, shifting him into a more comfortable position that didn't rub against the bruises on my shoulders. "Going to be able to be together?"

He nodded.

"We've hoped that once we're out of school, the leashes will loosen some. We'll have jobs and responsibilities. More leeway."

"More time to see each other."

"If we're careful," I said.

"And what's my role in all of this?" he asked.

"It was just supposed to be for the ritual," I answered honestly. "Your father, or someone in your family, is involved in all of this, but far lower down the rankings than Daren's and my families are. We all just..."

"Took a liking to me?" he chuckled.

"Are bad at following rules," I said instead.

Before Bellamy could ask another question, the door to Fletcher's bedroom slammed open and Daren stormed down the stairs, looking like he wanted to set the whole house on fire. His face was flushed, his hair sticking up in every direction like he'd been tugging it at the roots. Either that, or Fletcher had. I pushed that idea out of my head, adjusting myself up against the back of the couch without jostling Bellamy too hard.

"What's wrong?" I asked, beckoning him closer.

He looked at my outstretched hand and frowned. "The two of you need to go back home," he said.

"Fletcher can't be that upset," I said, moving as fast as I could to get out from underneath Bellamy, to get to my feet, to get to Daren. His features went taut, but when I reached him, he exhaled heavily and rested himself against my shoulder. I wrapped my arms around him and pressed my lips against the side of his neck.

"It's getting complicated," he whispered, sighing before pulling away from me. "I need to talk to Bellamy alone."

That tangled knot in my chest twisted tighter, condensing to a single, painful point behind my sternum.

"What?" I croaked.

Daren opened his mouth, but no words came out, and he gave me as apologetic of a look as I imagined he could muster.

"It's getting complicated," he said again, a plea.

"When am I going to see you again?" I asked.

Daren blinked hard. "I don't know."

I bit the inside of my cheek, nodding. I stepped back and Daren reached for me, but I maneuvered away before he could get his hands back on me. I thought I'd always known secrets were part of the deal, but I'd never thought they'd be between other people and not us. Daren loved me, I loved him, and we were in this mess together. We were trying to wait it out, to find our chance, and now...

"Whatever you want to say to me, you can say to him." Bellamy's voice was quiet behind me, gentle, soft as the press of his palm against the small of my back, steadying me. "I thought that...I thought there was something..."

He thought there was something between the three of us, the four of us.

Hell, the fucking five of us.

I'd thought the same.

"It's all right," I assured him, reaching behind me and brushing his hand off of my skin. I didn't want his assurances or his tenderness. I wanted to tear down the walls of Thorn Hill and bury Fletcher Sinclair in the rubble because I knew without a doubt whatever was happening was his doing, and his alone.

"I'll just tell him myself later," Bellamy said to Daren, which had both of us shaking our heads.

"You won't," I said, giving him a sad smile. "That's not how any of this works, and the sooner you learn the rules, the better."

"I wasn't raised for this the way you two were."

"So it's important you learn fast," Daren said.

I went to the door, hand on the knob before Daren was there behind me, spinning me hard and pinning me against the wall. He took my face into the cradle of his hands and crashed our mouths together, kissing me as deep and hard as a goodbye deserved. I fought to not melt into him because I had to take at least some part of my heart back to Rose Hall, and if I gave into him, I'd be lost forever.

"Don't hate me," he begged.

I swallowed hard and pushed him off of me. "I love you too."

Then I turned my back on them both.

CHAPTER 52

GIDEON

Bellamy and Luca showed up on the porch of the house looking miserable. Luca's shoulders were turned inward, his brow furrowed in contemplation. Bellamy's eyes were wide and nervous, his fingers twitching at his sides like he was seconds away from ripping off his skin.

"Where have you been?" I directed the question at Luca, even though I didn't need to ask to know where both of them had come from.

"Nowhere important," Luca spat, brushing past me and storming into the house. He banged around in the kitchen, then stalked upstairs to his room, slamming the door behind him. After the house fell silent again, Bellamy sighed, blinking up at me with tears in his eyes.

"Was this Fletcher's doing?" I asked.

Bellamy shrugged. "Can I stay here awhile?"

"What did Fletcher do?"

"I just don't want to be there," he said, taking a step toward me and flattening his hands against my chest. He walked us backward into the house, lifting onto his toes like he was chasing after a kiss.

Bellamy was a fucking siren. I'd known that since the initiation weekend, but there was definitely something more going on than met the eye. I snatched his wrists, both of them in one hand, and pushed him back. His eyes went impossibly wider and he gasped, pupils dilating into dark black pools in less than a second.

"I don't believe you," I told him.

"We're all on the same side," he whimpered, bones of his wrists slender and breakable beneath my fingers.

"I've known Fletcher Sinclair a very long time." I shoved Bellamy into the banister. "The only side he's on is his own."

"He's selfish," Bellamy agreed. "He's cruel."

I blew out an amused breath, hauling Bellamy around the corner of the stairs and up to the library room on the second floor of the house.

"I'm all of those things and worse," I warned, tossing Bellamy onto the floor. He landed hard on his ass, legs bent and hands splayed back behind him. He scrambled to his feet, chasing after me toward the door. His hands reached for my belt, for my hips.

"Gideon," he pleaded.

My body filled the doorway, and Bellamy pulled his hands away without having to be told. If I thought too long about it, I could remember his smooth naked skin beneath mine, the little breathy moans that left his throat when he was scared and aroused. It would have been easy to fall for a man like Bellamy. Far easier to fall for him than it had been when I fell for Fletcher the first time. But Luca was angry and Bellamy was too compliant for their arrival to have been anything less than contrived.

I was stupid for thinking things had changed, for believing that after all this time, Fletcher and I might finally be on the same page. I'd given him the last pieces of myself I had left, my body, my fucking virginity, because I'd never been able to say no to him. I'd never *wanted* to say no to him. But for the second time in our lives, he'd proven me a fool for believing his body over his words. Even though we'd sat together around a table and devised a plan, Fletcher was always going to make moves that suited *him* best.

He was no better than his father.

But I was.

"You can stay in here until you decide to be honest with me," I said, slamming the door closed in his face before he could look at me again with those desperate and horny doe eyes of his.

Just like the guest room Bellamy had stayed in his first night at Rose Hall, the door latched securely and automatically, ignoring his fists and his frantic fingers on the knob.

"Gideon!" he shouted my name until his voice cracked.

He yelled for me until Luca finally appeared at the end

of the hallway, wearing nothing more than a pair of low slung gray sweat pants and his glasses. His hair was damp from a shower, falling in clumps over his forehead. Water trailed down the sides of his neck, his chest, and I braced myself for another come-on. It was his way.

It never came.

Instead, Luca simply licked his lips, eyes flickering from the door to my face, then he pressed his back against the wall and slid down to sit on the floor. I didn't know if the two of them were both in on whatever Fletcher's little scheme was or if it was only Bellamy, but I wasn't sure I wanted to wait and find out.

"It's late, B," Luca rasped, dropping his head against the wall and closing his eyes.

"Then go to bed."

"I'm not tired."

"He's not to leave this room," I said, leveling Luca with a glare. "And you're not to go in."

"I don't have the key and you know it," he bit back.

I carded my fingers through my hair, shoving it off my face with a frustrated groan.

"What's he playing at?" I asked, pacing away from Luca, away from the library and toward the stairs that led to my bedroom.

"I don't know," Luca said, sounding as dejected as I felt. "Daren...didn't say."

"So he's no better than Fletcher."

"He's a thousand times better than Fletcher," Luca snapped.

I arched a doubtful brow, and Luca stretched his legs out in front of him.

"He's picked his side then," I said, cocking my head to the side and feeling more alone than I had in years. "Have you?"

CHAPTER 53

BELLAMY

Gideon kept me locked in the library for three days. There was no bed, but a door connected to the guest room bathroom, so at least I was able to take care of that on my own. Unfortunately, the pass-through door to the guest room remained shut. Luca came around three times a day with food, but he wouldn't look me in the eye. The anger he'd carried away from Thorn Hill was still boiling just beneath the surface, and I worried if I asked him about it, he'd explode.

Being isolated gave me more than enough time to think about how dramatically my life had changed since the summer and drew into sharp clarity that if I wanted to get control of things again, I'd have to take it. If I had to play Gideon and Fletcher against each other, I would. I just had to get out of this locked room.

Realistically, I knew he couldn't keep me locked away forever. My cell phone was dead. I had classes—which I'd already missed, and there was Vince. I knew Vince was the one behind my father's phone call the day after Daren took me out of the apartment, but how deep Vince's relationship with my dad went was something I still hadn't had a chance to figure out.

Before Fletcher exiled me to Rose Hall, he'd instructed me to get any information I could about Gideon North and his father's business dealings. He'd told me it was in my own best interests to cooperate, and I would have sworn his eyes had the hint of a plea in them when he said it. For as much as the four of them complained about being pawns, I was the true pawn, stuck playing a game I didn't even know the rules to. Fletcher had implied things with Gideon's family were not as they seemed, and I'd told him that was the case across the board.

The whole lot of them presenting nothing but rank and class to the public while drowning in lies and manipulation behind the scenes.

Even in the darkest parts of my lonely nights in the library, I couldn't imagine what it must have been like for Fletcher and Gideon growing up. Even Daren and Luca, knowing they were meant for this life and they had no say over it. They all seemed so resistant to it, but were four men enough to topple generations of a secret status quo?

I hoped so.

The lock on the door disengaged, and I turned from my perch on the chaise lounge I'd been using for a bed, expecting to find Luca, as usual, with a plate of food. Instead, I found Gideon, with bags under his eyes and a week of scruff grown out on his cheeks. He looked scarier than usual, with the shadows cast across his sharp features, the way he hunched his shoulders to step into the room.

"What do you want?" I asked, immediately recoiling at the vitriol I heard in my voice.

Gideon scrubbed a hand down his face and I sighed, climbing off my seat and closing half the space between us. His body swayed away from mine, so I stopped in the middle of the room.

"I came to see if you wanted to come have dinner with me," he said, not quite a question.

"Yes," I answered quickly, biting back anything else I had to say to him.

He turned and stalked out of the room without saying anything else. He left the door open, so I assumed I was meant to follow, which I did.

The formal dining room in Rose Hall was overstated and ridiculous, made of dark wood with ornate carvings of roses and thorns along the edge. There were twelve high-backed chairs, all matching. I found two places set, the end of the table and the seat beside it.

"Where's Luca?" I asked, using all of my strength to pull the heavy chair away from the table so I could sit down on the plush red cushion.

"Sulking."

"Seems to be a theme," I muttered.

Gideon took his seat with a huff, but it was hard to worry about him for long. Luca had been feeding me well, but the meal in front of me was the most delicious thing I'd ever smelled in my life. I was quick to grab my fork and knife, to slice into the pot roast and shove a forkful of it into my mouth. Gideon eyed me warily, face almost amused, but not quite.

We didn't speak through the entirety of the meal, but my pace had slowed to something closer to normal by the halfway point. The silence almost felt companionable, and by the time our plates were cleared, I was relaxed for the first time in weeks.

"Should I go back to the library?" I asked softly, folding my napkin and setting it on the table beside my plate.

"You can if you want," he said, pushing his chair away from the table and standing up. "Or you can join me in mine."

Of all the things I'd ever anticipated from Gideon, an invitation to his bedroom wasn't anywhere on the list. He'd been intimate with me, but I wouldn't have called what happened between us sex. I knew he hadn't slept with Luca, and definitely hadn't even heard rumors of him being with other students. Not in the way Fletcher was, at least. To the best of my knowledge, Gideon had only ever been with Fletcher, so the invitation was enough to make me choke on my own spit.

It felt like a betrayal to say yes.

Gideon was inviting me of his own accord, and my consent was solely to get out of the library, so I could get Fletcher the information he was looking for. I didn't want to hurt Gideon, but something had to give. Someone had to take action, and Fletcher was the only one trying to make moves.

"Bellamy?" Gideon said my name softly, unsure.

I licked my lips, my throat parched, and I looked up at him and whispered, "Yes."

CHAPTER 54

FLETCHER

Three days of Bellamy's week had passed, and I hadn't heard a peep from him or from Luca. Daren had spent most of the time giving me the evil eye, which I probably deserved. But at the end of the day, I was my father's son and the things he'd taught me were ingrained in my bones. The less people who knew what you were up to, the better. And if any of those people thought with their heart instead of their brain, they were a liability.

I envied Daren and Luca's love for each other, but it drove both of them beyond the point of control. I trusted Daren as much as I was meant to, but if Luca and I were both hanging off the ledge of a building and about to fall, I had no doubt who Daren would save. That didn't make him a bad man, but it made him a bad deputy. I would keep that secret for him, though. Because if anyone knew that about him, he'd be gone faster than the blink of an eye.

We were all replaceable. That was why we had to be careful with how we shifted power, how we gained control.

My father had called me every day, pushing me to get the dirt he was after on the North family. Earlier that morning, I'd finally snapped at him, reminding him that his time was going to be up soon and to get used to the fact I operated differently than he did. His shocked silence on the other end of the line had my blood running cold, but thirty seconds later he'd laughed into the receiver and called me a good boy.

I hung up on him.

I was getting antsy, and having Daren avoiding me like the plague was not making things any easier for me to manage. I didn't have anyone to talk to, no one to be around.

I was going crazy from the wait.

He'd left earlier that morning for class, leaving me to pace the house from attic to basement, which was where I was when someone knocked loudly against the front door. I thought the sound was imaginary, a figment of my brain after being isolated with my own thoughts for so long, but as I climbed the stairs to the main floor, I heard it again. This time, louder and more insistent.

I stalked across the room and yanked the door open, frowning when my stare landed on a man I didn't recognize. My heart sank, part of me wishing it had been

Bellamy, or maybe even Gideon. Maybe Luca, defying me again, all in the name of love. But, no. It was a dark-haired stranger, a flop of black hair slicked back from his forehead, his olive face angular in all the right places and his clothes hiding all the right designer labels.

"What?" I asked, voice barely more than a growl.

"What have you done with Bellamy Marchant?"

I raised a brow. "Excuse me?"

"You heard me."

Shocked at his bravado, I scrunched my nose and laughed at him. "Who's asking?"

The man cocked his head to the side, arrogant smile flashing across his face. "Me."

"Well, *me*. Since I don't know who the fuck you are, the answer remains none of your goddamn business." I moved to slam the door in his face, but he was quicker, shoving his booted foot between the door and the frame before I could get it latched in place.

"Let me rephrase that," he said, using his shoulder to push into the door. It didn't throw me off-balance, but it jarred enough of a crack open for him to get his body through. "I know he left this house three days ago, but I don't know where he went and he hasn't been seen since."

"He's not my concern," I lied, the words churning in my throat like bile. "Go take it up with student affairs."

"How about I take it up with your father instead?"

"My father cares less about Bellamy Marchant than I do."

Another lie.

I cared about Bellamy more than I would ever admit and my father cared about how useful he was. Nothing more.

"Are you going to make me spell everything out for you, Sinclair?"

"Don't call me that," I growled, slamming the stranger into the wall with my forearm pressed against his throat.

"That's a name for Gideon North, then. Is it?" He smirked at me, and I shoved my arm so hard into his windpipe, spit beaded at the corner of his mouth. Most men would have looked scared, but not this one. He looked...eager.

Exhilarated.

"Who are you?" I asked again.

"My name is Vince Angelini," he said, tilting his head against the door to alleviate some of the pressure against his throat.

"That name means nothing to me."

Another lie on the list. I knew exactly who the Angelini family was, but I wasn't about to let this cocky piece of shit know that. If his ego swelled up any larger, it would smother the both of us. The Angelinis weren't anyone as far as the Thorns and the Roses were concerned, but they had their own allegiances and their own rules...far outside the boundaries of the ways we ran.

"Then you're slow," he rasped. He might have known I

was lying, but he wasn't certain enough to call me out on it.

While I knew the family name, I had no idea who this arrogant little shit stain was. On the other hand, he clearly knew things he shouldn't have, and that was enough to have the hairs on the back of my neck standing up. I didn't know if he was a plant from my father to test my loyalty or what, but it was a rare thing for someone to have the upper hand on me, and I didn't enjoy the way it felt.

"I'll fucking bleed you out right here," I warned him, "if you don't start speaking in ways that matter."

"Use that pretty little brain of yours," he suggested, reaching up and tapping my temple.

I smacked his hand away, stepping back and letting him fall onto the floor in a heap. Vince sucked in breath after breath, then stood to his full height and gazed at me once again with that smug smirk that had found him against the door in the first place.

"Vince?"

Hearing the recognition in Daren's voice was the absolute last thing I'd expected.

"Pretty boy," Vince said, almost a coo. "Good to see you again."

CHAPTER 55

DAREN

I almost stumbled over my own feet when I saw Bellamy's roommate Vince standing in the middle of the living room, red-faced but otherwise unbothered. I was quick to regain my composure, coming to stand beside Fletcher as if there was no unease between us, no rift, no disagreement. Folding my arms in front of my chest, I tipped my head back to angle my chin up, giving myself as much height as I could manage. Fletcher let out a low and pleased-sounding hum after I took my place on his right, but my solidarity was a job. It didn't change anything between us.

"What are you doing here?" I asked.

"Looking for my roommate," Vince answered with a smirk.

"I told you the day I took him that he was our room-mate now."

Fletcher shifted the angle of his head, and there was

enough question in it that I knew he was simmering I hadn't mentioned Vince in any major detail. But when I'd met him, he hadn't felt important at all. Hardly worth a thought, let alone a mention.

"This is Vince Angelini," Fletcher murmured.

I immediately recognized the name. "Isn't that curious."

"Isn't it?" Vince mused, smoothing a stray lock of hair back into place.

"I don't have any business with you," Vince said to Fletcher. "I just need to know where Bellamy is."

"Do you have business with my father?" Fletcher asked.

Vince narrowed his eyes.

Fletcher licked his lips, rubbing the side of his finger across his nose with a disgusted-sounding sniff.

"I should have known," he said, turning away from Vince and stalking into the kitchen.

Vince eyed him, then looked to me. Fletcher had just put something together, but he wasn't going to share, at least not right away. Whether that was because he didn't trust Vince or didn't trust me, I wasn't certain. I hated the thought that it might be because he didn't trust me, but it was a feeling I hadn't been able to shake since the day he sent Bellamy and Luca away. Asking me to lie to Luca had been a bigger test of loyalty than whipping him raw, and I could tell by the way he leaned away from me before leaving the room that he wasn't convinced I'd done what he asked of me.

I had.

Even if it had killed me.

"Are you going to go after him?" Vince asked, jerking his chin toward the hallway that led to the kitchen.

"I haven't decided," I said, biting the tip of my tongue. "You wait here. I'll go."

"I'll make myself at home," Vince shot back, sinking comfortably into one of the couches. He spread his arms out across the back and propped his legs up on the coffee table, crossing them at the ankle. "I don't need a drink, thanks for asking."

"You're more arrogant than you have any right to be," I told him.

He winked at me.

I gave him the finger and followed Fletcher into the kitchen, finding him with both hands braced against the counter, head hanging low between his shoulders.

"What's going on?" I asked him quietly, resting my ass against his hand and re-crossing my arms in front of my chest.

Fletcher sighed. "Like you already know, my father thinks the North family is in debt. He bought Bellamy to use as a spy to find out for sure. Bellamy's father hand-picked his roommate, isn't that what he told us?"

"Right."

"You don't handpick the son of a mob empire if you aren't tied up in their dealings."

"It's below him," I mused.

"Quite." Fletcher righted himself. "But I'm not sure it's below Francis North."

"Are you saying you think Gideon's father is in debt with the mob?"

Fletcher grimaced. "I think my father is two steps ahead of me."

"You're not wrong," Vince said from the doorway.

Fletcher and I both looked up, and it was impossible to tamp down the annoyance I felt at seeing him there, leaning against the wall with such a casual brand of arrogance that should have been reserved for people with far more power and pull than him.

"Francis North is in debt to my father," Vince said, sounding bored. "But he's also in debt to everyone else. That's the evidence your father is after."

"Explain," I said.

"There were explicit rules to the loans my father gave, and if Francis has taken out money elsewhere and not paid back—with interest—what he owes us..."

"He's double-dipping," Fletcher said. "But how do you know what my father is looking for?"

Vince rolled his eyes.

"That doesn't explain your relationship to Bellamy," I interrupted, which felt more pressing than how the Angelini family had such deep insight into the Sinclair operation. I wasn't sure if that was Fletcher's priority, but just because he could pretend he didn't care about any of us didn't mean I could.

"I don't have a relationship with Bellamy," Vince said,

taking a step into the kitchen. "Which was the whole point of coming to this garbage school and having a roommate in the first place. But you *kept* him."

Vince enunciated the T harder than necessary and it made me want to hit him in the mouth.

"You're not here for Bellamy at all," Fletcher said.

"Smart and good-looking. Though it's a bit of an over-statement. I am supposed to be keeping an eye on your father's investment—"

"But also me."

"Also you," Vince confirmed. "Which has been decid-edly difficult since Bellamy hasn't been home to talk about you."

That explained the attitude Vince had the day I'd gone to the apartment with Bellamy to get his things. He was playing double duty, trying to make sure Bellamy stayed in one piece so he could get the dirt they all needed, and to make sure Fletcher was holding the company line. Fletcher was supposed to be using Bellamy to get dirt on the North family, which would in turn give the Angelinis the ammunition they needed to take them off the board entirely. The revelation somehow complicated every-thing, but made it easier at the same time. Vince was a new player who didn't even want to be part of the game. Just like the five of us.

"What does my father want to know?" Fletcher asked.

Vince shrugged, like he couldn't care less. "Everything."

CHAPTER 56
BELLAMY

Gideon snored quietly, the sheets kicked low around his waist, leaving little to the imagination. Part of me had known he wouldn't want to sleep with me, at least not right away, but his rejection after dinner had still stung. He'd kissed me softly against the corner of my mouth, stroking my hair away from my face, then he'd stripped down to his underwear and climbed into bed. I'd stripped down to my own boxers and settled in beside him, restless, until the soft huff of his breathing turned into a rhythmic metronome.

I had two choices. I could crawl out of bed and take what Fletcher wanted or I could stay in bed and take what *I* wanted.

Or at least a piece of what I wanted.

I wanted Gideon North. I wanted Fletcher Sinclair. I wanted Luca and Daren, and I wanted all four of them at the same time, a tangle of sweaty, rough hands and clashing teeth. I was desperate for a reprieve where they could all just settle into the things *they* wanted. The things *I* now wanted, even though I felt like an interloper in the intricate pieces of their relationships.

It was a weird and unexpected thing to have developed feelings for all of them, knowing that together they made a whole I'd never really be able to make sense of. Daren with his earnest devotion, Luca with his unbridled pursuit of pleasure, Gideon with his stubborn resistance, and Fletcher with his well-deserved concessions.

Then there was me, and what did I offer any of them?

As if in answer, Gideon murmured something in his sleep and reached across the bed, strapping his arm over my waist and pulling my body against his. I knew it was an accident, or at least unintentional, but the warmth of his embrace was so welcome after the isolation of the last three days.

How had he made it so many years on his own?

Gideon made a pained noise and buried his face into the back of my neck, hips thrusting his quickly thickening cock into the cleft of my ass. I moaned, arching against him and angling my head to give him more access to my neck.

"Sin," he rasped, voice hoarse and thick with sleep. His dick pulsed, nestled vgainst me.

"No," I said, using my shoulders to shift in his arms so I faced his chest. He was so much bigger than me there was no way to be face to face. I kissed his sternum and wrapped my arms around his broad shoulders.

"Bell," he corrected himself quietly, rolling me onto my back.

His weight was massive, all-consuming, and he rutted against me, thrusting his cock over the sharp angle of my hip bone until his pace stuttered.

"Come inside me," I whispered, pleading for his touch, for contact.

I spread my legs to make room for him between my thighs, the shift repositioning his cock closer to the hottest part of my body. Gideon groaned and went still, coming awake for the first time since he'd slipped me into his arms.

"You're not him," he said, burying his face into the pillow.

"No," I agreed.

"You remind me…" Gideon trailed off, kissing the side of my neck, my earlobe, my temple.

"Tell me."

"Of him," he said softly.

I hooked my ankles around the backs of his thighs and his whole body trembled as I opened myself for him.

"I'm not him," I reminded, tracing my fingers over the taut muscles in Gideon's shoulders, his back, his arms.

"Bell, I…" he trailed off.

"It's okay," I said, knowing what words were going to come next.

"What did you think I was about to say?" he asked.

I smiled and closed my eyes, even though he couldn't

see me. His lips were still warm against my skin, his body heavy and hard on top of me.

"Any number of things, Gideon. That you can't be with me, that you love Fletcher—"

"I want *you*," he interrupted, slanting our mouths together and slipping his tongue past my lips.

The confession was so unexpected, I opened for him on a gasp, and Gideon was quick to take advantage, deepening the kiss and pushing me down into the bed. Digging my nails into his back, the intensity of his kiss washed over me like a tsunami, and I had no idea how I was going to survive him, survive this thing between us. Gideon was so careful and calculating, and I was here under false pretenses. If he found out...

"Gideon, I—"

He cut me off with another kiss, stretching an arm away from me and coming back with a bottle of lube in his hand. My heart beat so hard against my ribs I worried it was going to explode.

"Do you not want me?" he asked.

He was fully awake now, also fully hard, and rocked back on his heels between my legs to coat his thick erection with a more than generous amount of lubricant.

"I do want you," I whispered. "But—"

"No buts." Gideon furrowed his brow and fell back above me, bracing one arm beside my head. The other held his cock, which he dragged past my balls and toward my hole. "Unless you want me to stop."

"I don't."

He pushed the tip of his cock into me first, crashing out mouths back together when I shouted in pain at the intrusion.

"Do you want me to prep you first?" he asked, biting my lower lip, sucking at it, kissing me again.

I shook my head, a cold sweat already beading against my temple. I didn't deserve for this thing I wanted to come easily. When I snuck out later and stole from him, Gideon would find out. He would know I took him into my body and he would think it had been meant as a distraction, but that wouldn't be the truth. I was falling in love with him, with all of them, and all of our secrets and the secrets of our fathers were going to tear all of us apart.

"What did he send you here for?" Gideon asked, sinking another inch of his erection into me. I spread my legs wider, but it wasn't enough. He was splitting me open with every slow pump of his hips.

"Gideon."

Another inch.

"Don't lie to me, Bell," he begged.

Another inch.

"Information," I admitted.

Another inch.

"About what?" Gideon shivered, like it hurt him to stop.

"Your father."

Another inch. He was going to tear me in half and it was the end I deserved.

"He could have asked me."

"He loves you so much."

Gideon seated himself fully, a trembling exhale ghosting across my cheek while his cock pulsed inside of me.

"I would have given it to him," he whispered.

"He couldn't ask you."

"He never asks me anything."

Gideon pulled out halfway and slammed back in. The force of the thrust pushed the breath out of my lungs, and he shifted above me to brace himself against the headboard.

"He's selfish," Gideon said, pounding back into me. "Cruel."

With every thrust, Gideon named off another way Fletcher had faulted him, and by the time his confessions had milked an orgasm out of me, we were both covered in sweat and tears, a hundred new secrets spilled between us and a promise that Gideon was going to save us all.

The problem was...

I didn't believe him.

CHAPTER 57

LUCA

Listening to Bellamy come his brains out from the privacy of Gideon's bedroom was the final straw for me. I shoved my feet into a pair of sneakers, grabbed a hoodie that probably at some point had belonged to Daren, then I stormed out of the house, slamming the door hard enough for them to hear. I had no direction in that moment or at all, but it was no surprise to find myself across campus with Thorn Hill in sight. The lights were on, but I knew better than to take that as an invitation.

It was just shy of nine at night when I flung myself down onto the curb, bending my legs at the knee and resting my forearms stretched out above them. More than anything, I wanted to call Daren. I wanted to see him, kiss him again, but my anger over our last goodbye was still too visceral of a thing for me to manage. He'd chosen Fletcher over me, chosen the Thorns over me. I shouldn't have been surprised, but I'd thought the love we shared surpassed his misplaced sense of familial loyalty.

Groaning, I stretched my legs out and leaned back, thinking of how hilarious my life had become. The one thing I'd been trying to do before I met Daren was get in the favor of the North family. It was the only way I could prove to my father I was worth anything, even though I only shared half his blood. And before I met Daren, that had mattered. It had meant everything. Now, with the sound of Bellamy's release still ringing in my ears, the memory of Daren and Fletcher taking me at the same time, everything that had come since...the favor of the North family—and my father—seemed insignificant.

I suddenly didn't want to tear anyone down. I didn't care about wrecking any foundations. All I wanted was to walk away unscathed and live a life on my own terms. I hoped that life could include Daren, but...

My phone vibrated in my pocket and I pulled it out with a sigh.

It was a text.

Bellamy: Where are you??

Bellamy: Gideon is looking for you.

I wanted to tell him Gideon could fuck himself, but the actions borne from years of trying to earn a place at his side weren't an easy habit to break.

Me: I went for a walk

Bellamy: U should come back.

Me: I will later.

Next was a text from Gideon that simply read *now*.

Jamming my phone into my pocket, I stalked back across campus toward Rose Hall, surprised to find a car I'd never seen before parked in the driveway. The lights were on and more than two figures milled about behind the sheer curtains. The door wasn't closed all the way, so I heard Daren's voice before I saw his face and, much to my dismay, all the anger I'd been building toward him evaporated as soon as he set his sights on me.

"Luca." He breathed my name and pushed past Bellamy, past Fletcher, past a man who looked vaguely familiar but not enough to matter. Then his arms were around me, his face buried in my neck, and my back was against the wall.

"What are you doing here?" I managed to ask.

He kissed my neck, breathed me in. "I missed you."

"That's not why you're here."

He pulled back slightly, scanning my face to get a read on why I wasn't returning his affection with the same level of fervor as he offered. I wanted to, but I was so far beyond tired. Instead, I gave him a small smile and reached for his hand, dusting a kiss across his knuckles.

"What's going on?" I asked, taking time to scan the faces of the men in the room with me.

"It's time to make a move," Fletcher said.

There was no chance of stopping the amused sound that built in the back of my throat. It tumbled out like the scoff I'd meant for it to be, and I dropped Daren's hand.

"Oh, has his majesty decided?" I sneered, narrowing my eyes.

"Luca," Daren warned.

"Don't defend him." I stabbed my finger into the middle of his chest, pushing him back. "Don't you dare come into this house and take his side."

"Calm down, Luca," Gideon warned, expression guarded. His hair was loose, a mess from the fucking he'd just given Bellamy no doubt. I wondered if he'd had a chance to finish before his boyfriend Fletcher showed up.

"I am calm."

"Things have recently come to light that are changing the plan," Fletcher said.

I mock bowed at him.

"Do I need to beat you senseless in the woods again to get you back on track?" he asked, a dark brow raised in my direction.

"I'd hardly call that being beaten senseless." I took a step toward him, shoulders squared back and ready to go. "You choked me while I had another man's cum in my asshole, Fletcher. That's admittedly my idea of a good way to spend a Sunday night."

Fletcher grinned, huffing out a quiet laugh.

"Are you done?" Gideon asked, the question directed at me.

"I'm beyond finished."

"It's honestly perfect that the lot of you are trying to ruin everything your fathers have built," the sixth man said, his bright eyes colored like the sky. "But I'm pretty sure you don't really need to try. You're already halfway there."

"And who the fuck are you?" I snapped.

"Luca," Gideon warned again, tone far more serious than it had ever been.

"Luca," Daren said, softer, like he meant to tame me. "Calm down."

"I'm Vince Angelini," the other man said, and a lightbulb flashed in my head. I recognized the name from information my father had shared with me years before. The Angelini family was far more open with their illegalities than any of our families were, and it was that brazen behavior that kept them a handful of rungs below the Sinclairs and the Norths.

"Good for you. I'm Luca Mandeville."

"Of course you are." He tilted his head to the side. "Bastard son of Ewan Mandeville who still hasn't been able to make the name his own."

"I'll fucking—" I lunged for him, but Daren must have known it was coming. He had both his arms around my chest, my back pressed against his front as he hauled me toward the edge of the room.

"What's gotten into you?" he whisper-yelled in my ear.

"Some common sense finally."

"This is cute and all," Fletcher said, rolling his eyes. "But it's getting late and it's time we laid all our cards on the table so we can finish this. Once and for all."

CHAPTER 58
GIDEON

Luca was spitting mad, and not much was going to calm him down. I poured him a glass of scotch, which he drank like water, using the back of his hand to wipe his lips after he swallowed.

"What's gotten into you?" I whispered, standing close to him while the others made themselves comfortable around the formal dining table.

"I'm tired of this," Luca admitted. "I'm just...tired."

I reached for his hand and pressed it flat against the now-healed brand he'd burned into the middle of my chest. Immediately, he winced and recoiled, but I held him steady until his fingers splayed out and dug into my skin.

"Don't let this be for nothing," I said softly.

Luca's jaw ticked, and he snatched his hand away, fidgeting with his glasses before stalking over to the table and taking a seat. I made my way to the head and sat down, staring at Fletcher who'd taken the opposite end. It was fitting, I imagined, for the two of us to share a table like this, in equal positions, equal rank. That was the way it always should have been. Our oaths and our lessons always meant to prove the Thorns couldn't exist without the Roses, so why had both tried for this long?

"So," Fletcher said, clearing his throat. "Here's what we know. One, we know Gideon's father owes the Angelini family well over five million dollars."

"What?" Luca choked, eyes going wide.

"Things you'd know if you were where you're meant to be," Fletcher told him.

"I went for a fucking walk," he grumbled.

"My father knows about the debt," Fletcher continued, unbothered.

"That's why he...bought me," Bellamy said softly.

"He what?" Luca asked, head jerking toward the other side of the table where Bellamy sat beside me.

"Maybe stop wandering off," I suggested.

Luca held up his hands in surrender and leaned back in the chair, lips sealed. I didn't blame him for his frustration, his exhaustion. I felt all of those things and more, but it was years of punishment and isolation from my father that had given me the tools to manage those feelings and not slit my own wrists. Though, it would be a lie to say that on more than one occasion, the bottom of the pool hadn't felt like a warm hug I never wanted to leave.

"I need proof that Francis North is taking money from

other families," Vince said simply. "Other places...then we can deal with him."

"When this is said and done, he's mine to deal with." Even to my own ears, my voice sounded deathly steady and nearly lethal.

"I'll put the request in."

"It's no request." I said. "If you want proof, he's mine."

Vince licked his lips and gave me a quick jerky nod of his head.

"What about the Sinclairs?" Daren asked, and all of us looked down the table toward Fletcher.

"We'll take care of it," Vince answered, glancing at Fletcher. "Unless you want to wring the life from your dear daddy's neck too?"

"I would rather he lose everything and live," Fletcher said, looking right at me. "I want him to lose the things he cares about most in this world so he understands just how much he's taken from me."

"This is..." Luca interrupted, shoulders tense as he shoved his chair back from the table. "This is too much, I'm sorry. This is laughable."

"Sit down," I warned.

Luca was half up, hands braced on the edge of the table and as he lowered himself back into his seat, the glare he shot me was sharp as daggers.

"We've all spent our whole lives sucking North and Sinclair cock." Luca gestured broadly, spit flying out of his mouth the angrier he got. "And now you just show up out of nowhere with the answer to all our problems? Where have you been for our. *Entire. Fucking. Lives?*"

"Luca, baby." Daren reached over and curled his fingers around Luca's wrist. Luca stared down at the connection point like it was a new development he didn't understand, but he didn't brush Daren off, which felt like a step in the right direction. Beneath the table, Bellamy kicked the side of my shoe, and I gave him a barely noticeable nod of agreement.

"Checks and balances," Vince said with a shrug. "Francis and Miller were taking things too far, going beyond the expectations that came with their status."

"And what? You show up to take them down a peg?"

"Our plan was to let them self-implode, if you want the truth." Vince smiled and spread his hands on the table. Luca sat up straighter, tension knotted up the length of his spine. "But after Sinclair had me put a tail on his son and his newest investment, I realized it could get a lot more fun if we didn't."

"So, what then?" Luca asked. "What happens now?"

"Now I give my father the information he's after," Fletcher said.

"My father is going to get spooked when his debt comes up for collection," I said, the next steps of the plan feeling like barbs in my mawth, even though it was a fantasy I'd held since the age of sixteen. "He'll come to me. He'll want me to move against Fletcher. Against the Sinclair family as a whole."

We'd already talked about this entire chain of events

while Luca had been out sulking on campus. We'd played through every possible scenario, every move, every action that my father and Fletcher's father could take when their very rickety houses of cards started to crumble. The conversation had been enlightening, but angering at the same time. I could see the same feelings mirrored in Fletcher's face as Vince made his suggestions about how we should act next. The both of us had spent so many years living in fear of retribution, when everything my father claimed to own was built on other men's money and his own lies.

"Your father will come to you," Daren said to Luca, who still looked like a panicked deer in headlights. "He'll tell you this is the chance you've been waiting for."

"You don't know that," Luca rasped.

"Men like your fathers are predictable," Vince said, reaching into his waistband and pulling out a pistol. "Men like us are not."

CHAPTER 59

FLETCHER

With everyone's eyes on Vince's Sig Sauer, I made sure my eyes were on everyone else. Bellamy was paler than ever, almost green and I worried he was about to throw up. As soon as the gun landed on the table, he reached for Gideon's hand, which had me wanting to crawl across the table and introduce him to the business end of that weapon in a far more intimate sense. Gideon, for his part, looked bored. Daren, for what might have been the first time since we'd all sat down, looked away from the gun to Luca, then to me. Luca looked from the gun to Gideon.

"What do you plan to do with that, Vince?" I asked, stretching my legs out in front of me.

"Nothing unless I have to."

Bellamy shoved his chair away from the table, cheeks puffed out like a chipmunk.

"I think I'm gonna…" was all he managed before covering his mouth and bolting for the bathroom.

Gideon moved to go after him, but I was faster. "You stay."

He looked like he wanted to argue, but for once, he swallowed his tongue.

I pushed my chair away from the table and found Bellamy on the floor of the second level bathroom, his face pressed against the cool porcelain edge of the bathtub. I turned off the lights and closed the door, folding myself down into the small space beside him.

"Are you all right?" I asked.

"None of this is all right," he said, closing his eyes.

"It was unfair of your father to bring you into this," I said. It was as much of an apology as I'd ever be able to give him.

"It's hard for me to be mad," Bellamy whispered, rocking his head side to side, cooling his cheek and forehead against the bathtub.

"I'd be fuming."

"I mean, I am. He…he fucking sold me off, Fletcher. Like, who does that?"

"A small man," I answered. "A scared man. A hungry one…"

"He knew what was going to happen to me." Bellamy blinked open his gorgeous eyes, staring up at me with a still and startling clarity. "With the initiation."

"If I'd known—"

He interrupted me, stretching his arm out until his

fingers grazed across the top of my knee. "You did what you were supposed to."

"Bellamy."

"I can't be mad about it now," he said softly.

I set my hand on top of his, engulfing his fingers, his palm disappearing entirely beneath my own. "You could."

"But I have you now. Don't I?"

A knot expanded in the back of my throat, and I grabbed Bellamy, hauling him out of the nook beside the toilet and onto my lap. He came easily, tucking himself against my chest, burying his face into my throat.

"Don't I?" he repeated.

I'd spent so many years of my life only wanting Gideon. Even knowing I'd never be allowed to have him, even expecting my father to force me into marriage with a woman, I'd wanted him. I'd fucked more people than I could count, but they'd never mattered. Not in the way Gideon had, but then there was Bellamy and Daren and Luca, and my entire life had flipped upside down.

Daren and Luca loved each other with such an intense ferocity, it was impossible to not get swept up in that in some way. Harder still to fight it after sharing a bed with them. Bellamy, though. The most unexpected addition of all, with his bravery and his tenderness...

The five of us couldn't have been more different, and yet together everything clicked. Just like the five-petaled oaths Gideon and I had taken that damned us to this miserable life, the five of us together had the potential to form something even stronger to break the curse of it all.

"You have me," I whispered into the top of his hair, kissing him and catching a whiff of Gideon as he moved to search for my mouth.

"Do you think I have Gideon too?" he asked, the question hot against my lips.

"You'd have to ask him."

"Do *you* want to have him?"

"More than anything," I admitted, slanting our mouths together and kissing any other questions out of his mind.

"What about Daren?" Bellamy asked, breaking to breathe. "Luca?"

"I'm a greedy man by nature, Bellamy."

"I think I like that about you." He smiled against the corner of my mouth and snuggled back into my arms.

"It's not an admirable quality."

"Would you sell me?" he asked.

A growl ripped out of somewhere deep and dark inside of me and my arms tightened around his slender frame. "Never."

"Because you're greedy."

"Selfish," I added for good measure.

"Very," he agreed.

I held him like that until my knee began to ache from the awkward folded shape I'd twisted myself into. Until I remembered where I was and who was waiting for me downstairs.

"We need to go back to the table," I told him. "We have to see this through."

"What happens when it's over?"

I dropped the back of my head against the wall and sighed, closing my eyes. I wished I had a better answer for him, but everything was unknown.

"Gideon's father is dead," I said quietly. "My father is removed from power."

"But what happens?" he pressed.

"Gideon and I do the one thing no one else before us has ever been able to do."

"What's that?"

"We bring the Thorns and Roses together as one."

CHAPTER 60
DAREN

An awkward silence lapsed over the table after Bellamy and Fletcher left, quickly broken by Vince's unnerving laugh.

"God," he said, scrubbing a hand down his face. "Are all five of you fucking?"

"Not directly," Gideon muttered.

"I'd love to know how you indirectly fuck someone, but you'll have to tell me about it another time. Until then." He returned his gun to the holster at the back of his pants. "I assume you'll give Fletcher whatever he needs to satisfy his father?"

"I will," Gideon agreed, glancing between Luca and me next. "Then he'll share what he knows with your father, who will call up the debt. After that, I expect mine to show up so it's important we maintain appearances for now."

I knew what that meant. We both did.

No more cavorting in the shadows. Back to pretending it was them against us.

"Can you manage that?" he asked Luca.

"As long as the end is in sight," Luca whispered.

"It's close," I promised.

"You can kill him whenever you want," Vince said, standing from his seat at the table and giving his clothes a quick pat down. "It makes no difference to me."

Gideon huffed out half of a laugh, tucking a loose bit of hair behind his ear.

"After that." Luca cleared his throat and fidgeted with his glasses. "Will...will you just...be the one in charge then?"

"That's how it works," Gideon said.

"Even if it's after a murder?"

"*Especially* if it's after a murder." Vince smiled like he'd murdered a few people on his own.

He wasn't wrong. Our families kept our dealings far more quiet than Angelini's did, but that didn't mean we didn't run in the same circles and do the same kinds of things. The Norths and the Sinclairs just did it better than most.

But not for long.

"And what about Sinclair?" I asked. "Not Fletcher. His father."

"I'll talk to him about it," Gideon said, joining Vince on his feet. "Let me walk you out."

Gideon gestured toward the front of the house, and Vince headed that way. The two of them left Luca and me alone at the massive dining table, sitting on opposite sides and facing each other head on.

"Will you forgive me?" I asked.

"Already did," he rasped, mouth twisting into a sad smile.

"Come here." I pushed my chair back, and Luca was around the table and in my lap before I'd even settled back into the seat. He was so lanky and tall, his hair so soft, his mouth so fucking perfect.

"This is killing me," he said, taking my cheeks into his hands and searching my face for an answer I wasn't sure I had.

"It's almost over," I promised, pulling him closer. "I love you. I love you. I lo—"

He cut me off with a moan and a kiss.

I arched away from the back of the chair, pushing my body closer to his and flattening both of my palms against his spine. Luca was so warm and so pliant, and three days without him had been too long. Any time without him was too long, but I had the sinking feeling things were going to start moving quicker than we'd ever imagined and when it was all said and done, we'd either be dead or we'd be together.

We'd be together either way, but one was more preferable than the other.

I kissed Luca with lazy and teasing strokes of my tongue, knowing we didn't have time to take things any further than a kiss. Bellamy and Fletcher would be back soon, and Gideon was only in the other room. Not that we had to hide ourselves from them, but this thing was bigger than us. Not just whatever kind of bizarre relationship the five of us had found ourselves in, but the situation with the families.

"How do you think it's going to go when Fletcher and Gideon have their little talk?" I asked, smiling as I traced my lips from Luca's swollen mouth to his ear.

"Bloody."

I chuckled, nipping at his earlobe.

"I love you," I told him again.

The front door closed.

"I love you," he whispered.

Gideon's footfalls were deliberately loud as he returned to the dining room. He took his seat, once again at the head of the table, expression entirely unsurprised to find Luca on my lap.

"I'm impressed you're not fucking on the table," he admitted, letting out a long sigh.

"Was that an option?" Luca asked, looking from him to me and back again.

"You know I like to take my time with you." I slid my hand up Luca's stomach and chest, wrapping my fingers around his throat until he tilted his head back with a breathy gasp.

"The two of you..." Gideon bit back whatever he was about to say, shaking his head instead.

"Make you sick?" I asked with a laugh, squeezing Luca's throat for good measure before letting him go.

"Give me hope," Gideon said, stare flickering up as Bellamy and Fletcher returned to the dining room.

Bellamy was flushed pink like a rose, spit shining on his lips. If I was a betting man, I'd have wagered it was from Fletcher's mouth, not any residuals from what had sent him to the bathroom in the first place.

Gideon stood, towering over all of us. "Bellamy, stay with Luca and Daren, I need to get some paperwork for Fletcher."

Luca stretched out his arm, wiggling his fingers in invitation for Bellamy to join us. It was awkward with Luca on my lap, but I managed to heft him up onto the table, and Bellamy hopped up beside him, resting his head on Luca's shoulders. He blinked slow and heavy, and I supposed he was as tired as the rest of us, if not more.

I looked from them to Gideon and Fletcher, finding them side by side, staring me down like they were both willing to burn me alive if any harm came to the two men in front of me. On their own, Gideon North and Fletcher Sinclair were imposing figures. Not only based on their size, but their presence, their power. The way they owned every room they wanted to own. Power had been spoon-fed to them since they were babies, and it showed.

"I've got them," I assured the two men whose shoulders barely pressed together on the other side of the room. The two of them were magnetized, much like how I felt about Luca.

Gideon would never warm to me...or Luca, though. Not in the way he'd warmed for Bellamy. And he'd never want any of us the way he wanted Fletcher, but somehow, that was okay. We were about to build a new world order and we could set whatever rules we wanted. Gideon could have Fletcher. Fletcher could have all of us. I could have Luca and Bellamy both.

I could have everything.

CHAPTER 61

BELLAMY

Luca reached his pinky finger toward mine, and as soon as I turned up my palm, he grabbed my entire hand and brought it to his mouth, kissing my knuckles. Gideon and Fletcher left, and Daren's shoulders deflated. He leaned against the back of his seat and covered his face with both hands.

"This sounds easy," I muttered, earning a soft smile from Luca against my fingers.

"I want to go to sleep for a week," Daren said, letting his hands fall into his lap.

"It's going to move fast." Luca pulled his phone out of his pocket and dropped it on the table.

"How long do you think we have until they're done?" Daren asked, glancing toward the stairs.

"I'd wager quite a while," Luca answered with a slow exhale. "They have a lot of talking to do."

"Talking." I snorted, thinking back to Gideon's whispered bedroom admissions. The way he'd been so honest and raw with me.. "Gideon is obsessed with him."

"Fletcher is the same," Daren said. "They're hopeless."

"I don't know." I gave a tired shrug. "They give me hope."

"For what?" Daren asked.

"Us."

I jumped off the table while the word was still on its way out of my mouth, pacing around the table toward the living room. Daren was the first to reach me, wrapping his arms around my waist and pulling me to a stop before I reached the couch.

"What about us?" he whispered into my ear.

"Something normal."

"There's nothing normal about this," Luca said, shouldering Daren to the side so he could get his arms around me too. "Nothing normal about anything we've done."

I thought about the reality of my own situation, separate of everything the other four men in my life had gone through. My father had sold me. That was why my mom had been so upset the day they told me about Rose Hill. She'd understood what I'd been signed up for...that there was no way out. And with everything that had come to light since that initiation weekend, the one thing I still didn't understand was why he'd done it. What was there for him to earn or receive by offering me up on a silver platter to the Sinclair family?

I wasn't going to find my answers in the middle of

Rose Hall, and I wasn't going to get any answers until all of this was said and done. My dad kept his secrets close to his chest, apparently, but there would be a time and a place for me to find out the truth. If it even mattered. There was no good reason for what he'd done to me. I was his son, his youngest son, and he'd given me away. And for what? Money? Power? Definitely not love, which I was learning with Daren and Luca was the most powerful force of them all. It was definitely a better motivator than the rest.

"Let's go upstairs," Luca whispered, dropping his chin onto my shoulder. "Enjoy the calm before the storm."

"You don't enjoy anything being calm," Daren said, turning and pressing his mouth against Luca's temple.

"Maybe just this once," he murmured, tangling our fingers together and pulling me toward the stairs. "I'll stockpile it until the end."

Daren snorted, but gave us both a push toward the stairs.

It was a tangle of exhausted but excitable limbs as we made our way to Luca's bedroom, and then a mess of shaking hands and flying clothes, and the three of us were bare in more ways than one.

Luca shoved Daren down onto the bed, crawling up after him. "I wish you had two cocks so you could fuck us both."

I joined them on the bed, my knees digging into the outside of Daren's thigh.

"There's three cocks between us," he said, guiding

both mine and Luca's hands to his swiftly thickening erection. "I'm sure we can figure something out."

"Seems like you're only worried about yours," I teased, wrapping my fingers around his thickness. Luca's fingers tangled with mine and we stroked him together, in tandem.

"It is the biggest," he gasped, arching off the bed as Luca and I gave him a squeeze.

Touching him wasn't enough, touching either of them...it was superficial and I needed a deeper connection. The coming days were a series of glaring unknowns, the biggest of which came from not even understanding how much my life mattered to people who had more power than I ever would.

Sinking down into the sheets, I covered the tip of Daren's cock with my mouth, tasting the salty tang of his arousal. He cursed under his breath and pushed Luca down to join me. Soon our tongues tangled around Daren's shaft, lips searching for purchase. Luca moved like he was desperate to kiss me and Daren's cock was nothing more than an impediment to his cause.

I grabbed the back of his head with one hand, sealing our lips as tight as I could manage with Daren's dick between us. And I kissed him.

I kissed him.

I kissed him.

Daren fucked his hips up off the bed, sliding his cock through mine and Luca's kiss, the moans and sighs growing louder with every pass of our tongues. It wasn't long before Daren's legs went tense beneath us and hot jets of cum shot against our cheeks and our lips. Luca opened his mouth and swallowed Daren down almost entirely. I used my mouth to cover the exposed base of his cock, and Daren shuddered, more cum leaking into—and out of—Luca's mouth.

After his orgasm faded into his bones and his cock softened and slipped out of our mouths, he pulled Luca and me down onto the bed. Half on his chest, he pushed the both of us together until our cocks pressed together, slick with our own arousal. He didn't need to tell us what to do next—our bodies knew. I moved against him, hooking a leg over his thigh and humping him until I spilled my release against the crook of his thigh.

"I need more," Luca whispered. "I'm sorry, I..."

Daren pushed us both off of him, rolling Luca onto his back and grabbing him by the throat before my orgasm had even finished. His grip on Luca's throat was so tight I could see the whites of his knuckles, and when Luca gasped out a terrified breath, my dick ached with a deeper arousal than I'd ever felt before.

"Help him," Daren said to me, and I reached between them to grab Luca's cock. His arm flailed out and he grabbed mine, jerking me to milk the rest of the cum out of me while I stroked him toward his own end. His face turned pink as he gasped for breath, the admiration and fear and love in his eyes enough to send another wave of pleasure through me. Luca blinked slowly, fingers absently clawing at Daren's grip, and then a burst of heat coated my fingers as he came onto my hand. Daren didn't let him go until I pulled my hand away, and even after that, Luca kept his hand on my sticky cock, even if his hold was looser than it had been before.

Above us, something crashed, and Daren let out a long suffering breath.

"Maybe they'll kill themselves and this whole thing will be finished tonight," he said.

Luca hummed and rolled onto his side, tucking against me like that wouldn't have been the worst outcome, but as I stared up at the ceiling, I wasn't so sure.

CHAPTER 62

GIDEON

Fletcher followed me to the library, making himself at home on the chaise lounge while I opened the bottom drawer of my desk. Things were out of place, which meant Bellamy had already done his snooping and come up empty-handed. I'd known, buried balls deep inside of him, that he'd been sent to spy. That he'd been here on a mission to steal from me, all for Fletcher's gain. For Fletcher's whims.

For Fletcher.

"Bellamy didn't check for the false bottom," I said, unlatching the secret compartment in my desk that kept the copies of my father's financial records safe. I pulled the whole stack out and set them on my desk. "Everything your father will need is there."

"I can't believe your father trusted you with all of that," he said, lips pursed. "Mine would never."

"We have different relationships I think, Sin." I kicked

the drawer closed. "Has your father ever tried to kill you with his bare hands? Because mine has."

"Not with his hands, no."

I walked around to the front of my desk and rested my ass against the edge, crossing my arms over my chest and staring at the way he'd spread himself out against his seat. The way he looked from the books to me with a calm and calculated kind of interest. These moments were our last together in this version of our life. Once his father had the records of my father's financial dealings with the Angelinis, a bomb would go off. I wanted to kill my father—and I was going to—but I had no idea what Fletcher planned to do with his.

"He's known all along," Fletcher finally said, almost under his breath.

"What?"

"About the Angelini debts...and a hundred other things."

"How do you know that?"

He shifted from his recline, dropping both of his feet on the floor and bracing his forearms against the tops of his knees, staring down at me like the answer should have been as simple as me knowing the sky was blue or the grass was green, or that I loved him more than my own life.

"Why do you think I did what I did?" he asked me, bottom lip pushed into a dangerously kissable frown. "Back before, I mean."

"Because you're a Sinclair."

His eye twitched.

"You had me, Gideon. You know that, right? You had me convinced that we were bigger than we thought. That we could change things."

"We are," I reminded him. "We're doing it now."

"But then, I mean. I thought..." He swallowed and caught me in his stare, eyes dark but clear. "I thought loving you was going to be enough."

"Sin."

He shook his head, tracing his tongue across the front of his teeth. Climbing to his feet, he stood tall, still shorter than me, but taller than most. He closed the space between us, coming to stand between my spread legs. The position giving him a few inches on me and, for the first time in years, he stared down at me.

"He was going to expose your father back then," Fletcher said. "Not because he wanted to hurt your father, but because he wanted to hurt me."

"What? Why?"

"Because I loved you then, because I wanted... because..." He exhaled and tipped his head back, exposing his throat. "Because united families was never something *he* wanted."

"What are you saying?"

"He knew about us. Somehow. Or maybe it was a guess and my actions confirmed it for him. I don't think I'll ever know. He was going to ruin everything. He was going to ruin *you* and I couldn't..." Fletcher's voice grew thick, and he swallowed hard. "I couldn't let him."

"So you did it yourself instead?"

"I thought I was doing the right thing," he whispered. "I was in love with you, and I wanted you, and I thought I was keeping you safe."

His words hurt more than the brand in the middle of my chest ever would, but I rubbed my hand across it like I was capable of easing the pain and the history between us with my fingertips.

"Is that what you still want?"

"United families?"

My throat was drier than the desert, and I rasped, "Me."

Fletcher opened his mouth and closed it again, all his features going soft like he was on the cusp of crumbling.

"Gideon, I..." His tongue stuck to the roof of his mouth and he shook his head. Slowly he let his hands fall to my legs, fingers splayed out against the top of my thighs. He touched me tentatively, like he had no right to it.

There was a flash in his eyes, a fleeting moment, where I worried he was going to say no. Worried he was going to tell me things had gone on too long and too far for us to find a way out of it. And in that flash, I imagined strapping myself to my father and taking us both down to the bottom of the pool because if the resolution of this stupid game left me alone again...

I didn't want any part of it.

I pushed up from the desk, standing at my full height, towering over him. Fletcher tilted his head back and stared up at me, his jaw the only tight part about him.

Our toes touched and we were sixteen again, except this time it was my hand in his hair, my mouth driving the kiss. I crashed our mouths together before he could answer because he'd taken long enough and I was tired of waiting.

I'd never realized how often I caught the smell of chlorine in my nose. How often my nightmares of my past held me prisoner in the present. But with Fletcher's tongue in my mouth and the smell of him wrapping around me like the most delicate, golden ribbon, all of that was gone. I didn't think about dying, didn't think about revenge or power or money.

I thought about the only thing that had ever mattered in my life.

I thought about Fletcher Sinclair. I thought about him coming downstairs, fresh after fucking Luca and Daren. Thought about him rutting Bellamy into the forest floor on initiation weekend. Thought about all the other people he'd had over the last six years while I'd had no one before him.

"Do you still want me?" I asked again, pressing the question into the corner of his mouth with my swollen lips. My fingers tightened in his hair and he looked me dead in my face and told me the truth I'd been running from my entire adult life.

"No."

CHAPTER 63

FLETCHER

"No," I said, shaking my head and moving my mouth back over Gideon's. "I fucking need you. I'm never walking away from you ever again."

The relief that rolled over us both with my confession was palpable, and Gideon kissed me so hard, our teeth clacked together. He was so much bigger than me, so much stronger, and he had me turned and lifted onto his desk before I'd even managed to lick my way back into his mouth to kiss him back.

"Are you really going to kill your father?" I asked, fear and arousal wrapping around my spine and snaking through me while we kissed. Gideon ripped me out of my pants, and I toed off my boots to help him along. I rucked my shirt up beneath my chin so I could stare down my chest and get a better view of my cock, of his...once I got him out of his jeans.

"Yes," he whispered. "I'm going to wring his neck at the bottom of the pool."

I took Gideon's thick cock into my hand while he spoke, feeling him burn and throb with every word that left his mouth.

"I'm going to crush his windpipe with my bare hands. I'm going to watch him die in the place he tried to kill me and failed."

Precum leaked out of his tip and smeared against my finger.

"You're so fucking turned on right now," I murmured, using his cock like a leash to yank him closer. It was hard work to get both our dicks into my hand, but I did the best I could. The feel of his hardness against my erection had me falling backward over the desk, the culmination of years of fucking *want* too much for me to fight any longer.

We'd fucked before out of rage and desperation, but the heat between us now sat differently. It was solid, unbreakable. Even when Gideon put space between us to get lube from his desk, the strings were still tied, the connection ever present. It had always been there, I imagined. Like cord tightened around my wrists at sixteen, being told I had to break not just Gideon's heart, but my own. And the distance between us, the time and the years, it simply wound around me. Day after day, tighter and stronger with every pull. There was no escaping the power Gideon North had over me, and that didn't scare me anymore.

The future he'd come so close to convincing me that

we could have was actually within my reach. His father would be out of the picture, and that was enough of a break in the foundation for me to strike against mine, but I wouldn't have to do it alone. Gideon would be with me. Maybe even Daren and Luca...maybe Bellamy too.

I watched, rapt, as Gideon slicked his dick and lined up with my hole. I spread my legs and lifted off the desk to give him room, crying out when he pushed into me with no prep and no warning.

"Hush now, Sin," he whispered, falling forward over me and brushing my hair back from my face. "This is nothing, it's nothing."

Another inch.

"It's everything," I bit out.

Emotion welled up in my throat. It was anger, and love, and desire, and rage all at the same time. Everything I'd ever felt every time I'd ever thought of Gideon North converged on my heart at the same time, in the same breath, and he was all the way inside of me for only the second time in our miserable lives, but somehow he'd been there all along. Being with Gideon was like coming home.

Like finding peace.

"Oh, God," Gideon groaned, hiking one of his legs up onto the desk to sink even deeper into me. His eyes rolled back and his entire body shuddered, and I slid my hands down his back to steady him.

"It's nothing," I whispered, closing my eyes and just letting myself *feel*.

Gideon snapped his hips hard, using his body to make liars out of both of us. He slanted our mouths back together, burying his length into me over and over and over until I was lost to the man I loved, the man I'd made. Above me, inside of me, Gideon transformed into the beast everyone else knew him as. With a wet and snarling mouth, he snapped his teeth inches away from my throat, using his cock to mark ownership of me from the inside. He reached past me, bracing himself against the far edge of the desk to get deeper, to fuck me harder.

Everything hurt and it was perfect, and the folder of papers that were going to save all five of us crashed to the floor as he went rigid above me with a deafening roar. Gideon's cock thickened and pulsed, spilling burst after burst of cum inside of me. He was so deep it was hard to breathe, and I gasped helplessly against his mouth, fingers scrabbling at his arms for support.

He grunted and moved, reaching between our bodies and curling his massive fist around my erection and squeezing tight enough I saw stars, he milked my own orgasm onto my stomach.

After minutes—or hours—of catching my breath, Gideon dropped his head beside mine on the desk, breathing hard against my ear.

"If you ever try to leave me again, I'll fucking kill us both," he warned, biting my ear hard enough blood began to run down the side of my neck.

It was far from an empty threat, but it was one that would never need to be realized. I was going to fight for

Gideon with everything I had. Every trick and trap my father had ever taught me, I'd now use to make sure that nothing would ever tear us apart again.

"I'd expect nothing less, Gid. Nothing less."

CHAPTER 64

LUCA

It took two days for Francis North to show up at Rose Hall. He came like we'd all expected, furious and full of bluster. He slammed the door open with so much force it rattled the house, but I didn't have it in me to flinch. I closed the book I was reading, a tattered copy of *Hamlet* that belonged to Gideon. I'd picked it up the night we'd all been together last, reading it slower than normal to drag it out. It had been impossible to pay attention in class, so I'd given up trying, instead choosing to focus on the way the paper of Gideon's book was rough and worn against my fingertips.

Sometimes, I wondered what they'd both been like as kids, he and Fletcher. Had Gideon always been so quiet? Had Fletcher always been such an asshole? I'd only known Daren as an adult, and he'd only known me as the same. What must it be like to have that much history bearing down on your heart at all times?

Maybe one day, I'd know.

"Where is Gideon?" Francis asked from behind me, the door still swinging open.

I shifted my positioning on the couch so I could get a look at him, his face red and his hair falling out of place. He looked positively frantic.

"He's at the pool," I answered, closing my book.

"I need to speak with him; he's not answering his calls."

"Probably because he's at the pool."

"You're terribly insolent for a bastard," he spat, shoving his hair away from his face.

As if he'd somehow been summoned, my cell phone started to vibrate across the coffee table, an incoming call from my father.

"He agrees," I said, swinging my legs around and picking up the phone. "If you'll excuse me. My father doesn't take kindly to being ignored."

Francis North huffed an indignant noise in the back of his throat, and I answered the call on my way upstairs to my bedroom.

"Hello?"

"Where is Gideon?" my father asked.

I sighed, closing the door to my room behind me and resting my back against the sturdy and cool wood. "He's at the pool," I said. "Why?"

"There's been...some revelations as of recent."

"Like what?" I asked.

"Just...just stay away from him for a few days."

I laughed, the suggestion the most ridiculous thing he'd ever said to me. The tattoo in the center of my chest burned like it was a brand. "I can't just *stay away from him*, Father."

"I don't want you to get hurt."

"I didn't think you cared." I rubbed my palm across my sternum, trying to imagine it was Daren's hand, or Bellamy's...their touch replacing the permanent mark of a loyalty my father had forced me to wear.

"There's been revelations," he said again.

"Is one of them that you care about me after all?"

"Watch your tone with me, Luca."

"Francis North is downstairs right now looking for his son. He also looks like he just ran a marathon. If there's something I need to know, I suggest you tell me now."

My father was quiet on the other end of the line, and I wondered how much he knew, how much he was willing to tell me. We'd wagered, even with Vince in on the game, there was a chance the Angelini family would descend like vultures, ready to pick Francis off at first sight. There was a chance, albeit small, that Gideon was going to get caught in the crossfire, though we all hoped it wouldn't come to that. The timing was everything.

"Keep your distance from Gideon until Francis is gone," he finally said. It wasn't an answer, but it was a hint. Someone was after Francis North, they were close, and he'd brought them right to our front door.

Adjusting my glasses and pushing off the door, I made a promise to myself.

I'd spent weeks trying to get Gideon into bed because I was bored, because I thought it would benefit me somehow in the end to have his loyalty in my pocket. Gideon was a smart man, a calculating man, and he had to have seen right through me. Had to have understood my intentions were...selfish at best.

My father had taught me at a very young age that sex equaled power, whether you were the one having sex or orchestrating it. And that wasn't the same kind of thing as what I had with Daren, with Bellamy. What Fletcher had with Gideon. There was love in it, and...that changed my loyalty entirely. Even if Gideon never wanted to take me to bed, he had those feelings for people *I* had those feelings for, so somehow...that left us tied.

"I don't think I will," I said to my father, opening the bedroom door and heading back down the stairs.

"You're making a mistake," my father warned.

"I don't think I am."

I disconnected the call and slid my phone back into my pocket. Francis was still in the living room, staring down at his phone and tapping out a message. His brow was knit tight above his nose, and he looked so different from how I remembered him, so much smaller than how he'd always existed in my mind. I wasn't bloodthirsty. He hadn't harmed me in any direct way, but I had the fleeting thought of killing him myself. It would be a gift to the men I cared for, but no...there was too much to say between Francis and Gideon, and I would never take that away from him.

"Can I get you a drink, Francis?" I asked, giving him my most insincere smile. "I should have asked upon your arrival. My manners must have left me."

"Did your father talk some sense into you on that call?"

"He made sure I was aware of where my loyalty belonged."

That made Francis look proud in a sick and twisted way I never wanted to see again.

"No drink," he said, palming his phone and stepping back. "I'll go find him at the pool."

"The waiting is killing me," I said to Fletcher, leaning against the kitchen counter and eating leftover rice out of a white takeout container. I'd been trying to get a hold of Luca, who was stressed because Gideon had gone to swim and wasn't answering his messages. Luca had texted to let me know Francis had shown up, angry as the devil with Gideon's name hot on his tongue. Luca had sent him after Gideon to the pool, but I hadn't heard a single peep since then.

"You have no idea." He closed the fridge with a bottle of beer in his hand, letting out a long and steady sigh.

"Do you want to talk about it?" I asked.

He gave me a perturbed expression. "About what?"

I took my rice to the table and sat down, Fletcher coming in after me and dropping down into the seat beside mine.

"About Gideon. About…anything."

A lifetime of loss flashed across his face in the blink of an eye, and he chased it away with a huge swallow of beer. "Not particularly."

I traced my tongue across the front of my teeth, stabbing my fork down into the rice and pushing the container toward the middle of the table. My appetite had been borderline non-existent since our meeting with Vince, my attention span even worse. I'd given up going to class, knowing that it wasn't relevant to whether I graduated or not anyway. There was no longer any point in holding up the facade of everything because it was all going to change before mid-terms.

"My father, he..." Fletcher paused and frowned. "I suppose he's no better than Gideon's."

"Gideon's dad locked him into solitary confinement at sixteen," I said.

"Mine did the same, just...in plain sight." He took another swallow of beer. "He says my heart is my biggest liability."

"I doubt that's true."

"It's the reason we're all here," he said, finishing his beer and immediately turning his attention to picking off the corner of the label with the sharp edge of his fingernail. "He sniffs out the people I care about and..."

"And?"

"He threatened to out you," Fletcher said, eyes dark. "And Luca."

Adrenaline raced up my spine, fight or flight kicking in even though the threat was already well on its way to being neutralized. I wasn't sure how my parents would react to finding out I was bisexual, but for Luca...it would have been devastating.

"That's why I had to send Bellamy over. I had to do what he wanted to..."

"To protect us," I whispered.

He glanced up at me, lips pursed like he was ready to argue about my word choice. But as far as I was concerned, there was no more room for argument. Fletcher cared, and not just about Gideon. He'd acted to save Luca and me...and even Bellamy. There was a time when I'd found him stoic and selfish, and he was anything but.

"Anyone who gets close to me becomes leverage," he said. "It's better to keep people away, but..."

"Luca is pretty irresistible," I teased, leaning back in my chair and stretching out my legs.

Fletcher barked a laugh, rolling his eyes. "He is, but it was more than that this time. I didn't have it in me to break my own heart a second time, a third, a fourth."

Fletcher cleared his throat and pushed away from the table before I even had a chance to comment. I supposed there wasn't anything that needed to be said. The dynamic of whatever was developing between us was far out of the range of normalcy, but I didn't hate it. I loved Luca and the more people who loved him, the better. It was the least he deserved and the most I could give him. I'd never keep him locked away when he was so willing to light up the lives of everyone he came into contact with.

Even his name, his status in his family, Luca was an open book and a kind heart. Besides Bellamy, he was the best of us; I knew that.

Everything he did was to gain favor, not power.

Everything I did was because I was scared of losing both.

"Fletcher." I reached out before he could leave, catching his pinky finger with my pointer. It wasn't anything more than the hint of a touch, but it stopped him in his tracks just the same. "What happens after?"

"Assuming Gideon doesn't get arrested for murder?"

I snorted, curling my finger around more of his hand, grazing it across his palm and the bends of his fingers. "Assuming that."

"We unite the Sinclair and North families," he said.

"That...that takes your parents out of the way, but what about Luca and me? What about Bellamy?"

"Your fathers will fall in line or they'll be taken out of it entirely."

"How?" I asked.

"Angelini ties run deep, Daren," Fletcher answered, turning his palm so our hands connected, both of us staring down at a new and tentative connection between us. "I'm starting to think they have more sway than Gideon's and my father combined."

"Then why don't they take power?"

"Power comes with visibility." He shrugged, letting my hand fall away. "And responsibility."

I hummed, thinking of the possibility the Angelini

family had been pulling strings before we'd even understood we were puppets.

"All three of you, four of you, five of us, whatever… we're all getting out of this and getting our lives back. You can be with Luca and—"

"So can you," I interrupted.

Fletcher swallowed, cocking his head to the side like I'd propositioned him. In a way, I supposed I had, but with so much uncertainty swirling around both of the houses, it would be nice to know what was waiting for me on the other side of this war.

Before I could ask for clarification, the moment was interrupted by the sound of tires crunching on gravel. We didn't need to look to know who it was.

Miller Sinclair had finally arrived, and Fletcher was about to get his reckoning.

CHAPTER 66
GIDEON

"You never seem to learn from your mistakes."

My father's voice dripped with vitriol, and I was quick to leverage myself out of the pool to meet him toe to toe. I'd been swimming laps for half an hour and my muscles were finally starting to loosen and get warm. Two days for him to show up after the Angelinis were given proof of his double dipping had seemed like an eternity, but here he was now. Dressed as impeccably as he always was, but his face was flushed, his cheeks unshaven, his hair disheveled.

"What do you mean?" I asked, not bothering to dry off.

My fingers itched, so I balled them into fists at my sides instead of throwing him over the edge of the pool before I had a chance to say my piece.

He closed the space between us, heels of his expensive shoes clacking against the wet concrete pool deck, and when he was close enough to reach, he slapped me across the face. His signet ring had turned toward his palm, immediately breaking open a cut on my cheekbone. The pain was barely noticeable, but I pressed my fingertips against the wound to still the bleeding.

"Don't play stupid."

I chuckled. "I've been doing a lot of work behind your back, Father, so I'm going to need you to be more specific in this instance. There are at least half a dozen indiscretions you could be accusing me of right now."

He growled, but he was so small and so scared.

"Is this because I'm fucking Fletcher?" I tilted my head to the side and smiled at him. "Or because I'm fucking Bellamy Marchant."

"You're a fool."

"Is it because I don't wear this with enough pride for you?" I patted my hands against the brand on my chest.

"It looks better on me, better on anyone who isn't you."

"I'm such a letdown."

"Do you have any idea what you've done?" He loosened the knot on his tie, which felt preemptive and futile, but he'd find that out eventually.

It was an unreal moment, almost out of body.

There'd been so many times in my life, especially my teenage years, when I'd daydreamed about killing my father, but I'd never thought myself brave enough to see it through. Or worse, if I killed him, what then? It would spiral me into another unknown. Maybe one that put

Fletcher's father in a place of power and I'd find myself dead beside my father. I didn't know.

My freshman year of high school had been the first time I wasn't living in fear. The way Sin made me feel, the way his skin burned against mine and the way he kissed me like he had every right to my mouth. He still kissed me that way, and I was man enough now to know it wasn't a feeling I could ever walk away from again. Not from him and not from Bellamy, not from Luca and Daren who were brave enough to risk everything not just for themselves, but for us.

"Again, I'll need you to be more specific."

"You handed over our financials to the Angelinis?"

"Technically, I handed them to Fletcher."

"They're going to kill me, Gideon," he warned. "They'll kill you."

"I'd like to see them try to kill me." I swallowed, taking a step toward him. "You, on the other hand...that's nothing you have to worry about."

"You stupid little shit, you have no idea what you're talking about."

"They're not going to kill you," I told him, closing the space between us so I could whisper his fate directly into his ear. "Because I promised them I would."

"You insufferable and arrogant—"

I didn't want to hear the rest. I didn't need to hear it. It was more of the same garbage he'd spewed to me my entire life, that for so long, I'd believed. I collared my hand around his throat and lifted him off his toes, turning us both and carrying him back toward the pool ledge. He kicked out at my legs, shocked by my strength or my determination. Maybe both, but it didn't matter.

"Go on," I prompted, holding him over the water. I couldn't keep him up for long, but I didn't need to. He was fully dressed and I was in my swimsuit and, for the first time in my life, I believed I held the upper hand.

He opened his mouth to say something to me, and I dropped him into the water. I went down after him, knees banging against the ledge so when he came up, I was there and I was ready. He broke the surface, gasping and sputtering like a drowned rat, and I shoved him back beneath the water.

"Do you remember doing this to me?" I asked when he fought his way back up for air. He couldn't see, blinded by the chlorine, so his flailing arms didn't do him any good. "Do you remember all the times you tried to drown me? When you held me down? When you tied me up and tossed me in?"

"You won't go through with this," he choked out, and I laughed.

I laughed loud enough I knew he could hear me with his ears plugged with water. He was making such a fuss, and I was in too deep. I needed to watch the life leave him, and I hoped that didn't change me as a person. But it had been so many years of torture and torment from him and his threats, his promises. The isolation had turned me into the man I was, and it was time for him to see what he'd made of me.

I let him push halfway out of the pool. Even as my hands encircled his throat, he screamed and cursed my name, but it was only fuel for my fire. I took us both over the edge, wrapping my legs around his waist after the water covered my back, holding my father's stare a we both sank down to the bottom.

Only one of us was going to make it out of that pool alive.

And it was going to be me.

CHAPTER 67

FLETCHER

I sent Daren after Bellamy, hoping the both of them would keep quiet and out of sight. Daren's door had barely closed before my father threw open the front door to the house, a smirk on his face.

"You did good, son," he said in lieu of a greeting. He wrapped me up in his arms and clapped his hands against my back, ignoring the way I went rigid beneath his touch.

"I told you I would."

My father stepped back from the hug and nodded at me like he was proud, like ruining the lives of his enemies was the best thing I'd ever do.

"We should go celebrate."

I swallowed, thinking of Gideon at the pool with his father and the radio silence that had ensued. "What did you have in mind?"

"I was thinking we could go to Rose Hall and share a

toast in front of Gideon North." My father grinned. "Let him know who's in charge of things now."

"I'm surprised you don't just want to call in a bulldozer while they're all asleep over there," I said.

My father hummed a thoughtful noise in the back of his throat, probably debating the merits of my suggestion. "I'm proud of you for coming around, Fletcher."

I swallowed thickly again, nodding and gesturing toward the front door. "Why don't you drive?"

My father rambled on about some nonsense the entire drive across campus, and my silent phone burned a hole in my pocket the entire time. When we pulled up to the house, Luca was pacing the porch, golden eyes worried behind the frames of his gold glasses. He stopped and straightened when he saw us roll up the driveway, and I offered him a fleeting and apologetic glance before my father had a chance to open his mouth.

"Where's North?" my father asked, brushing past Luca and not even giving him an opportunity to answer.

"He's at the pool," Luca said, following us into the house.

My father gave the room a disapproving onceover, then turned his attention on Luca.

"Where's his office?" my father asked.

"The second floor," Luca answered. "The only door."

"We'll wait for him there."

Without another word, my father headed upstairs. I glanced at Luca, lowering my voice.

"Still no word?"

The footsteps overhead went silent, and Luca shook his head.

"Okay," I said.

Gideon's absence didn't change what I was supposed to do. I had to have faith that he had his own father under control, and that I could take care of mine. Killing him, while an enjoyable thought, wasn't necessarily my plan. I'd lost sleep over the prospect of it, knowing if it came down to it...

I might not have a choice.

"If he comes back, send him upstairs."

"The door is locked," my father shouted.

I closed my eyes and sighed. "Bellamy stole the key, Father. I'll be right there."

Bellamy hadn't stolen anything. Gideon had given me a key two days before, in case of emergency. But my father didn't need to know that. He'd find out soon enough.

"Be safe," Luca whispered, brushing his knuckles against mine.

I nodded, the most assurance I could give him.

Climbing the stairs, I made my way to the office, finding my father pacing in front of the locked door. I swiped the fob across the lock panel, barely holding my balance as my father brushed me out of the way.

"Where did Marchant find the financials?" he asked, almost giddy.

"A false-bottomed drawer."

He trailed his fingertips across the ornate edge of the desk, and it took all my control to not tell him I'd just had my ass in the same spot, getting stuffed full of Gideon North's beastly cock.

"I'm glad he was worth the investment."

I slid Gideon's keys into my pocket. "I've been meaning to ask. What did Bellamy's father get out of that deal with you?"

"What did he get out of it?" My father laughed. "Nothing. He got the honor of doing business with the Sinclairs."

"No return?"

"It depended on how useful I found his son."

"And?"

"And I won't make him give me the money back," he said.

I'd wanted more information. I wanted more of an answer for Bellamy, but it seemed the only thing he'd been offered up for was opportunity.

My father made himself at home behind Gideon's stately desk, and I went to the other side of the room, behind the chaise lounge to the small balcony door. It was, of course, locked, but I had the key. With a quick beep, the lock disengaged and I pulled open the door, stepping onto the narrow iron balcony.

"I'm glad we're here," I said to him, "In Gideon's private space."

"This is a lesson, Fletcher." He splayed his hands across the top of the desk. "On the importance of maintaining the upper hand."

"You're not wrong," I agreed. "That's why I want to tell you a secret."

He arched a curious brow.

"I'm in love with Gideon North," I said simply.

My father's mouth twitched into a smile that quickly fell away, turning into something darker that I hadn't seen in years. He pushed the chair back and stalked toward me, backing me against the railing with a furious glare.

"It won't save him."

"I think it might."

"It will be the end of you both," he warned.

I tried to straighten to my full height, but my father was too close, too broad, too overpowering. He always had been, and I was that scared sixteen year-old again, listening to my whole world unravel at the sound of his voice.

"It's the end of *you*," I whispered, words trembling as they left my mouth.

"Do go on, Fletcher. Tell me what you think you've done."

"Right now, Francis North is at the bottom of a pool," I said. "His lungs are full of water, his face is blue. Gideon's hands are wrapped around his throat."

"One less North for me to manage," he sneered.

"I'm glad you feel that way because it's time for things to change."

"What are you on about?"

"I'm doing the one thing you never could." The words

shook as they left my mouth, and my father heard it. He laughed in my face, his breath smelling like stale scotch.

If I closed my eyes too long, I could see Gideon's teenage face when I told him Gideon North and Fletcher Sinclair were the only things we'd ever be. Neither of us understood, back then, that was enough. That was everything.

"I'm the one taking control of the North empire," my father said. "The Angelini family—"

"The Angelini family doesn't want to see you in charge anymore."

A flash of doubt on his face. "You don't know what you're saying."

"I know exactly what I'm saying, but you're not listening," I said, forcing my spine to straighten, bringing us face to face. "I have stronger allies than you. I'm the one who's a step ahead."

"Fucking the heir of a displaced dynasty isn't worth shit, Fletcher."

"I'm not fucking him; he's fucking me."

"You're disgusting."

"He fucked me on that desk," I said, voice low. "He fucked me there after he handed over the financial records and the keys to his house. I told him I loved him and promised I wouldn't make the same mistakes a second time."

"The Angelinis won't—"

I didn't care what he had to say or what he thought they would or would not do. I had Vince's word, and between him and Gideon and myself...we'd decided things were going to change. We were done letting other people pull the strings.

"You're too much work," I said with an unimpressed shrug. "You aren't willing to bend when flexibility is required so, in the end, you're going to break."

"What have you done, Fletcher?"

I didn't need to tell him because he knew. He lunged for me, both of us limited by the small balcony, but the railing was my leverage in more ways than one. I ducked and twisted, and it was enough for my father's hip to launch over the wrought iron railing, a tangle of roses and thorns meant to confine in the ways it always had. It wasn't enough anymore, and with a high-pitched yell, he was on his way down.

I didn't push him over the edge.

But I didn't reach for him as he fell either.

BELLAMY

It was nearly midnight before Fletcher stumbled home and over the threshold, a dark purple bruise casting his right eye into shadow and claw marks down his forearm. Daren was up from the couch before I'd even fully registered the sight of him in the doorway. We'd stayed together in his room until Fletcher and his father had left, and then we'd waited.

And waited.

And waited.

Then we'd heard the sirens and we'd waited some more.

"What happened to you?" Daren asked, reaching for Fletcher like he was a worried lover, a concerned partner.

Fletcher didn't fight him off.

He went still in the entry of the house, exhaling slowly as Daren checked him over for other wounds.

"Luca," he muttered, blinking slowly.

"What?"

"So it…so it looked more like self-defense," he said, gently shaking Daren off and heading for the couch. I hadn't moved, so I opened my arms and let him sink down into my embrace.

"What happened?" I asked.

Daren settled in beside him, getting closer than I'd ever seen Fletcher allow. I didn't know if things had well and truly changed, or if he was just tired and didn't have it in him to fight us off.

"He…he would have thrown me over the ledge if I…"

"It's okay." I kissed the top of Fletcher's head, stroking his hair flat so I could see Daren, whose stare flickered between mine and the door. "What about Gideon? Where's Luca?"

"No one is answering my messages," Daren said.

"Luca is at the police station with Gideon," Fletcher murmured. "He's being questioned about his father's drowning."

Daren sighed heavily, closing his eyes.

"What about you?"

Fletcher moved halfway out of my arms, stretching out his legs and thumping his boots down on top of the table. Instead of being held by us, he pulled Daren and me against him, eyes unfocused on the wall ahead of him.

"My father attacked me," he whispered, sounding rehearsed. "There's proof. He just…we were on the balcony, and…"

"Okay." I pressed my hand against the middle of his chest.

"I didn't mean for…"

"Fletcher, it's okay."

"I asked him about you," Fletcher said to me directly.

"What did he say?"

"I wish I had more answers for you, Bellamy."

I grimaced, shaking my head for him to stop. I'd sat for weeks with the possibility my father had offered me up as something disposable, and I'd made my peace with it. Being with Daren and Luca had shown me what real love could do, and it wasn't an emotion my father had ever held for me. It wasn't something I could worry about or linger on because I'd never get resolution from it. I was the youngest son. The accident or the afterthought. I was the bartering tool for him to get more for himself. Thankfully, the men I'd fallen in love with would never treat me the way my own blood had.

"It's okay," I assured him, meaning it all the way down to the marrow in my bones.

All three of our cellphones vibrated at the same time, breaking the tentative peace of the moment. Fletcher moved so quickly I almost fell onto the floor.

"It's just Vince," Daren said before Fletcher could even get his hand into his pocket. "He says Gideon and Luca will be on the way over soon."

"Was he charged?" I asked.

Daren shook his head and tossed his phone onto the table beside Fletcher's feet.

"Vince said it was laughable for us to even worry about such a thing."

"The Angelinis have more power than we realized, don't they?" Luca asked.

Fletcher barked out a laugh that quickly tapered off into a sigh. "They're the puppeteers, that's for sure."

I bit the side of my thumbnail. "What happens now?"

Fletcher scrubbed a hand down his face and immediately grunted in pain when he pressed his fingers against the dark bruise beneath his eye. Luca had really laid into him to sell the self-defense thing, but I also imagined Luca had been saving up some animosity toward Fletcher for quite a while.

"Literally now or the long term now?" he asked.

"Long term now."

"Gideon and I need to meet with Vince," he said. "Establish a new order."

"This is all so unbelievable," I murmured, burying myself back into the crook of Fletcher's side. "Like a story or something."

"One of those ones you get told as a child so you act right," Daren said.

"Clearly worked out well for the two of you," I teased.

"What now, though?" Daren went on, still half-focused on the door. "In the immediate sense?"

"Gideon and Luca come home." Fletcher closed his eyes. "And we sleep for a week."

"I like the sound of that." Daren's fidgeting turned unmanageable, and he finally pried himself up off the couch to pace the porch while the three of us waited for Gideon and Luca to make it over. The pace of his footfalls was hypnotic in its monotony, so to keep myself awake, I nosed my way up the side of Fletcher's throat.

"Even now you're a horny little thing," he rasped, tightening his arm around me. "Just like Luca. You're perfect for them."

"What about for you?"

Fletcher hummed, hauling me onto his lap. The bags under his eyes were heavy and dark, even through the bruising, and he looked like he hadn't slept in days. I supposed none of us had.

"You're unexpected," he said softly, closing his eyes as I traced my fingertips across his cheekbones. The stubble on his jaw prickled against my fingers. "But far from unwelcome."

"Just unconventional."

Fletcher straightened up and softly pressed our mouths together. "I'd say your fetishes around adrenaline and fear are quite unconventional, Bellamy, but Daren and I are most certainly happy to oblige you."

The words were like a drug against my mouth, and I leaned into him with a whimper.

"Daren too?" I whispered.

"All of us, somehow," he promised. "I'm tired of letting people take away the things I want most in life. If they want to paint me as a villain for being selfish and holding onto what's mine, then I'll gladly play that part for them."

"Is that what you did for Gideon?" I asked, kissing the corner of his mouth.

"For years," he said, licking across the seam of my lips.

"There's nothing I wouldn't do for him. Nothing I wouldn't do for any of you."

A shiver raced up my spine, followed by the slow chase of Fletcher's hands.

There wasn't anything he wouldn't do...

Including cover up a murder.

CHAPTER 69
LUCA

Six hours after he'd been hauled in by the police, Gideon North was free to go. While he was being questioned, I was on the phone with my father, who still hadn't heard the news of Francis North's untimely passing. I'd save that for another day because I didn't have it in me to play politics with him. My real family—the men who mattered the most to me—were spread across town, and I needed then back together, first and foremost.

Stretching my legs out in front of me, I found as much flexibility as I could in the hard and cold plastic waiting room chair. The coffee was burned, the vending machine empty. I was cranky, tired, and alone, but I wasn't going to leave. Regardless of what came of the Sinclair and North dynasties after today, I was still Luca Mandeville and I was still second to Gideon North. I would stand by as he needed until he told me not to.

I was loyal in ways my father never would be. It was that loyalty, that *devotion*, that gave me the foresight to get clothes for Gideon before running to the police station. He'd been brought in directly from the pool in his Speedo and a towel, and the jumpsuit they offered him at the top of the first hour was too small in every way. I'd forced them to give him the clothes I brought, and when they'd finally had their fill of interrogating him, Gideon emerged from the bathroom looking weary, but well dressed.

"What's the verdict?" I asked, fidgeting with the frame of my glasses.

"It was self-defense," he answered.

I didn't think I'd ever know if the cops truly believed him or if the Angelini family had a hand in paying someone off to make Francis North go away with as little fanfare as possible, but I was a smart enough man to know it didn't matter.

"Seems to be going around," I said, gesturing toward the door with my head.

Gideon furrowed his brow, but followed me outside, waiting until we were safely across the street from the station to ask for clarification.

"What do you mean?"

"I heard them talking while you were in the interview room." I scrubbed a hand over my mouth, unsure if I should be the one to deliver the news or if it would be better served coming from Fletcher's mouth. "Miller Sinclair is dead too."

"Is Fletcher all right?"

"I had to give him a black eye over the whole thing—"

Gideon rounded on me like he was ready to throw me into traffic, and I backpedaled, holding up my hands in surrender. "Hey, hey, he asked me to! He asked me to!"

"Why?"

"He pu—well...his father attacked him and ended up falling off the balcony in your office during the scuffle."

"He atta...he fell??? *My office?*"

"We're going to Thorn Hill," I told him. "You can get caught up, and besides, the three of them are probably worried sick about you."

"And you," he offered.

"Daren is, I'm sure."

We made a turn, walking across campus toward Thorn Hill. My car was at the police station, but the air and the freedom was more than welcome after hours cooped up in the poorly ventilated police station.

"Bellamy too," Gideon said. "And probably Fletcher."

I snorted, glancing up at him to gauge his seriousness. "Fletcher only has eyes for you."

"He's fucked you."

"I said eyes, B. His cock is far less discriminating."

Gideon chuckled, and something tangled uncomfortably in my stomach.

"Does that bother you?" I asked, knocking my hand against his. "That we've fucked?"

"I'd be a hypocrite if it did."

"No one's perfect."

"Fletcher and I have come too far to not have everything," he said quietly, Thorn Hill coming unto view at the end of the road.

"Does this mean I'm finally going to get a shot at you?"

Gideon dragged us both to a stop and took my face into his hands. I'd never felt so impossibly small as I did with my cheeks cradled in his massive palms. I shivered, knowing those hands that touched me so tenderly had just caused a man to lose his life. The power Gideon North carried was far more than hypothetical. It curled and coiled in every inch of his muscular form, barely restrained and only so because he chose to.

"I love the way Daren loves you," he said softly, thumb dragging across my cheekbone. "And I love the way Bellamy fits into your pocket."

I reached up between us, pushing two of my fingers against his mouth to stop him from saying the rest.

"I'm just not your type, B," I said, pressing against his lips before letting my hand fall away. "I get it."

"I'm invested in you, Luca." Gideon dipped his chin toward his chest, searching out my stare with imploring green eyes. "As much as I am in Fletcher. I don't need to sleep with you for that to be true."

Swallowing, I blinked hard a couple of times, unsure if the unexpected swell of tears was a result of the rejection or the absolute kindness that somehow meant more than getting Gideon into bed would ever mean.

"I love you too, Gideon," I said, huffing a breath out of my nose and breaking his hold on me. "But don't worry, it can be our little secret."

He snorted, rolling his eyes at me in the same casual way he used to do and, for the first time in weeks, every-thing felt right in the world.

We walked the rest of the road in silence, and as we crested the steep driveway that led up to Thorn Hill, the first thing I saw was Daren. He paced the porch, fingers tangled in his hair and his posture crooked like a tree. I should have called out for him, should have put him out of his misery. Gideon could have done the same, but instead we continued our ascent in silence. We couldn't have been more than fifty feet away when Daren saw us, his eyes going wide and his shoulders deflating, and then he was off.

He jumped off the porch at full speed, closing the space between us in seconds, and I was in his arms. With my face smashed against his chest, it was impossible to breathe, but I could have died happy like that. My last gasping breath being nothing more than the smell of the man I loved.

"I'm here," I said, words muffled into the crook of his neck.

"He's safe," Gideon said. "We all are."

And then he carried on without us, leaving Daren and

me in the middle of the driveway, chests pressed together and arms wrapped around each other.

"Are you okay?" he asked, pulling back and checking me over for injury. I imagined him doing the same to Fletcher, to Bellamy, to...maybe not to Gideon. But that was okay. Daren and I loved each other openly; there was room for more between us. Things with Fletcher and Gideon were different, and rightfully so.

They deserved that peace.

"I'm perfect now that you're here," I promised, lifting onto my toes and slanting our mouths together. I'm sure my tongue tasted like stale coffee, but Daren didn't seem to mind. He threaded his fingers through the hair at the back of my head and held us together, his tongue dipping deep into my mouth and kissing me until my knees didn't have the strength to hold me up any longer.

CHAPTER 70
GIDEON

The last fifty feet to the house might as well have been a mile.

I walked in and found Bellamy on Fletcher's lap, his head thrown back like he was on the cusp of an orgasm and jealousy burned hot and thick in my veins.

"That's enough," I said from the door.

Bellamy jumped ten feet into the air, and Fletcher was up before Bellamy even hit the ground.

"Luca is outside with Daren," I said to Bellamy, not taking my eyes off of Fletcher. "I'm sure he'll be excited to see you."

He took that as I meant it, not as an insult or a dismissal, but an invitation to explore the other side of whatever unconventional relationship the five of us had found ourselves in. I understood I was the odd man out, my focus very nearly singular, but that didn't mean I wouldn't share, that I didn't want them to enjoy...it simply meant that when I wanted Fletcher, I wanted him. I wasn't going to magically become a different version of myself just because my father was out of the picture. I'd always be his son, no matter how much I hated that.

Bellamy made a soft sound in the back of his throat and headed for the porch, grazing his fingers against the top of my hand on the way. Fletcher arched a brow at the touch, and I ignored his pause.

"Are you all right?" I asked, sizing up the black eye Luca had given him. It must have hurt, and I imagined there was slightly more intent behind it than cover when Luca delivered it.

"My father is dead," he said.

"So is mine."

"I didn't intend..." Fletcher trailed off, licking his lower lip.

"I did."

He nodded. "Is it enough?"

"I think so." I held out my hand and he came toward me, around the couch and right into my arms like he'd always been there. "If it's not, I'll make it enough."

Fletcher sagged against me with a weak laugh.

"So many years lost, Gideon," he whispered into my neck.

"So many years left," I reminded him, fisting the hair at the back of his head and pulling him away so I could see his face, so I could see his mouth. "So many years, Sin."

He almost whimpered, slanting our mouths together

without another word between us. Fletcher kissed me like it was the first and last time, pouring years of apology and love into my mouth and I gladly swallowed it all down and took more. I would take everything from him and I would consider it repayment for the pain I'd suffered while living without him.

He bit my lower lip until it bled. "I fucking need you."

The pain lanced through my mouth, and I swiped the blood away, painting it down his cheek with steady fingers.

"You have me," I promised.

We made it to his bedroom and onto his bed. We managed to get out of our clothes and then I was on my back, Fletcher on top of me with his head thrown back like the most beautiful angel I'd ever seen. He fucked himself on his hand and made me watch, then he lowered himself down slowly onto my dick. Inch by agonizing inch, he took me into his body. With a trembling hand, Fletcher cradled his cock and balls in his palm, lifting up so I could see the place I entered him.

It was too much and somehow also not enough.

With a growl, I raised off the bed and threw Fletcher onto his back. Propping one of his legs against my shoulder, I sank deeper into him, relishing the way he winced at the depth of my reach.

"You have me," I told him again, setting a punishing pace that had my own muscles burning for how hard I fucked him. Thrust after thrust, Fletcher's moans and grunts drove me deeper and harder until I spilled so much cum inside of him, it leaked down his balls and the backs of his thighs.

But I wasn't finished with him yet.

I was so far from finished.

"Come on, Sin," I coaxed, moving us to get comfortable. My cock slipped out of him with a wet pop and I pressed the bottle of lube into his hand.

"You want..." he looked from my spread legs to the liquid in his hand.

I nodded.

"Oh, fuck."

He moved quick after that, like I was going to change my mind, but I would never. He didn't need to know that, though. Something about the urgency and the importance had my spent cock quickly thickening back to life.

"I love you," he whispered against my mouth, settling between my legs with slippery fingers sliding up the crack of my ass. "Have you..."

"No." I shook my head. "Never."

"Look at me, Gid," he rasped, and we were teenagers again in the darkness of my dorm room, playing with feelings we had no business toying with. This time one finger entered me, then another, but even as I arched away and choked on my own breath, Fletcher was there, his stare and his love solely focused on me. "Just like that. You're... just like that."

He replaced his fingers with his dick, and my vision went black. Stars around the edges, impossible to breathe, but his mouth was on mine and the world was whole again.

"I'm not going to last," he murmured against my mouth, hips skittering against me as he fucked into me, a little deeper every time.

"We did it, Gideon," he said, kissing his way up my jaw to my ear. His mouth and breath burned against my ear, and when he came inside of me, cock impossibly thick and pulsing, I cried out.

"We did it," I whispered back to him, petting my fingers down the bumps of his ribs, tracing the bone and muscle as it curved down to his hips and his ass. "We did it, Sin."

He huffed a quiet laugh, forehead pressed beside my head.

"*Sub rosa,*" he murmured, a long forgotten promise that existed between us. "*Sub rosa. Sub rosa.*"

"Not anymore," I said, wrapping my arms around Fletcher's back as a shudder ripped through him, violent enough to shake his softening cock right out of me.

Another burn, a desperate gape and need for him to always be with me.

"We don't have to hide anymore, Fletcher," I promised. "I refuse. The curse of our names, the fucking thorns and the roses... it ends here. It ends now."

CHAPTER 71
DAREN

"**N**o more sex. I need to eat," Luca murmured, half asleep and half lust drunk.

I quieted him down by feeding my soft cock into his mouth, pushing it into the back of his throat and leaving it there to harden. His lashes fluttered and he groaned, eyes flying wide when Bellamy sank down onto his lap, stretching himself around Luca's hard dick.

"Eat this," I whispered, brushing Luca's golden curls away from his face and angling my cock deeper into his mouth.

Obediently, he sealed his lips around the base of my shaft and sucked. The groans that Bellamy ripped out of Luca's mouth with the quick thrusts of his hips vibrated up my cock, pushing me close to an orgasm I wasn't even sure my body could handle.

It had been two days since the police had correctly determined there were no charges to press against

Fletcher or Gideon around the untimely deaths of their fathers. Two days since Vince had texted us a thumbs up, then gone radio silent. Two days since I'd locked Luca and Bellamy in my bedroom and hidden their clothes. I'd gotten them coffee and sandwiches, but most of the hours had passed in a blur of tangled limbs, sleep, and sex.

Luca sucked my cock like it was his job, and I leaned down his body, grabbing Bellamy around the back of his neck and hauling him closer so I could kiss him. Spearing my tongue into his mouth while Luca swirled his around my cock, Bellamy let out a high-pitched whine as he shot long ribbons of cum across Luca's bare stomach. I groaned, pushing him back enough for me to breathe, giving Luca room to grab Bellamy by the hips and fuck up into him with enough force to bring him his own release.

With the two of them panting and spent, I swung a leg over Luca's face so I straddled him. One knee on either side of his head, I tipped my weight down and sank as far back into his throat as I could reach, shooting my load straight toward his stomach. He sputtered and choked around me, face going red as I filled him with cum, and then gasping for breath when I gave him room to breathe. Collapsing on the bed beside him, Bellamy fell half on each of us, his hair damp with sweat and tangled from the way I'd been using it as a leash.

"That was great and all," Luca said, voice slurred, "but I think I could use a fruit or a vegetable."

Bellamy's chest lifted and fell with what might have been a laugh, but there was no sound behind it.

"Can the two of you manage a shower?" I asked, patting Bellamy's hip.

He nodded, and Luca nodded, and I freed myself from the weight of their joined bodies. Bellamy tucked himself against Luca's side and Luca kissed the top of his head, and I wanted to cry for how perfect it was.

"Can I take a picture of you two?" I asked, digging around in my nightstand for my phone. "Like this?"

Luca gave a dismissive wave that I took for consent, and I snapped a quick series of photos of the two of them, blissed out beyond comprehension. I set it to my wallpaper, put on a pair of pants, and headed downstairs. I tripped over my own feet when I walked in on Fletcher and Gideon standing together in the kitchen, both half-dressed like me, with cups of coffee in their hands. They stood close together, Fletcher's head tilted back with a small smile on his face while Gideon whispered something down to him that I'd never be privy to.

"Good morning, sunshines," I said to introduce my arrival.

Gideon started, but Fletcher was clearly used to me. He tilted his head to the side and glared at me, no doubt for interrupting whatever they'd been talking about.

"Thought you fucked those poor boys to death," he said to me, rolling his eyes.

"I sure tried."

Gideon laughed at that, then pulled Fletcher out of the way so I could get to the coffee pot.

"What time is it?" I asked, not even sure if coffee was

the appropriate drink anymore, but knowing I had two men naked in my bed which also felt somehow inappropriate.

"It's eleven," Fletcher said.

"In the morning," Gideon clarified.

"Thanks." I pulled three mugs from the cabinet and set them on the counter, filling them one at a time and wondering how I was going to get all three of them anywhere.

Without warning, the gravity of our new reality hit me in the face like a freight train, and I bent forward over the counter to catch my breath. Gooseflesh prickled up the back of my spine, and Fletcher stepped alongside me, gently pressing his fingers against the small of my back.

"What happened there?" he asked.

"It's a lot," I said.

"It's not." He brushed a fleeting kiss across my temple. "It's just real."

I dropped my head into my hands, the shape of Fletcher's mouth still hot against my skin.

"You're not alone in it," Fletcher said gently. "This is... not even between us, but it's equal."

I knew what he meant.

The five of us were not involved in all the same ways together, but we were all on the same level, carried the same weight. Bellamy was more a part of Luca's and my relationship than he was Fletcher and Gideon's, but Fletcher wasn't wholly removed from my bed either. Gideon was as close to a man alone as our group seemed to have, but the way he looked at Bellamy had me wondering how long that would last. Bellamy was a soft contrast to Fletcher's hard lines, a delightful break from Luca's intensity. He was a balance I don't think either of us knew we'd needed, and the irony of having Fletcher's father to thank for that gift wasn't lost on me.

"Have either of you heard from Vince?" I asked, clearing my head and managing all three mug handles into my grip.

"That's why we're down here," Gideon said, shifting his weight to lean against the counter. "Vince is on his way over right now."

CHAPTER 72
BELLAMY

In the shower, Luca and I washed each other with our bare hands. Soapy fingers slipping and sliding across valleys of bare skin until my cock was half-hard again and my back was pressed against the wall. Luca kissed my neck, water racing down over both our heads, and I sighed at the perfection of it all.

My father may not have wanted me, but this man did.

Daren did.

Fletcher did.

Gideon...in the ways he was able...did.

"You're addicting," Luca murmured against my skin.

Someone—Daren, I assumed—cleared his throat from the doorway. "I said shower, not fuck again."

Luca turned toward Daren with a sly smile on his face and water drops beaded against his forehead.

"Will you punish me later?"

I turned off the water and reached past Luca for a towel.

"You won't like the way I punish you," Daren said, taking a second towel and holding it open for Luca, who stepped readily into his arms.

"Tell me more," Luca hummed.

"I'll tie you to a chair and fuck Bellamy until he cries."

I shivered, and not from the temperature change that came with getting out of the shower.

"We'll deal with that later, though. We have to get dressed and go downstairs. Vince is on his way over."

"I liked it better in bed." Luca grumbled something else under his breath, then put his glasses on, blinking both of us into focus. A tired smile flickered across his face and Daren pulled him in for a kiss.

I left them to it, rummaging around in the bottom drawer of Daren's dresser until I found a clean pair of underwear and a fresh set of clothes. It was weird to have clothes on again, to not have a cock inside of my ass or my mouth, but real life was waiting and that was going to be the real test.

"Do you think I'll be able to graduate?" I blurted, leaning against the door and trying not to drool while the two of them got dressed in front of the bed.

Daren looked up at me, mouth twisted into a frown. "Why wouldn't you?"

"Oh, I don't know. Probably because I haven't been to class more than three times since the semester started."

"Just because Miller and Francis are dead doesn't

mean the Sinclair and North names don't carry weight. It doesn't mean the Angelini family couldn't call in a favor to handle any absences so far this year," Luca answered.

"Vince did seem rather fond of him," Daren teased.

My cheeks burned. "Would you stop?"

"Did you want to fuck him?" Daren grinned, coming toward me. "Before all of this."

"He's not my type."

"What's your type, then?"

"I think I like a good villain." I gasped as Daren sucked a bruise into my neck, Luca smiling at me over his shoulder.

"Villains, are we?" Luca mused.

"Not you two."

"Always Fletcher," Daren muttered into my skin before licking his way up to my ear. "Do you think about him when I'm fucking you?"

"Only when he's fucking me too," I promised.

Downstairs, voices raised in greeting, not confrontation.

"Yes," Luca answered my earlier question. "You'll be able to graduate, Bellamy. You can go back to class whenever you want."

"Are you two going to?"

"I don't know what I want to do." Luca shrugged. "For so many years, all I've cared about was earning my father's favor. I never stopped to think what mattered to me."

"It's obviously me," Daren said with a crooked grin. "Us, I mean."

He hadn't meant it as a slight, and it didn't hurt. I was new still and they had history. Nothing would erase the connection between Daren and Luca, and I wouldn't have wanted it any other way.

"Whatever you want, I support," I said, grabbing Luca by the front of his shirt and yanking him toward me. Lifting onto my toes, I pressed our mouths together, smiling as Daren laughed at my brazen maneuver. Luca hummed happily, licking his way into my mouth to deepen the kiss.

"Hey now," Daren mock-whined, pulling Luca away from me and kissing him. Inches away from my face, I watched Daren lick my taste off Luca's tongue. The two of them melted into each other and melted into me, coming close enough for me to taste them together on my own lips.

"I completely forgot I brought you two coffee," Daren murmured, chuckling under his breath.

Sure enough, there were three coffee mugs on top of the dresser, still fresh and steaming. They would have to wait because, downstairs, heavy chairs from the dining room were being moved around. The three of us sobered, back from our momentary reprieve where the only thing we had to do with our days was kiss and make promises.

"Are you ready for this?" Daren asked, taking my hand, taking Luca's hand.

"Are you?"

"I have to be," he said simply, jerking his chin toward the door in invitation for me to open it. "I always have been."

We went downstairs together, Vince's eyes sparkling like diamonds when he saw our proximity. Gideon and Fletcher sat side by side at the table, their chairs pulled close enough together so they could touch. It was as much of a statement as they'd ever made in mixed company and my heart swelled at the quiet sight of it. The three of us took our seats, and together the five of us mapped out the course for the rest of our lives. On our own terms and with our own rules. The dynasty was finished, the thorns and the roses were united, and together...we were free.

CHAPTER 73

GIDEON

After two hours with Vince, I sent him and the triad out for lunch, leaving Fletcher and me alone in the house.

"What do you think about burning both of the houses down?" he asked me casually, not like he was suggesting the addition of another felony to our list of uncharged crimes.

"Here I was going to suggest we put on a movie and get comfortable."

"I didn't mean right now." Fletcher shoved his chair away from the table and pulled me to my feet. He wrapped his warm arms around me and walked me out to the living room, sat me down on the couch. "We've never watched a movie before. We've never been comfortable."

"I have to admit, Fletcher, I'm not sure how to live if I don't hate you."

He grinned and pulled me half onto his lap. "You can still hate me sometimes if you want to."

I let out a long breath and tucked him into my side on the couch, stretching my legs out and propping them on the coffee table. He mirrored the pose, threading our fingers together and turning our hands a couple of times. I wondered if he was committing the sight of our fingers twined together to memory or if that was just me.

"What do you think about the agreement with the Angelini family?" I asked, knocking the side of my head into his. It was comfortable and it was casual to be with Fletcher like this, even if the conversation was anything but. At the end of the day, we'd barely begun to scrape the surface of knowing just how deep the treachery of our fathers ran, but we knew even less about the stretch of Angelini money. Fletcher and I both were under the distinct impression our fathers felt they had wielded far more power and control than they actually did. There wasn't a string the Angelinis couldn't pull, not a single tie they couldn't cut.

So in the end, we'd made it easy for them.

The Sinclair and the North families would no longer run in opposition to one another. They were interwoven now as one with the full financial and political support of Salomon Angelini—Vince's father. Fletcher and I had both agreed to give the Angelinis anything they wanted, since they were fully capable of taking it anyway. It also gave us a chance to strip rank and bank from Daren's and Luca's fathers, as they both deserved. There was a special payback for Michael Marchant, but neither of us had made up our mind yet how that was going to go.

The wonderful thing about it all, though, was...we had time.

There were no races, no more alarms, no deadlines.

There was no one making the decisions except for us. And that was even a stretch. We were merely figureheads for people with a lust for control that stretched much further than ours ever would. Vince had found it laughable at first, how much we'd been willing to walk away from in order to find peace, but it hadn't taken more than one long look at all of our faces to understand the exhaustion caused by a lifetime of competition none of us had asked for.

"I think it's flawless." He closed his eyes and rested against the back of the couch. "But I do think we should torch both houses. I hate what they stand for."

"And where would you have us live?" I asked.

"A place with bigger beds," he murmured with a soft smile.

"My bed is not open to your little throuple of fuck toys, Sinclair."

Fletcher laughed, and I pulled him onto my lap. He was so long and heavy and he was so very much mine. I didn't think I'd ever seen him laugh, not when we were kids and certainly not now. Reaching up, I tapped my fingers against the corners of his mouth, touching the places that showed the marks of his happiness.

"You like Bellamy," he teased, licking the tip of my finger. "And you're fond of the other two."

The other two, like they were dismissible and replaceable when we both knew they were anything but. Luca, especially, who had fought so hard for his father's approval when he didn't even need it, and Daren who never even knew better until Fletcher showed him the way of it.

"I care about all three of them." I hooked my thumb over the top of his bottom teeth and brought him in closer so I could kiss him. "But it's you that I love."

"You're soft for me," he whispered.

Lifting my hips off the couch, I wanted him to feel just how much of a lie his words truly were.

"I'm anything but." I pressed my mouth against his. "But you, Fletcher Sinclair, you are soft for me, aren't you?"

He hummed, licking a hot stripe across my lower lip that had my blood burning so hot I grabbed him by the throat so he didn't dare move away.

"I'm whatever you want me to be," he said, eyes rolling back in his head. "Whatever you see in me, Gideon, I'm certain it's there."

"You're mine," I said. "That's the only thing you need to be."

"I'm so glad you were brave." He let out a soft moan and my fingers curled tighter around his neck. "So glad you were brave when I couldn't be."

"You were almost there," I reminded him. "But you're here now."

"I'm here," he said, and it was enough.

CHAPTER 74
FLETCHER

I'd lived a hard life, but Gideon had—somehow—always given me a place to be soft.

Even back in high school when we'd been two kids with more hormones than sense, more dreams than we had any right having, he'd seen my rough edges and he'd grabbed them with both hands and ripped them wide open.

Gideon was the only person, the only place, where I was allowed to exist safely.

If I was angry, he would be my defense.

If I was scared, he would fight.

If I loved him, he would yield and he would let me.

I'd made myself the villain in both our lives because it was the only way I knew to save him, and even though it took us years to get there...

He let me do that too.

And now...finally...it was time to be his hero.

Acknowledgments

Thousands of thanks for EM Denning for never letting me give up on this one, even when the polycule was poly-culing way too hard for me, to ML promising me it didn't suck, and Alethea for helping me know what needed to get thicker and when. And also, my endless love and affection to the always diligent, Kate Hawthorne Fan Club...I hope you find a new kink in this one, too.

Necessary Time

Duality

Dual Destruction

Dual Surrender

Dual Defiance

Two Truths and a Lie

A Real Good Lie

A Cold Hard Truth

A Matter of Fact

Room for Love

Reckless

Heartless

Faultless

Fearless

Limitless

A Very Messy Motel Brothers Wedding

Relentless

Secrets in Edgewood

A Taste of Sin

The Cost of Desire

A Love Made Whole

Secrets in Edgewood: The Complete Series

The Lonely Hearts Stories

His Kind of Love

The Colors Between Us

Love Comes After

Until You Say Otherwise

<u>STANDALONES</u>

Rebound

One for the Road

Daybreak - Vino & Veritas

Unfettered

Dreams

A Thousand Lifetimes

<u>COLLABORATIONS</u>

With E.M. Denning

Irreplaceable

Future Fake Husband

Future Gay Boyfriend

Future Ex Enemy

A One-Time Thing

With J.R. Gray

May the Best Man Win

About Kate Hawthorne

Kate Hawthorne is an author of character-driven LGBT romance, known for crafting emotionally intense stories with high heat and a kinky twist. Creating worlds where passion and angst collide, Kate's books bring you complex protagonists in fearless pursuit of self-exploration and happy—if not sometimes unconventional—endings for everyone.

Visit her website
http://www.katehawthornebooks.com

Sign up for Kate's newsletter
http://www.katehawthornebooks.com/extra

facebook.com/authorkatehawthorne

instagram.com/kate.hawthorne

patreon.com/katehawthorne